Renee's Renegade

La Patron's Den, Volume 3

Sydney Addae

Published by Sydney Addae, 2017.

This is a work of fiction. Similarities to real people, places, or events are entirely coincidental.

RENEE'S RENEGADE

First edition. November 16, 2017.

Written by Sydney Addae.

Dedication

Book 3 of La Patron's Den

Renee's Renegade

I never thought life would change, that I'd see it in dull, neutral colors. All my life things were vibrant, bold, strong. Nothing could happen to change the absolutes I saw around me. Then, one day, the impossible happened. Daddy died. It was just for a few seconds in time. Not only did it tear my heart, learning such a thing could happen ripped at the fabric of who I thought he was. Who we all are. Something fundamental changed inside me. Something I hope to regain one day.

Everyone wants to know if I'm okay. They ask what's wrong. I can't explain this sense of loss, of emptiness I feel inside. They have mates and share their burdens. One day that will happen for me and maybe then things will change, I don't know. Until then I place a smile on my face to keep my family happy and move through life like a machine. Saying and doing the right things, while crying inside.

-Renee Knight

<<<<>>>>

Renee's Renegade

It's time for the annual art show at the Art Museum Renee manages. Pack from all over the country has sent their work for this prestigious event hoping to make names for themselves as well as money. Renee's lack of enthusiasm doesn't dampen sales or attendance, her beauty and being the last unmated daughter of La Patron attracts attention.

Niklas Storm is on a mission of vengeance to destroy everyone remotely connected to the death of his beloved Alpha. His quest takes him from South America to the States where he meets more than his quarry, he slams into his destiny. How can he hope to attract the attention of someone so different from him? As a half-breed he can walk away, but at a high cost.

This is the third book in the La Patron's Den Series.

Thanks to my Facebook group, La Patron's Den. This book celebrates all we've been through together for the past four years. Thanks for your support.

Thanks

Sydney

CHAPTER ONE

MOONLIGHT SLIPPED THROUGH the thick overhead branches, offering dots of lights along the long, dim, twisted path. Dressed in black patent-leather ankle boots, black jeans with a matching jacket tied around her waist and a yellow tee-shirt, Renee pushed low hanging branches aside as a sense of urgency gripped her.

"He's here somewhere. I've got to find him," she murmured as she quickened her steps. Low growls disturbed the quiet. Turning, she looked over her shoulder, expecting to see David or Adam, her litter-mates. Instead, darkness and silence greeted her.

Afraid, she ran.

Leaves slapped against her face, pulling her long black ponytail loose. Hair spilled across her back and shoulders, all but blinding her as strands flew in front of her eyes.

"I don't need this," she murmured. Where were the others, she wondered as she stopped to catch her breath? Someone was coming. Her beast growled. She tipped back her head to scent the air. Frowning, she looked over her shoulder again. The scent was unfamiliar, that wasn't good.

"David? Adam? Jackie?" she called, her siblings through their link.

No answer.

"*Really guys? I need some help here.*" Tentative, she moved forward, listening and searching for the way out of this madness.

The sounds grew stronger. Closer.

Renee swallowed hard and ran. Desperation locked with fear came out of nowhere and choked her. Her breaths were short sips. She needed more air. Breathe, she told herself as she sought safety.

"Daddy!" she yelled as she tripped over a rock and fell forward, rolled a few times and hit a fallen log. Unbearable pain shot through her head, back and legs. She couldn't move.

The growls multiplied, came closer.

She struggled to get up. Pulling on the energy from her beast she rolled to the side and stood slowly. It hurt to breathe. Blood covered her hand and she wondered where it came from.

"There she is." The voice had a sinister quality that skid across her arms. "What do we have here? A black wolf alone in the woods."

Although she couldn't see the entity, it smelled of rotten eggs and sour wine. Heat brushed against her arm.

She jumped back and looked in the direction of the voice. "Who are you?" Inwardly she groaned. Did the bastard's name matter? No, not really.

Focus, Renee. This thing followed you for a reason. Prepare to defend yourself. Remember your training.

"You don't know me." It said and paused. "Yet. But you will. We will become well acquainted."

"What?" She stepped back, but kept up her guard for an attack.

"No matter. We do what we must." It leapt forward.

All Renee saw was a ball of darkness come at her. Instinctively she leapt high, avoiding contact, pivoted and kicked the back of it. Her foot made contact. Pain radiated up her leg as she landed on the other side watching. It swerved and came at her again.

This time she went low to sweep its legs from beneath it and encountered sharp claws that pierced her fashionable boots and pinned her to the ground. Stunned, she lay still for a few seconds trying to disengage her foot.

She screamed as the pain from the impaled claws raced through her body. *"Daddy!"* she called again. *"Mama!"*

"No one will help you. You're too weak. An embarrassment who can't even defend herself," it said.

Tears ran down her face as the pain increased. *"David! Reese! Rone!"*

"No one will help you." It's hot, fetid breath scorched her neck. Long, thick, yellow incisors appeared out of the darkness and came closer to her face.

Renee screamed and shot straight up in bed. Shaking, she looked around her room and exhaled.

Safe.

Rapid knocks hit her bedroom door. "Open the door, Renee."

"Mama?" Renee glanced at the floor, her things were tossed everywhere. She hadn't bothered cleaning up in a while.

"Now, Renee or I will open it myself. Believe me, you don't want that," her Mom said in a tone meant to be obeyed.

Sleep forgotten, Renee jumped out of bed, ran to the door and opened it. "What's wrong, Mama?"

Jasmine stared at Renee for a few moments. Dressed in a pair of boy shorts and tank top, Renee wondered if she should've put on a robe or something.

"Shower, you stink. Comb your hair, get dressed and come to breakfast. You've got 15 minutes." With that imperial decree, her Mom turned and stalked down the hall.

Renee glanced at the clock. It was almost ten. How had she slept so long? Rather than waste time on questions she had no answers for, she closed the door, and headed for the bathroom. As the hot water pelted her skin, she wished she could linger but knew better. Something was bothering her Mom and it was best not to aggravate her.

Stepping out the shower, she grabbed her wide tooth comb and set about detangling her long hair. Once again, she thought of cutting it into a more manageable style, but the idea of doing more than a ponytail or bun kept her from doing it.

Tangle free, she pulled her hair back and secured it with a band. Moments later she had on clean clothes and was out the door. She made it to her parent's suite with two minutes to spare.

HER MOM OPENED THE door as she arrived and greeted her with a small smile and kiss on the cheek.

"Something smells good," Renee said entering the foyer. Mama had been baking, something she rarely did anymore.

"When was the last time you ate?" her Mom asked watching her.

"Yesterday?" Renee tried to remember, but couldn't which was strange.

"Where? Not here. I asked, you were here all day, but didn't get anything from the cook or Adam and Bella's kitchen." Mama her arms and stared at her.

"My appetite's been off," Renee murmured. Unsure what was going on she edged toward the kitchen.

Her Mom moved, blocking her. "Are you on drugs? Illegal drugs?"

Renee blinked. She couldn't have heard what she thought she heard. "I'm sorry, what did you ask me?"

"Are you on some kind of illegal drugs? Something that's changed your behavior lately."

Taking a deep breath, Renee counted to ten. "No, Ma'am. I've never done drugs." It hurt her Mom would think she'd do something like that.

"Then what's going on with you?" Frustration and love tinged her mom's voice.

"Nothing..." the look in her Mom's eyes stopped her from giving her normal response. Renee exhaled and shook her head. "I don't know. I'm not sure what's going on."

Several seconds passed with Renee staring at the ground. Her thoughts flew in several directions. Things she didn't want to look at closely edged to the surface. She took a deep breath to combat the nausea.

And another.

Warm arms enfolded her, settled her stomach and mind. Inhaling deep, Renee breathed in her Mom's familiar scent, allowing it to fill empty spaces and comfort her.

"Come eat, we'll talk."

Renee followed her mom to the kitchen, grabbed a cinnamon biscuit and took a bite. Two bites later, her appetite waned, and she placed the remaining portion on a plate. "Where's Daddy?" She hadn't sensed him when she arrived before her Mom blindsided her with that question.

"Work. He's working with Lucian, the Honduras Alpha to get their school and medical facility open. He and his brother are coming soon for a tour of our schools, and businesses. This way they have an idea of what can be accomplished." Mama sat at the table with her plate.

Uninterested in anything that had to do with Honduras, Renee nodded as she took a seat.

"You're not hungry?"

Renee looked at her plate and the lone half-eaten biscuit. She placed a slice of bacon and a link sausage next to the biscuit. Breaking the bacon in half, she nibbled on it while her Mom ate in silence. Idly, she wondered what Jackie was up to. She and her mate, Quinn, had been assigned to assist in the building of the new medical facility, but if the Alpha was on his way here, maybe Jackie was as well. It was something to think about.

"Higley and his mate, Emma, sent word for you, Adam, Bella and David to come to his new club tonight or tomorrow. Everything I've heard about it sounds good. Cameron and Lilly are happy he's moved closer. They missed their oldest son."

Renee nodded. Higley had a voice that could hit any pitch and could sing so good, he'd make you cry. It was unfortunate the human world would never experience his gift. But with their long-life spans, it was too risky to become a pop star.

"Sounds good." She wasn't sure she felt up to attending. Even if the music wasn't too loud, she wasn't up to being around a lot of strangers.

Someone tapped the front door.

"I'll get it," Renee said, standing and heading to the foyer. On the other side of the door, she sensed David, and a few others. She opened it and stepped back. "You're in time, Mama's been baking."

David looked at her for a long moment.

"What?" she snapped as Adam, Tyrese and Tyrone followed him.

"She's been baking for three days." He closed the door and watched her.

"Really?" How had she missed that? "I didn't know."

"Exactly. Come on, let's go inside."

Seeing her brothers sitting in the living room, she stopped and looked at her Mom. "What's going on? Y'all not here for breakfast?"

Mama walked over to her, took her by the hand and walked into the living room. Adam moved as Renee and Mom sat on the love seat, side by side.

"What's going on?" she asked Adam and David.

"Wait for Mom," Adam said as he pulled a chair in from the kitchen.

"Renee, I'm concerned by the change in your behavior over the past two-weeks. At first, I didn't think much of it when you missed training with the others, or an occasional meeting at the museum. But things have gotten worse. You don't go to the museum at all and I know you love working there."

"Love's a strong word, Mom," Renee said to lighten the mood. Mama didn't bite.

"You love art and none of us have seen you do any drawings this past week." Mom leaned back. "When was the last time you sketched or saw something that you wanted to draw?"

Feeling the weight of five pairs of eyes, she looked at the floor. "Maybe there's nothing left to draw."

"What's going on, Renee?" Adam asked softly. "Like Mom, I didn't think much until I didn't see you drawing. I can't remember a time when you didn't have a pencil or crayon in your hand and you weren't drawing something."

"Nothing's wrong," she snapped and then closed her eyes. Shoulders slumped, she shook her head. "Sorry, Adam. I don't have an answer."

"Are you sleeping okay?" Tyrone asked.

"Sometimes," she said, looking at her hand clasped in her Mom's hand.

"Nightmares?" Tyrone prompted.

Her head flew up. How'd he know? "Sometimes." More like every night, which was why she fought going to sleep.

"Do you remember them?" Tyrone asked. "Your nightmares or dreams?"

Frowning, she tried to recall and couldn't. "No. I just wake up scared, shaking sometimes." She glanced at her Mom and then back at their joined hands.

"Can you recall how long you've been having these bad dreams?" Tyrone asked.

Again, Renee tried to recall and couldn't. "No. I don't know."

"It's been a couple weeks at least," Adam said.

"So not before Dad came home from Honduras," David said, his gaze locked with hers.

Renee closed her eyes to block the memories of that nightmare. Daddy had died. She'd thought him indestructible. But he wasn't and that turned her world upside down.

"That was three months ago," Tyrone said slowly. "We all talked about it during that time."

"I don't know if you experienced his death," David said. Renee met his gaze. "It was a difficult thing to fathom and go through. But I, we felt when he stopped breathing."

"Yeah, freaked me out," Adam said.

"I didn't know that," her Mom said slowly. "None of you ever said anything. Is that what's bothering you? Feeling your Father..."

"Mom," David said softly. His gaze flitted between Renee and their Mom. "Everyone's mated and could share their grief with their mates. Believe me when I say it was a real mind-trip and physical experience going through that." He sighed and looked at Renee. "I shared with Sarita, she helped soothe the burned images and pain."

"I had Bella," Adam said slowly.

Renee met her Mother's tortured gaze. "It was the worse feeling in the world. The link burned, disappeared. In an instant he was gone. It hurt like nothing I've ever experienced," she whispered as tears ran down her cheeks.

"Oh baby." Jasmine pulled Renee close and held her tight. "I didn't know. You can't hold that in, it's destroying you. All your creativity, your bright, bright light has gone dim."

"I didn't realize... not until David just said...it hurt so bad, Mama. It hurt so bad." Renee sobbed on Jasmine's shoulder for several moments.

Jasmine's heart broke. It never occurred to her that the kids felt his death at the explosion in Honduras. As the Goddess' wolf his life was spared, but for a few moments Silas had died.

"What's wrong?" Silas asked.

"Renee... I'll tell you later. We've got to help her, she's been suffering."

"On my way."

Jasmine didn't bother telling him not to come, he needed to know. She stroked her daughter's head and rocked her gently. Adam's glassy eyes said how much this all affected him.

David sat with his head down, she could only imagine what was going on his mind. She hoped he didn't blame himself for this. They all missed it. Since David was determined to claim Sarita, Renee was the lone wolf in their den and had no one to help her through a deeply emotional, physical and spiritual catastrophe.

"I'm sorry, Renee," David said, his voice a ragged whisper. "I didn't think, didn't remember that you'd need... Goddess, I can't believe you've been dealing with this alone all this time."

Renee turned and extended her hand to David. He fell to the floor and crawled forward, taking her hand and kissed the back of it.

"Forgive me, please," he said.

"Nothing to forgive. Neither of us knew. I thought I'd dealt with it," Renee said.

"I'm sorry too, Renee," Adam said and then exhaled. "I didn't realize Bella helped me through it until just now. Still learning this mating stuff. Whatever you need to get through this, I'm... we're here to help."

The door opened.

"Renee?" Silas' voice cut through the room as he entered and stopped. "What's the matter, Princess?" He stood next to Jasmine. *"What's wrong with her?"*

David stood and looked at Silas. "She never dealt with your death. Didn't have anyone to help her through it is a better way of explaining." He waved toward the others. "Everybody else had mates that helped deal with the separation and pain. Sarita helped me."

"*Separation?*"

"They felt you die. It was quite painful," Jasmine said softly.

"No," Silas said sounding horrified.

"*Yes. Renee's been having nightmares and lost interest in life,*" Jasmine said, stroking her daughter's hair.

"How can I help?" he asked, while staring at Renee.

David ran his hand through his hair and took a step back. No one spoke for several moments.

"*Remember what happened when you returned from Honduras? How desperate I was to make sure you were okay? To feel alive again?"* Jasmine asked slowly. "*Every mated pair made love with their mates to reconnect to life. I can only imagine what David and Sarita did long distance.*"

Silas shook his head slowly. *"There has to be a way to help her through this. I cannot abide seeing her so... so despondent like this."*

"Renee are you afraid?" Jasmine asked in a soft voice.

"Not right now."

"You wake up scared and shaking, are you thinking of your Daddy dying again? Is it possible that's what the nightmares are about?" Jasmine asked watching the sorrow on Silas' face.

"I don't know. I call for him, but he doesn't answer. None of you answer when I call." She gasped and sat up. "I remembered that." She looked at her brothers. "I called for you to help me." She pointed at them and then looked at Jasmine. "You too, Mama." She looked at Silas. "I called you the loudest." Renee wrapped her arms around her waist tight. "No one came to help me." She sounded so lost it brought tears to Jasmine's eyes.

"Well you know that was a dream, Peanut," Tyrese said in a harsh whisper. "Nothing would stop me from ever coming if you called and needed me." He pointed at Renee. "Got that? Nothing would ever stop me from coming to you. So, the next time you call, and I don't answer, say this is a fucking dream because my brother would never, ever, leave me hanging. Never," he said again, his voice breaking, leaving no doubt how her words affected him.

"I know, Rese. Right now, sitting here talking about it, I know none of you would have left me hanging." She shook her head. "It's just... Daddy wasn't supposed to... you know. I always thought it couldn't happen to him. When it did, something changed." She tapped her chest while looking at the floor. "In here. Something happened."

"Same here," Adam said. "An uncomfortable realization for sure."

"Death comes to everyone at some time, Sis," Tyrone said. "For us, it's delayed, that's all."

"I know," Renee said and released a long sigh. "Maybe that's it. I just never thought of Daddy that way." She looked at her parents. "You're my superman, always have been. Mom's your kryptonite. In my mind you've always been totally indestructible." She took a breath. "What happened that day, what I felt, I can't imagine what it was like for you. When Mom explained what happened, I couldn't believe it. She told us over and over you weren't... gone, just unavailable while you healed."

"The pain had lessened by then, so we knew you weren't dead," David said. "But feeling you being ripped from me... I don't want to ever experience that again."

"Me, neither," Adam said.

"I had no idea and don't know what to say at this point," Silas said sounding baffled. "I want to help you through this, Princess. I miss you. The bright, colorful you, who sees beauty in the most unlikely places.

Renee snorted and mumbled. "The world isn't as beautiful anymore."

"Maybe not, but you are," Silas said reaching down, he pulled her up from the sofa and hugged her. "You're still a bright light in my world and I need you to continue to blaze bright for me. For all of us. Tell me what you need. If you're afraid of someone, train with Adam and David again like you used to until you feel invincible like your Mom."

"Silas," Jasmine said with a slight smile.

"It's true," Silas teased. "Everyone knows I'm just the figurehead around here."

Jasmine shook her head at his antics but didn't speak since Renee was smiling.

"Sounds good," Adam said. "We can go through the paces later today, make sure you can kick... defend yourself while asleep or awake."

"Thanks, I'll let you know," Renee said.

"Nope, not good enough," David said standing. "Today, me, you and Adam in the gym, working out. I'll feel better once I see what you can do. It's been a while." He looked at his watch. "Two hours from now?" He met Renee's gaze.

No one spoke.

Renee sighed, but didn't leave her Father's embrace. "Okay. Two hours we meet in the gym."

"Great, that'll give us some time alone," Jasmine said.

"What else do you need?" Silas asked Renee.

"Just be here, anywhere, as long as you're here," Renee said softly.

Silas kissed her forehead. "Promise to do my best."

Renee's smile didn't reach her eyes, but her countenance looked better than it had when Jasmine knocked on her bedroom door this morning.

"When are you going back to the museum?" Silas asked Renee. "Don't you have some sort of event coming up?"

"On the 18th," Renee said as she returned to the seat next to Jasmine.

"That's next weekend," Adam said.

"Is it?" Renee frowned.

"Yes. Which would explain the frantic calls for you from the museum. You blocked Edmund and Crystal?" David asked.

Renee sighed but didn't answer.

"Do you want to cancel or push back the date?" Jasmine asked, growing concerned over Renee's lack of interest in the annual show.

"I don't know. Once I see what's been done, I'll make a decision," Renee said looking at the floor.

Jasmine met Silas' worried gaze. Renee had been working all year on this event. Students and artists from packs all over the country made arrangements to be in attendance. Every room within 15 miles had been booked for months. Not to mention all the Alphas and their mates who planned to attend the scholarship ball the second day of the event. To cancel or make changes now would disappoint a lot of people.

"Forces of Nature, right?" David asked watching Renee.

"That's the theme for the art exhibit this year," she said.

"That's you. A force of nature. You'll get through this, Renee. You just need your second wind. Grab something to eat, and meet us in the gym in a few." Bending, he placed a kiss on her forehead, and walked toward the door.

"I guess that's the cue to leave you and Mom alone," Adam said and winked. He kissed Renee and Jasmine and left.

"I'm invisible today?" Silas asked Jasmine.

"No, they just remembered you died and are dealing with it the best they can," Jasmine said.

Tyrese walked to Renee, pulled her from the sofa and hugged her tight. They remained that way for a few moments. "I love you, Renee. Never doubt that for one minute. I don't talk as much as Rone, but I'm here if you ever need me for anything."

Renee nodded and wiped the moisture from her eyes. "I know, Rese. Love you too." She looked over his shoulder and chuckled at Rone's frown. "Love you too, Rone."

Tyrone wrapped his arms around her, while pushing Tyrese out the way. "Such a hog," he murmured before placing several kisses on her forehead. "Love you, love you, love you. My door is always open, and I don't talk more than Rese, just want to clear the air with that." He looked over his shoulder at his twin.

Renee laughed. This time it reached her eyes.

Jasmine exhaled as she watched the three of them toss jokes back and forth.

"I didn't know they experienced that with me," Silas said as he placed his hand on Jasmine's shoulder.

"Me neither. They never mentioned it until now. Wonder if the twins experienced it?"

"No," Silas said. *"I asked them. Just the four and maybe you?"*

"Nothing like what they explained," Jasmine said. *"Lots of angst, pain, but not the ripping thing."*

"*Good, I didn't want any of you to experience that.*" He paused. "*She'll be okay?*"

"*Yes. I think so. I was so worried I didn't know what to do. I asked her if she was on drugs.*"

Silas chuckled. *"I could've told you the answer to that or you could've scanned her yourself."*

"Now you tell me." Jasmine groaned.

"*The most important thing is you noticed, we discussed it and now she can recover. I'll make sure David takes her into town to the museum tomorrow. She needs to be around her work,"* he said.

Jasmine agreed and stood to walk with the twins to the door. When they left, Renee took Jasmine's hand.

"Thought they'd never leave, I'm starving," Renee said.

Jasmine grinned. "Good. Eat first. Then go clean your room, it's filthy."

Renee smiled as she headed to the kitchen. "Yes, Ma'am."

"I'll see you later, Princess," Silas called to Renee as he wrapped his arm around Jasmine's waist.

"Bye, Daddy and thanks."

"*I'll see you for dinner,*" he told Jasmine.

"Indeed you will," she murmured against his lips.

CHAPTER TWO

RENEE SAT IN THE FRONT seat of David's late model Ford truck on her way to the museum. Fight or fuck. That had been Adam's explanation on how he dealt with the trauma of their dad's death. David hadn't been as direct but agreed with Adam. He refused to explain how he and Sarita, Hawke's daughter, were able to accomplish either since she was on another continent.

Yesterday, she had met her two brothers in the gym and they'd taken no mercy on her. Maybe it was because Asia's two sons, Kayden and Wyatt were nearby working out with Angus' two younger sons, and they didn't want her to look bad.

Even though Asia's boys were only 12, they won every fighting competition they entered. Tall, muscular, they looked much older and carried themselves like young men instead of high school students. Whether it was Asia's extra something she got from Nicromja through her dad, or Hawke's black wolf heritage, everyone knew their sons were Alpha material and not to be taken lightly.

Fortunately, Bella, to whom Renee would always be grateful, stopped the training when she came for Adam. Once Adam left, it was easier to deal with David. They talked more than trained. He'd really been worried about her. Feeling everyone's eyes on her, she fought harder than normal and, in her opinion, she didn't do a bad job. Which was why she fell into an exhausted sleep last night.

This morning she woke refreshed. The world still had ugly spots, but spending the bulk of yesterday with her Mom and brothers reminded her of a lot of good things.

"When are you going to trade your car for an upgrade? It's about time, right?" David asked as they passed the large car dealership Cameron and Lilly owned at the entrance of Pack lands. Tyrone and her father implemented a lot of incentives to keep Pack money within the Pack. Every Alpha was required to have at least one car dealership in their state where Pack members could buy quality transportation at cost. If they required financing, it came through pack-owned and operated credit unions.

"Maybe later this month or next when I have time," she said after a few moments.

They turned onto the highway and headed to Charleston. "Think you'll be able to have the art show next week?" David asked breaking the silence.

Renee had been thinking about the event all morning. There was no way she could cancel. Too many pups and Pack members already made arrangements to come. This event would span two days, making it larger than last year or the year before.

"Yeah, we'll get it done. Crystal may be ready to quit, and Edmund might be swinging from the chandeliers, but we'll get it done." She smiled at him, grateful he hadn't pressed on the car or any other issues they'd discussed.

"Does that mean you won't make it to Higley's club tonight? We didn't go last night, I think this is the last night."

Renee had forgotten.

Higley was Cameron's oldest son. He and David had always been close. She appreciated his love of music, another form of art and wanted to support him.

"What time?"

David told her.

"I'll be there." Rather than drive, she'd have a driver pick her up an hour before, so she could eat, dress and make it to the club on time.

"Good. Adam and Bella are going. I think Rese and Rone went last night with Rose and Danielle. Nana watched the kids."

Renee laughed. "Rese' four, Tyesha, Tyanna, Tylena, and Tyrell are 13 and in high school. They probably watched Renita and Rebecca, Rone's kids while Nana supervised. No telling what those six got into. Nana may miss having kids in the house, but she doesn't do a whole lot with them."

David agreed. "Rone said Ryan and Ryder were headed to Hawaii for some surfing competition."

Renee missed her oldest nephews who were a few years younger than her. They all grew up together. The twins played sports in high school and college. After college, they'd done some traveling, spent time on the west coast and apparently took up surfing.

"Must be nice," Renee said as they sped along the highway.

"Aunt Renee's hosting the Jewels next week. Nana's flying out to meet them."

Renee looked at David. Why was he giving her the family newsletter, something he never did?

"Is she?"

He nodded.

"Does Nana know you call her babies "the Jewels?" Renee used her fingers to form quotation marks for the nickname given to her Mom's younger sisters.

He shrugged, not caring in the least. "Diamond, Ruby, and Jewel, is a mouth full. Easier to just call them "Jewels" which they are." He added with a smirk.

Victoria and Jacques never hid the fact they were spoiling their pups, the jewels. The three girls were brats around everyone except Renee's parents. Once, Diamond forgot her manners and snapped at Renee's Mom. Before anyone could respond, Tyrese lifted her by the shoulders with feet dangling above the ground and gave them all a stern lesson on how to talk to La Patroness. Trembling, Diamond begged forgiveness and never misspoke to her older sister again. Pity they couldn't all handle the "Jewels" that way.

Renee crossed her arms over her chest and continued watching him. "What's with the family briefing?" she asked when he didn't say anything else.

"Olivia, Sophia and Amelia, want to enter something in the art show. Lilly called twice this week to ask if there could be a local artist corner or something like that."

Renee frowned. She had no idea Cameron, her father's godson and State Alpha, wanted his three youngest pups to be a part of the show this year. Lilly, his mate, never mentioned the girls interest. "They're into art? I've never seen anything they've done."

"They're 14 and looking for ways to express themselves I suppose. Mom asked me to tell you since she forgot."

Everyone knew how particular Renee was when it came to art. This art show highlighted the best talent in the Nation and already had over a hundred entries. For Lilly to ask to have her kid's work included at the last moment rubbed Renee wrong, but she couldn't muster the energy to get angry over it.

"I don't know." She looked out the window as they exited the highway to a less populated area where the museum stood as a lone bright star. Her heart caught as the tall, building came into view.

Architects created a steel, glass and concrete masterpiece on the outskirts of a nearby small non-descript town her father owned. It took a year and a half to build. Her father walked her through the floors, the outer and inner courts for sculptures, the basement and vaults, a week before she graduated college. Working here, corralling artist from all over the Pack had been her mission. Since then, a few Alphas opened art museums in their states, highlighting the importance of various forms of expression.

David parked in one of the reserved spots set aside for her family and they went in through the employee entrance.

Dressed in a sleeveless cobalt blue, form fitting dress that rested mid-thigh with matching shoes and accessories, Renee strode to her office and unlocked the door. She needed a few minutes to go over her notes to see where she'd left off a couple weeks ago.

"Two weeks?" she groaned as realization of how much time she had lost hit. She had a backlog of emails, most with urgent marks which she tackled first.

Crystal tapped on her door and stuck her head in. "Good to see you're feeling better. When you have a minute, I'll brief you on what's been happening."

Renee waved her in. "Thanks. Lock the door behind you."

Crystal, a short, bubbly half-breed with long dreads, numerous bangles on her wrists and a collection of colorful beaded necklaces around her neck, nodded. Renee hired her after her first week as manager of the museum and never regretted it. Crystal was smart and loyal with a quirky sense of humor. "Got it." She waited until Renee sat back and looked at her.

"First off we have a squabble on ownership rights for the Hunter collection sent from Washington." She paused. "The one you wanted on the first floor near the entrance."

Renee recalled the beauty of that statue done in steel of a wolf hunting a deer. She hadn't met the artist or researched him, something they always did before accepting the submission.

"Who created it?"

"That's the problem, we don't know. Two others have come forward claiming ownership," Crystal said.

"Came forward? All three are here? In town?" Renee asked.

Crystal nodded.

Her father could determine the owner, but she hated to bother him over this. Asia could do it as well, Hawke too for that matter. Could Tyrese determine who was telling the truth? She wasn't sure but would run it pass him, otherwise she'd ask Asia to meet them at the club tonight and discover who owned the sculpture.

"Contact them, have them meet me tonight at this club." She gave Crystal the address and time.

"That's on Pack lands, they're from out of town, will they need a pass?"

"Probably, take care of that for me, please." Renee glanced at the email on her screen and then looked at Crystal wanting her to continue.

"Edmund agreed to create a local, up and coming artist corner. He place it on the second floor but is looking for a spot on the first floor. I reminded him he couldn't move anything but if he found a clear spot to let you know." She looked up at Renee with a twinkle in her dark brown eyes. "There is no space available on the first floor and he knows it. He's trying to earn brownie points at Alpha house."

Since Renee was aware of what Lilly wanted, she was relieved Edmund handled the matter.

"Good luck with that," Renee murmured.

Crystal's smile widened. She continued discussing vendor concerns and complaints, artist demands and complaints and finally staffing issues. Renee gave instructions that cleared up most of the problems. The rest she would need to handle personally with a call or visit. Nothing major. Things weren't as bad as they could have been.

"We'll need additional staff for the event, the high school art department pitched the idea of art students working to gain insight, and so did the college in Kentucky since they're sending two bus-loads of students. Both would solve our shortage problem."

Renee liked the idea. "Have the college and high school send over candidate information for you to review and select the ones we'll use."

"Me?"

Renee smiled at Crystal's shocked expression. Renee always personally selected everyone who had anything to do with her events. It was her way of making sure everyone understood her vision. Today she wasn't feeling it.

"Yes, you. I trust you to choose the same people I would, or better." She smiled and looked at her emails again.

"Thanks for your vote of confidence, I think," Crystal said shaking her head. "One last thing. We haven't received the contract for the entertainment. They've been changing the terms, asking for more concessions. Basically, becoming a real pain in the ass."

"I saw that." Renee thought a few minutes.

"They're good, probably the best the full-blood band in the Nation," Crystal said. "And they know it. Bunch of pussies."

"Cancel them. We won't ever use them again for any La Patron events." Renee decided. Tonight, she would plead her case with Higley, he would know someone who needed a boost in their career.

Crystal clapped her hands as she laughed. "Hallelujah! I can't wait to send their agent the message."

Renee smiled. "What? No phone call?"

"They don't deserve it." Crystal stood. "That means you have to find someone else to perform at the ball." Smiling she unlocked the door and left.

An hour later, Renee emerged from her office with her electronic notepad to begin a tour of the building. She started on the first floor.

Each art selection for the event sat in a specific location which had to be given to security and the insurance company. Paintings in every medium, highlighting the artist' interpretation of "forces of nature" filled the walls, columns, niche's and small areas. Sculptures, ceramics, baskets and tapestries with various depictions were grouped together upstairs. Several photographs lined the staircase and were in the elevators.

Proud they of the displays of Pack talent, Renee took her time making sure each item was in its proper place.

Hours later she finished the first floor and headed upstairs. Edmund, a half-breed talented artist she met in college caught her before she reached the second-floor landing.

"Renee, it's good to see you. How're you feeling?" he asked as he joined her. Edmund stood a few inches taller than her, with a slighter build and sandy blond hair. He would be the first to say he was no fighter, more a lover of women and art, although not in that order.

"Better thank you." Glancing at her tablet she turned right.

"There's been a few changes," he said.

She shook her head. "I didn't authorize any changes." She continued verifying the location of each piece.

He cleared his throat. "I know. You were out, and Alpha's bitch asked if we could add a local corner for Pack members in the area. I told her I'd ask, she called a few more times and came here yesterday."

Renee stopped and looked at him. "Lilly came here?"

He nodded and stuffed his hands in his pocket. "With her three youngest in tow. Let me show you what they created." He turned and walked past the ceramics and photograph sections into what was really a small corner. Six drawings of people on the beach, running or having fun outside sat on pedestals with the names beneath.

Edmund remained quiet while Renee battled the urge to toss the drawings into the trash. Everyone could draw, speaking through pictures was a basic form of communication. She inhaled and beat back the nasty demon that would turn her into a snob. This exhibit was for the Nation. If the host Alpha wanted his youngest involved, so be it.

"This is a good spot, Edmund. You've done well." She turned to finish her audit.

"Renee?"

She looked over her shoulder at him. "What?"

"Are you okay? I mean, I know you were sick for the last couple weeks. Is everything alright?" he asked walking toward her.

Had she been a tyrant? Yes. When it came to this museum, her museum, she had high standards and never gave an inch.

After this past week, no... longer than that, she realized life was too precious, too fleeting to get hung up on small stuff. "I'm fine. If you had put that any place else I would have you move it. But it's in a decent spot and will make Lilly and Cameron happy." She shrugged. "No big deal."

"That's what I thought, but I wasn't sure. I had to make a snap decision and... well it was nice helping the Alpha. Can't hurt." He gave her a boyish grin and winked.

When they met in college, he asked for a date and was a good sport when she told him about Tomas. Since he was as dedicated to art as her, they became friends. Sculpting was his preferred medium and two pieces of his work were in the museum courtyard, another at her father's Compound. He hoped to sell a few pieces and secure commissions for more during the art show.

Renee smiled and continued checking the artwork. "You're right."

CHAPTER THREE

LATER THAT NIGHT, RENEE stepped into Club Nu, Higley's nightclub dressed in a short emerald green dress that clung to her body with a short hemline. She wore her long, thick, wavy black hair parted on the side and let it hang down her back. Getting away from work to listen to Higley sing had been the light at the end of the tunnel for her all day.

The early part of her day had provided a false sense of calm. All the artwork was in place, which made her think they were on easy street to meeting their deadlines for the art show.

Wrong. Crystal and Edmund took cues from the past and approved nothing on their own.

Several vendors she and Crystal hadn't discussed, had complaints, lacked direction and hadn't ordered necessary supplies to meet their contractual obligations. Renee had spent hours hunting suppliers to expedite flower orders, salmon from Washington, prime cuts of beef and other food stuffs for the caterer and choosing outfits for the waitstaff, and ushers.

The most liberating thing she did today was turn Crystal and Edmund loose to handle the formal event. Initially, they couldn't believe she wanted them to present a plan to her in two days how the ballroom should be decorated. After reminding them of their deadline to have something on her desk they got busy.

Instead of her remaining at work after hours as normal, she left those two in the office pouring over ideas.

"Renee," Adam yelled, waving at her. "Over here." He sat next to Bella who was dressed in a beautiful gold and cream dress that highlighted her curves and natural beauty.

Pleased they saved her a seat, Renee pushed through the crowd to greet them. "This place looks great. Higley and Emma did a fantastic job. Feels like a big-time club in New York or LA," She said.

"That's the feel we were going for," Higley said as he reached their table with a bottle of champagne. He leaned forward and placed a kiss on Renee's cheek.

Gone was the shy youth that avoided people and preferred to remain at home. Once Higley left for college, he studied business and never looked back. Successful, mated and polished, he owned a club in Texas and from what she heard had petitioned the Illinois Alpha to open one outside Chicago.

"Our clubs are on Pack lands, and just for Pack members. We deserve the best," Higley said as he poured glasses.

Adam took two glasses and handed them to Renee and Bella before taking his own. "And it keeps Pack money on Pack lands, creates jobs for Pack and we can party without worrying about humans."

Higley smiled. "You read my application for the club."

"No. David did. He helps with that stuff," Adam said. "But it's all true. Daddy says the Alphas are building strip malls, shopping centers, art galleries, all kinds of things on Pack lands to help keep money in the Pack and create Pack jobs. Makes good long-term economic sense to me."

"We already had the structure in place with our schools. Now we're expanding commerce all over. Only Pack can shop or work on Pack lands where prices are much lower, it's an extra incentive to register and be counted," Renee added.

"True." Higley hugged her. "It's good to see you. How're you feeling?"

"Better, thanks for asking." She inhaled his woodsy scent. It was good to see him again, she was glad she came.

"Thanks for allowing the three terrors have a place in the art show. I know how particular you are and am pleasantly surprised by your generosity." He chuckled. "I think mama counted on you saying no, now everyone will see what those three can do."

"Everyone can draw," Renee said.

"So you've always said," Higley replied as he squeezed her arm and turned to Adam. "I haven't met your mate."

"My Bella," Adam said. "Bella this is Higley, my cousin."

Although they weren't technically cousins, it was easier to make that claim than to explain Renee's father's guardianship over Cameron. She hoped Adam explained it all to Bella later rather than getting into it now.

"Hello, Higley, this place is great. The acoustics are unbelievable."

Higley's brow rose. "Are you a musician?"

Bella's smile dipped.

"Forgive me, I've been gone and don't know much of what's been happening outside of my parent's large home. Ten siblings require a lot of catching up, not a whole lot of time to learn everything else," Higley said with a slight smile.

"She has an amazing voice," Renee said. "Very few can match her gift."

Higley, an excellent singer, met Renee's gaze. "That's high praise, coming from you."

Renee smiled. "She's that good. Before I leave tonight, I need to talk to you. Asia is meeting me here in an hour along with three guests from another Pack. Hopefully you can give me a few minutes."

"Anything you need," he said and waved the waitress over. "Give them whatever they want, place it on my tab."

"Yes, Sir," she said and took their order.

"Is Hawke coming? Haven't seen him in a while," Higley asked.

"I don't know. I need Asia to handle a dispute for me." Renee told them the problem regarding the statue.

"Good idea having Asia handle it. Saves a lot of time," Adam said taking another sip.

"Excuse me, it's time for the performance." Higley looked at Bella. "Afterward, I'd like your opinion on it."

Bella smiled and nodded.

Renee sipped her drink while watching Bella and Adam. She understood why her brother was so captivated by the genuinely good-hearted beauty. Bella never intruded but was a solid shoulder to lean on if needed. She loved Adam unashamedly and accepted all his quirks. She was gifted but you'd never know it. She was quiet, comfortable in the background, while Adam couldn't remain hidden if he tried. A real yin-yang match.

The lights dimmed.

Emma, Higley's mate, dressed in an elegant, white, flowing gown, walked to the front of the small stage and spoke to the audience. Welcoming them to the new club, explained why they were on a mission to provide quality entertainment to Pack on Pack lands, just as Renee had brought other art forms to the Nation.

Surprised by the comments and further when she received a standing ovation, Renee nodded her thanks to Emma and the crowd. When Emma started singing "Ain't no mountain high enough," Renee knew the show was going to be good.

As expected, Higley came out singing the next verse. He was in his element and it showed how much enjoyment he received by sharing his musical gift.

Renee glanced at Bella. The woman sat on the edge of her seat, eyes glued on stage, entranced by the performance. Adam met Renee's gaze and then looked at his mate.

David slid onto the seat next to Renee. "*Sorry I'm late.*" He poured a glass of champagne. "*They sound great.*"

"*Yes they do.*"

"*Look at Bella, I think she wants this,*" Renee said to David thinking how cool it would be if Adam and Bella remained in the states.

"*Possibly. Adam said she didn't want to be a star like Whitney Houston, maybe this will fit her needs. Not sure how it'll work with Adam's schedule though.*"

"*Maybe he'll give up his dream for her to find hers,*" Renee said.

"*Doubtful, but maybe,*" David said.

Higley's wife left the stage, leaving him to perform. His wide range of talent left the crowd breathless and clamoring for more after an hour and a half.

"I need a break, but I'll be back. Welcome to Club Nu, everybody!" Higley yelled and threw a kiss to the crowd as he left the stage. A DJ played popular songs for people to dance. The floor filled quickly.

"That was unbelievable. He's so talented," Bella gushed. "Did you hear his ranges?"

Smiling, Adam nodded.

Bella looked at Renee. "That was the most... the best performance I've ever heard. I can't... I can't believe it."

Renee understood. "He's always been that way. Higley could hear something once and sing or mimic it exactly, even when we were kids. He could compete with anyone in the world and win, hands down."

"But he's ours," David said. "A gift from the Goddess to the Nation, just like you Bella. I hope you'll sing tonight."

Bella's eyes widened. She looked at David, then at the stage and then at Adam.

"If you want to, I'd love it," Adam said. "This is all Pack. No record companies or labels. Try it, see how it feels."

Bella bit her lower lip, but Renee saw a glimmer of excitement in her eyes.

"Asia is here. So are your three guests," David said.

"Excuse me," Renee said pushing back from the table. She picked up her glass of champagne and walked toward the entrance.

Asia and Hawke stood just inside the door talking to a few people.

"Renee, these three says they're meeting you here?" the doorman asked.

"Yes." She looked at the two men and lone female. Full-bloods. "Is there a place we can talk briefly? I promise it won't take long." She waited for the doorman to point them in the direction of one of the small VIP rooms.

Moments later someone approached her. "This way please." He walked toward the hall.

"Asia, Hawke, please come with us." Renee looked at the couple.

Asia nodded. Dressed in black pants and a matching top, Asia looked every bit as dangerous as rumors proclaimed her to be. For decades she had been a top assassin in various countries until she met La Patron. Renee's Mom and Asia were best friends. Renee had known Asia all her life and like the rest of her litter mates, thought of the woman as her godmother.

Inside the room, Renee wasted no time. She asked each person if they were the creator of the steel statue. All three claimed the masterpiece.

Asia frowned. Looked at Hawke and then walked to each person, placed her hand on their shoulder and asked the question again.

"The creator of the sculptor is dead. Each of them assisted him at some point, but none of them are the owner." Asia pointed to the female. "This is his mate."

"And the rightful owner of the statue," Renee said seeing the relief on the face of the woman.

"Thank you. We have pups, I wanted to tell them their father's work was being displayed in the museum. It means a lot to us, to his memory."

"Does he have other work?" Renee asked.

The woman's eyes brightened. "Yes, yes, he does. Would you like to see them?"

"If it's alright with you, I'll send my assistant, Edmund to look at the pieces. If there's enough, we could do a special showing for his work," Renee said, liking the idea.

The woman broke down crying. "Thank you, thank you so much. Beaver wasn't a fighter, didn't have much to do with our local Pack and was ostracized. We've been slowly getting help but it's been hard."

The timing wasn't right to ask questions regarding her mate's death and their situation, but Renee would make sure Edmund got the whole story. She took the woman's hand.

"No need for all that, we're Pack. Pack looks out for each other." Renee bent forward. "Especially artists."

Asia and Hawke chuckled. The two men looked pissed that they lost their claim, and left the club. Renee escorted the woman inside as her guest and gave her a glass of champagne.

"This is nice. We don't have anything like this on our Pack lands."

"I'm sorry, what's your name?" Renee asked.

"Lacy."

"Lacy, this is my brother, David." Renee introduced her to everyone at the table and waved at Hawke and Asia who sat at another table in the back.

Higley had come to the table, and spoken to them in Renee's absence. The second set was beginning. Dressed in a purple and silver pantsuit, Emma greeted the crowd, told a few jokes and then started singing an Anita Baker song.

Higley joined her on stage for a few numbers. Then he took center stage and blew them away again with a wide array of music from country western, to R&B, to pop and everything in between. He held the audience in the palm of his hand, inviting them to remember where they were when they first heard certain songs. Considering the long-life spans of most Pack members, this approach met with a howling success.

He had been performing for an hour when he called Bella on stage. Pleasantly surprised, Renee watched Bella release Adam's hand slowly and head for the stage. Bella received applauds because of her mate who was generally well liked.

Higley introduced her and the two of them sang "Baby, come to me," a song recorded in 1982 by Patti Austin & James Ingram. Before the end of the song, the audience was on their feet swaying with the rhythm. Higley bowed and walked off stage.

Bella's gaze locked onto Adam as if he were the only one in the room as she sang Whitney Houston's "Run to You". Some of the notes sent chills down Renee's arm. Couple's pulled each other closer, kissing and moaning as the song continued.

While Bella made love to Adam through music, people slow danced, or gyrated against others on the dance floor. When Bella finished "Run to You", she sung Whitney's "I will always love you" and pointed to Adam whose eyes were glassy. The audience went wild, clapping and screaming as she pointed repeatedly at Adam.

David placed his hand on Adam's shoulder as Bella hit notes that caused the glasses on the table to shake. Renee's throat tightened from holding back tears that flowed from Lacy and several others in the audience.

Mates. The gold ring in their world. Everyone in this room wanted what Bella and Adam had. Renee glanced at Asia and Hawke, they were locked in a hungry kiss, as were many couples in the club.

Higley and Emma stood on the side of the stage, smiling as Bella walked from the stage while singing to Adam. Her voice carried throughout the room.

It was heartbreakingly precious to see the love shine from Bella's eyes to Adam as she extended her hand to him. He took it and they walked back up on stage.

Higley placed two stools in the middle and waved for them to sit amidst raucous applauds.

"I can't sing," Adam said as he took a seat. The audience laughed. "My Bella, she's... she's unbelievably talented. Higley's the only person I know who comes close."

The audience clapped and whistled as Higley, holding his mate's hand, bowed graciously.

Bella started with the "Power of Love," by Celine Dion, and worked her way through Adele's "Rolling in the Deep," and ended her mini-concert with Whitney's "I Am Nothing." Adam grabbed her and kissed the last note from her mouth.

Renee, along with the crowd stood clapping and whistling.

Higley and Emma returned to the stage, wiping their eyes with large grins. “A lot of pups are going to be made tonight,” he said, gaining more applauds.

Adam stood holding Bella around the waist. “My mate everyone, the incomparable, Bella Knight.”

The crowd stood while clapping.

Renee looked at David. *“Still think he won’t change his plans for her?”*

“Maybe I spoke too soon. She’s… beyond words. I had no idea she had all of that inside,” David said continuing to clap.

CHAPTER FOUR

"COME ON, NIKOLAS, WHY do we need to leave now?" Barbie Lopez complained as she and her bodyguard were hustled out of a popular full-blood nightclub in Brazil.

"It's Storm," he snapped. "Your flight has been sitting at the airport for an hour waiting. If you don't want to be hauled away like an infant, act like an adult." His gaze swept the area and recognized full-blood security ahead.

"Stop," a full-blood called from behind them.

Barbie's face brightened as she turned. "Stefano, can I stay with you?"

Storm cursed and glared at Vicks, the bodyguard hired to keep Barbie safe.

"Come on Barb, your father sent the plane, it's waiting. We should go," Vicks said.

"I'm not ready to go." She extended her hand to Stefano. "I want to stay a little longer, with Stefano and his friends."

Stefano's glance swept over Storm and then landed on Barb's oversized breasts. "She stays until she's ready to go." He reached for her hand, before he made contact, Storm moved to stand between them. The movement was so fast, Stefano stepped back and looked at him again.

"Who are you?" Stefano demanded.

"The man her father hired to make sure she gets on that plane. What she does after that..." Storm shrugged.

"Tell daddy I'm not ready to leave," Barb whined.

"Tell him your damn self," Storm snapped without taking his eyes off Stefano. "You shouldn't be here anyway." Humans were not allowed in dual-natured clubs or homes, this was a clear violation of most Alphas policies.

Stefano straightened. "She came as my guest."

Storm stared at the man, letting him see that he was aware of the lie.

"I would like her to remain, and would make it worth your while to allow it," Stefano said in a sly tone.

Storm didn't care for liars. Or bullies. Or drug dealers. Stefano was all three. "I'm under contract." There was no need to say more.

Stefano held his gaze a few moments longer and then shrugged. "Big mistake," he said softly.

Storm shrugged, turned and ushered the women out the club. The two full-blood guards had stood silently in the background until he reached them. "Rather than go out front, go through the side door, there's more room," Storm.

Surprised they warned him of the pending attack, Storm nodded.

"Can't we stay a little longer?" Barb asked again, obviously drunk or high.

Storm whirled around. "Call your father now," he demanded.

Her cheeks pinked. "I don't have my phone," she lied.

Storm whipped out his and handed it to her. She didn't take it. He dialed her father's number and waited for the man to pick up.

"What's wrong?"

"Your daughter doesn't want to leave and has requested local assistance to help her remain," Storm said, watching Barb. "Talk to her or I will leave her right here." He pushed the phone beneath her nose.

She snatched it, took a deep breath. "Papi?

Storm listened as her father cursed her out and told her to get her ass on the plane. Tears filled her eyes as she begged to stay longer and made all sorts of promises. Fortunately, her father didn't budge and demanded she leave now. She wiped her face before returning the phone.

"We good?" Storm asked her father.

"For what I'm paying, we damn well better be. Spoiled brat," he muttered.

Storm clicked off without responding. The man had himself to blame for his daughter's behavior. If the old man hadn't heard his only daughter had fallen in with a disreputable group known for kidnapping and blackmail, Storm wasn't sure he'd be on this rescue mission. "When we go outside, stay behind me with your back against the wall." He looked at Barb's mulish face. "Your life depends on obeying me. I made that clear to your father. I am not going to search for you if you're taken after disobeying me. Are we clear?"

Vicks pulled out a gun. "Crystal clear. I'll shoot her if she tries to leave."

"What?" Barb yelled.

"He's about to have his hands full because of your childishness. I'm not searching for you either if they kidnap you."

"You're fired," Barb said.

"Too late, I quit. Told your father two days ago. He asked me to stay until he could send someone to get you." The female held the gun so Barb could see. "If you try to run or leave, I promise I'll shoot you." Vicks hard gaze said she meant every word.

Barb swallowed hard. "Let's get this over with so I can be rid of both of you."

Storm opened the door and walked out. Head tilted up, he listened to determine the direction of the attack. A dart whizzed by and embedded into the ground. Storm jumped and missed the next shot. Ruining in a zig-zag pattern he leapt forward and landed on the shooter. After a couple hits in the face, he took the rifle, broke it and tossed it aside.

A shot was fired, followed by screams.

He ran back to the club to see Barb on the ground screaming and holding her arm.

"She tried to run," Vicks said.

Storm shook his head. "Let's go."

"Our car or yours?" Vicks asked as she pushed Barb between them.

Both were probably compromised by now, Storm thought, but they had little choice. "This way."

Inhaling, he separated scents until he located his vehicle. It had been tampered with. He searched for a clean car and headed forward. It was a jeep of some kind.

"I've got this," Vicks pulled out a pouch of tools. Seconds later she opened the door, and started the car. She stepped out so Storm could drive and she sat in the back with Barb.

"Buckle up," Storm said looking in the rear-view mirror before spinning out of the lot.

A car pulled out after them.

Unsurprised, Storm floored the gas and shot off down the street, switching lanes and barely missing pedestrians before he turned onto the highway leading to the private airport.

Would these fools use guns? Or would they attack as wolves? Storm wasn't sure and needed to plan for either. A bullet hit the back of their car answering his question.

The car swerved as the next bullet took out a tire. "I can't believe they plan to do this in the open," Storm murmured as he pulled the car over on the shoulder.

The other car pulled up behind them. Stefano stepped out holding a gun as he strode forward. Storm glanced at a wide-eyed Barbie and then at Vicks. They were about to witness something forbidden for them to see.

He waited until Stefano was close to the car, opened the door and leapt on Stefano. The gun went off.

The momentary burn in his side alerted him that he'd been hit. Storm snatched the rifle and beat Stefano with it, smashing in the full-blood's head. Two others in the car jumped out and ran forward.

Storm tossed Stefano's weapon across the highway, and twisted Stefano's head, breaking his neck before he could heal. He jumped up, avoiding the two men who charged him. They hit each other and spun around.

Storm grabbed one, twisted his neck and grabbed the other before the first one hit the ground and twisted his neck. Without a backward glance, he left the three crumpled on the side of the road as he drove to the airport in silence.

When they reached the airport, Barb jumped out the car, lost the contents of her stomach and then ran to her father's plane.

Vicks shook her head. "At least she waited until you stopped."

Storm shrugged, turned and walked off. He placed his hand on the spot where the bullet entered, it had healed after pushing out the bullet. Just another fucking day at the office, he thought as he strode toward his vehicle to head home.

CHAPTER FIVE

LATER THAT NIGHT, STORM leaned against the shower wall as hot water ran down his body. Out of habit, his hand rubbed the long, jagged welt high on his thigh. His body was riddled with various scars but this one, this one changed his life in ways he couldn't begin to count.

He refused to think about it and finished his shower. Alpha Romano knocked on the door before Storm finished dressing or ate his supper. With a towel wrapped around his waist, he opened the door and stepped back allowing Romano to enter.

"Nice place, very nice," Romano said, looking around the condo Storm used when his work brought him to this country. Romano walked to the windows that overlooked the city. "You have a great view."

Romano hadn't come to discuss Storm's living quarters or the view, they both knew that. "Enjoy the view while I finish dressing." Storm returned to his bedroom and pulled on a pair of jeans and a short-sleeved shirt that stretched across his chest. He slid his feet into a pair of comfortable slippers, ran the comb through his dark, shoulder length hair and returned to his guest to finish their business.

Romano sat on the sofa sipping a beer he'd taken from the refrigerator. "American beer, nice." He held out the can as if Storm didn't recognize his own purchase.

"Yes, it is." Storm sat across from Romano and waited.

Romano wore his blond hair pulled back in a short ponytail. He stood under six feet with a slender build. His smaller stature belied the tenacious fighter beneath. Many challengers discovered Romano was a full-blood with hidden depths and an uncanny ability to zero in on his opponent's weaknesses. Few lived to share the news.

"I hear the package was delivered," Romano said.

Storm hadn't thought of Barb since he left her at the airport earlier that day. "Good. The price has been paid." That rescue was payment of a debt he owed Romano. Storm had no idea what Barb's father paid Romano.

"She was wounded."

Storm shrugged. There was no need to explain, he was sure Romano knew the particulars of the case.

Romano placed the can on the wood and glass coffee table in front of him and leaned forward. "We are good."

Relief flowed through Storm. He hated owing anyone anything, but Romano had been the only person willing to share information on the death of his Alpha. Storm bartered his services to go after those who defiled his deceased Alpha's den. The massacre of the pups and his Alpha's mate, along with his Alpha, ate at Storm until he went mad. For months he heard their screams in his sleep. Even asleep he raced to save them but was too late to help.

Furious, he attacked those he suspected of being involved. It didn't matter if they claimed their innocence, he became judge and executioner. Bounties were placed on his head and he welcomed all challengers, anything to eradicate the pain and the guilt for failing to protect the den.

Alpha Romano had been a close friend of his Alpha and offered to help. Initially, it was a few names here and there. Those individuals never pleaded innocent, but they begged for mercy. He gave them the same mercy they showed his Alpha's pups.

None.

The last name Romano gave him came at a price. A favor for a favor. Storm hadn't complained and thought it fair. He'd found the assassin in Brazil a week ago. The full-blood remained to himself and wasn't easy to take down, which made the final kill all the more satisfying. According to Romano there was only one more.

"There is one more," Romano said slowly, almost hesitant. "This one was not directly involved." Frowning, he paused and then continued. "However, the deed could not have been accomplished without him." He looked at Storm.

"Explain." Storm sat forward.

"Niklas, everything is not in black or white."

Storm held up his hand. "Do not call me that. It is my Alpha's name for me."

Romano's nostrils flared. They stared at each other for several minutes. "Why do you not join my Pack?" Romano asked.

Storm didn't want to go through this again. "I do not want to join another Pack, I've told you this."

"We all need Packs," Romano said.

Storm waved down his comments. "Tell me of this last person involved in the massacre of my Alpha's den."

Romano released a long breath. "Before I tell you his name, we will discuss terms."

Storm's beast grew agitated at the delay. Neither he nor his beast would rest until he avenged his Alpha's den. "What do you want?" he didn't bother hiding the bite in his tone.

Romano's nostrils flared again. For several moments they looked at each other. "Terminate the new Alpha in Honduras."

"No." Storm's answer was immediate and definite. He would never terminate an Alpha, Romano knew that. "What else do you want?"

"Lucian and his litter-mate, Duke, murdered their Tio, Ricardo, who was the Alpha at the time, so he could take his position."

Storm frowned. He hadn't heard of another Alpha's death, but he didn't get involved with packs. "How do you know this is true?"

"Several Alphas from El Salvador and Panama have told me this."

"Why do you care? Is this a job from a client?" Storm asked, watching the man. Romano didn't get involved with much outside his Pack, so there had to be a reason for wanting this Alpha dead.

"He killed his Alpha, his Tio, that should be enough."

"In Honduras?" Storm allowed his skepticism to bleed through. "You care about what's happening there?"

Romano eyed him for a few seconds. "If he killed his uncle I want to know. If it is true, I want him terminated. Is that better?"

Storm didn't like the idea of terminating Alphas, it left a vacuum in the Pack, which harmed many. Besides, this last person Romano would give him wouldn't be worth the fall-out of taking on an Alpha.

"I won't terminate him." Storm stretched his long legs wishing this conversation was over. He had others searching for anyone related to his Alpha's death and needed to speak with a contact who left a message earlier.

"I will send someone else." Romano stared at the floor for several moments. "There is a package in Mexico I need retrieved and brought to me when you finish in the States."

"States?" Storm had no plans to travel to America.

"Yes. That's where this last full-blood lives." Romano's lip curled. "He lives in a Compound in West Virginia. A scientist, one of the best in the world. He invented the poison administered to your Alpha."

Storm sat forward. "How do you know this?" He'd long suspected Romano was involved or knew who crafted the plot to wipe out his Alpha's line but couldn't prove it. The man knew entirely too much about what happened that day.

"Liege."

Storm stiffened but remained silent.

"He worked in their laboratories for decades, creating devices to enslave us. From what I hear, he did it willfully, stood by and watched as others were used as tests for those bastards. Ask around, his name and what he did is well-known."

"And he created the poison that incapacitated… Alpha?" Before his Alpha was torn apart, he'd been drugged, a coward's way of battle. Storm's Alpha had called him through their link, asking him to save his pups, telling him about the poison and their location. Storm had been too late to save any of them.

"Yes, it was his formula or a variation of it. But he was the originator, I'm certain. Ask his Alpha if you doubt me," Romano said with disdain. "Hawke is a traitor to every full-blood that walks this earth and should have been eliminated."

"Why wasn't he?" Everyone had heard of La Patron. The Alpha wasn't stupid and didn't put up with fools.

Romano shrugged. "He mated with one of La Patron's soldiers."

That made no difference in Storm's opinion. "So?"

"I do not know the answer to that question. You can ask yourself."

"Hawke lives with La Patron?" He wanted to be sure.

"Yes, I have said this already," Romano snapped.

Storm stood and looked down at the Alpha. He would not be disrespected in his own home.

Romano waved his hand. "Many apologies. It's this whole thing. Alphas being attacked, replaced. There's no honor anymore." He looked up at Storm who remained standing.

"Hawke is a skilled fighter; you may not win the challenge."

"I pledged my life to protect my Alpha's den, his mate and pups," Storm said, wondering where Romano was going with all of this.

Romano sighed and shook his head. "I know. It's just...things are changing. Our way of life, how we live as packs, it seems to be slipping away. There is little respect or honor these days." He stood and met Storm's gaze. "I understand you will do as you feel you must. No matter how many times I have told you not to feel guilty, I know it burdens you that you were too late to save them. If Adolfo were here, he would tell you the same himself."

Storm tensed at hearing his deceased Alpha's name but said nothing.

Romano released a long sigh. "I will contact La Patron on your behalf; alert him of your intent to challenge Hawke so that you can cross into their territory."

Storm frowned.

"The States has a hierarchy and a set of protocols that must be followed. La Patron's Pack is the largest in the world; do not test him by entering his lands without permission. Your petition is honest and if handled correctly, it will be acknowledged."

Storm knew each state had an Alpha and that they were well organized, but he hadn't realized he would need to meet La Patron to destroy Hawke.

"Do you understand what I'm telling you?" Romano stressed.

"I appreciate your assistance, once La Patron agrees to allow me to enter his territory I will leave from here."

Romano nodded slowly. "Good. I will contact him in the morning and let you know what he says. Once the challenge is met, fly to Mexico. I will give you instructions once you're there."

Storm nodded.

"What will you do when you finish?"

Storm's brow rose.

"After you've destroyed everyone involved with Adolfo's death, will you start living again? What are your plans?"

"I'll let you know when I know," Storm said as he walked toward the door to let Romano out.

"I'll see you after Mexico," Romano said as he left.

ROMANO LEFT STORM'S condo with a heavy heart. Over the past year he had grown fond of the half-breed. Things had changed and didn't seem to be getting better. Every man had to wrestle with his own conscience, do what was best for him and his den. Downstairs, his beta, Cris, opened the outer door and followed Romano outside toward the waiting car.

Inside, Cris handed Romano a case filled with cigars and waited. Romano collected his thoughts as the car pulled onto the road.

"He is going after Hawke."

Cris shook his head. "Fool. He'll be killed. If not by Hawke, then by his mate, Asia."

"I didn't tell him Asia was Hawke's mate." Romano looked out the window but saw his Beta's surprised expression in the glass. "He would go after Hawke regardless, so I didn't say. They don't know each other."

"No, but we've all heard of Asia," Cris said.

"If he survives, he will go to Mexico. They want him."

"Pity he wouldn't join us," Cris said sounding disappointed.

Romano wished a thousand times Storm would join his Pack, it would have made things much easier. "Agreed. But he's too dangerous to be free. How much is the bounty on his head now?" He looked at Cris.

"Twenty-five million. I'm surprised the humans haven't joined the search. That kind of money would set them up for life," Romano said.

"Several lifetimes."

Romano nodded. It would also help thousands of Pack members in Brazil. "I offered to call La Patron, explain what's going to happen."

Cris nodded.

"Hand me the phone." Romano extended his hand. Cris gave him a throw away cell they purchased for this deal. "You have the number?"

"It's programmed into that phone."

"Si, I see it." Romano removed the cigar and placed the call. He spoke to two people before someone named Jacques came on the line. Romano explained the purpose of his call and that he'd like to speak to La Patron. Jacques said he'd deliver the message and someone would get back with him.

Satisfied, he'd stirred the pot, Romano turned to business. "When is the next shipment coming in?"

An hour later, Romano sat at his desk sipping bourbon when the call from La Patron came through.

"Hello?"

"Alpha Romano, this is Silas Knight, you called earlier with a request for one of your Pack members?"

Romano's heart raced. He never thought he'd speak to La Patron. "No, Sir. Niklas Storm, that's his name. His Alpha, Adolfo was a good friend of mine. Unfortunately, through foul play, Adolfo, his mate and his pups were murdered several months ago. Storm has tracked down every person connected to the massacre and destroyed them."

"Hawke has been here, he had nothing to do with Alpha Adolfo's death," La Patron said.

"Si. I know. However, he created the poison that was used to paralyze the Alpha who watched his den destroyed before he himself was ripped apart." It still pained him to repeat what happened that fateful night.

Neither spoke for several moments. Romano's respect for La Patron rose when the man didn't deny Hawke created the fatal brew.

"I will speak with Niklas Storm."

Romano hadn't expected that. "He's not here. I have a number that he collects his calls from. You'll have to leave a message, he'll call you back."

"There's no direct way to contact him?"

"No. When I need to speak to him I leave a message. He's aware I'm speaking to you on this matter and is waiting for permission to come to America for a formal challenge."

La Patron swore.

"If I may share something with you." Romano waited.

"Go ahead."

"Do not be fooled by his appearance. There are many full-bloods much larger in human form, when Storm shifts, I have not seen any bigger than him.

He is the fastest wolf I've ever seen and has survived many assassination attempts. Even now there is a huge bounty on his head. There are not many in this world as good as him. Do not take him lightly."

"Is that a threat?"

"No, Sir. You have no idea of what he can do. He has no fear of Hawke or Asia or anyone who was involved with the death of his dear Alpha. Guilt rides him hard. He was too late to save them. He will not stop until he believes justice has been done."

"I see," La Patron said. "Are you acquainted with Alpha Lucian in Honduras?"

"Hell no. I want nothing to do with that murdering bastard." Romano wasn't sure if this was a trick or if La Patron was serious. Either way he intended to make his feelings about the despicable man, known.

"Why call him that?"

"He killed his Alpha, his Tio, for that position. He is beneath my contempt."

La Patron released a long sigh. "He did not kill his uncle. I knew Ricardo and oversaw the Alpha challenge in Honduras. Lucian had nothing to do with his uncle's death."

Romano sat back in his seat, mouth agape. "You were in Honduras? How long?" Why had no one told him La Patron was that close.

"Long enough for an Alpha challenge. Ricardo was murdered during the challenge but not by Lucian. I was with Lucian at the time Ricardo died. I trust you will pass this correct information to those in error of the truth."

"Si. Yes of course. I'm very glad you've told me this, I did not know. Did you discover who killed Alpha Ricardo?" Romano asked.

"I handled the person who ordered the deed, the Pack eliminated two more. We are searching for the remaining three who escaped to nearby countries. Bounties are on their heads as well."

"Si. Gracia's for explaining. I will pass it all along. Although..." he paused, weighing his words. "Storm could find them quickly if he was motivated. No one tracks as well as he."

"Storm?"

"Yes, he is very good, reliable if he agrees to the task. You may want to mention it to him when you talk," Romano said. "Please tell him I suggested it. I passed on bad information to him regarding the Honduran Alpha."

Silence met his comments. "Is Storm going to attack Lucian?"

"No. He wouldn't do that, not after what happened to his Alpha. He is an odd one, but not a fool. His code of ethics are... well you judge after speaking with him." Romano grew tired of the conversation. Soon, Storm would be on another continent, someone else's problem.

"Question."

"Si?"

"If I tell Storm he cannot come to the States, that I refuse the challenge, what will he do?"

"He will come to the States and seek a way to administer the challenge or kill Hawke."

CHAPTER SIX

"WHAT DO YOU MEAN HAWKE has been challenged?" Jasmine asked Silas. He took her hand, pulled her into their bedroom and closed the door. Inside, he looked into the light brown eyes of his mate, read her worry and squeezed her hand. He would need to tread carefully with this.

"An Alpha, Adolfo I believe his name is, was murdered a few months ago. They used the poison Hawke created for the blue birds. It paralyzes its victims. Angus was infected, it took me a while to push it out, so he could function."

"I know that, Silas." Jasmine crossed her arms over her chest. "It happened years ago. Why is this person coming after Hawke now? Better yet, why are you considering it? We have a lot going on right now with the military, Canada and Mexico; this isn't the time to have Hawke distracted."

"Time makes no difference, Jasmine. Hawke admits he created the poison. The challenge is based on that premise alone. If the Alpha hadn't been poisoned, he could've protected his mate and pups who were slaughtered in front of him."

She opened her mouth and then closed it. "They killed his pups?"

"Yes. I suspect that is the driving force to destroy anyone involved with the murder. From what I understand, Storm has traveled three continents taking revenge."

Jasmine frowned. "Storm?"

"His name is Niklas Storm. He prefers Storm."

She looked at him for a few seconds. "Why is this challenge bothering you? Hawke is one of our best fighters. He's linked to your Sword, Asia. You don't think Hawke will lose, do you?"

Silas sat on the bed with his elbows on his thigh. "Something about this disturbs me. I spoke with Storm. He's no braggart, he stated his case simply and his desire to terminate Hawke for what he did."

"What?" Jasmine moved to stand in front of him. "Did you say terminate?"

Silas nodded. Being human, his mate would never accept or understand fully their brutal, bloody manner of solving problems. Storm reminded Silas he was within his right to call out Hawke for past crimes against full-bloods. It didn't matter one bit that Hawke had been a victim, forced by a computer chip in his brain to go along with the Liege. If his mate hadn't found and released him, Hawke would probably be a prisoner today.

"Not terminate, Silas. No. No. No."

He sighed, took her hand and pulled her down next to him.

"I mean it Silas. I don't want to hear any death talk."

"When the bomb went off and I died, Angus told me every last one of my pups demanded he terminate the bastards."

Jasmine jumped up, pointed her finger at him. "Don't you dare bring that into this conversation. That was different, and you know it."

"I'm an Alpha. If what happened to his Alpha, and we verified it did happen, if it happened to me or Cameron or any of my Alpha's, we'd all challenge the individuals involved."

"Is Angus going to challenge the inventor of the explosives used to kill you? Is that what you're saying? Because that's the equivalent—"

"No, it's not. That explosive wasn't created to hurt or destroy full-bloods."

Her mouth opened, and she shook her head. "I can't believe we're having this discussion. Hawke and Asia are our friends. Loyal and trustworthy. Why are you allowing this?"

"You think Hawke will be killed?" Silas asked watching her intently.

"No. But you think there's a chance he could lose. That bothers me."

He nodded.

"Asia will help him if he's losing."

"Storm's aware Hawke's mated, although he was surprised to discover it was Asia. He's heard of her."

Jasmine snorted.

"She hasn't heard of him. But the Liege never sent her to certain parts of South America. In fact, they forbid her to travel anywhere near where Storm lived for decades."

Jasmine frowned. "Oh."

"Like I said, there is something about this. I have this gut feeling I have to let it play out. Even when I tried to say no to the challenge, my wolf balked."

Their gazes met.

"Have you discussed it with the Goddess?" Jasmine asked, retaking her seat next to him and taking his hand in hers.

"No. I've asked for an audience." He shrugged. "Honestly, I don't know what to do. I agreed to the fight but not to the death. I explained there was too much unrest and I needed Hawke's services. If the fight wasn't enough to satisfy him, I offered to stand in Hawke's place."

Jasmine gasped.

"He didn't accept either. Storm wants Hawke in the same condition the poison left his Alpha. Problem is, if it were anyone other than Hawke, I'd probably agree with him."

"But it is Hawke. And Asia. I'm linked to her. If anything happens to her, I'll be fighting to save them both. I refuse to ever feel her die again, Silas. I can't do it. Don't ask me not to interfere, like it or not, Asia and I are linked. In good and bad times."

Silas cursed. He'd forgotten his mate and Asia's connection. Would Jasmine be pulled under if anything happened to Asia? Would she feel Asia's pain? He wouldn't allow Jasmine to die or suffer with Asia, not now, not ever.

"Thank you for reminding me of that. I'll be sure to tell Asia and Hawke."

"No, Silas. That may handicap them if she's worried about me." She placed her finger beneath his chin and turned his face to hers. "Promise me you won't mention it to them."

"Jasmine."

"This is important to me. Promise me, Silas."

"I promise. Just know, as your mate, I will break that connection between you and her if you're in danger."

She nodded and then smiled. "No way can anyone win against Asia and Hawke."

"I believe you're right, which is another reason I don't want this fight to end in death. The loyalty Storm shows his deceased Alpha is admirable. We need more Pack members like him in the world."

Jasmine snorted.

Silas chuckled at the stubborn tilt of her head. "I would hope my Alphas would be as tenacious as he is in seeking justice for me should anything happen."

She glared at him. "Don't say that. I'm tired of almost losing you. I don't like it."

His hand tightened on hers when she pulled away. "Jasmine, I know our ways are violent to you."

"Not all, just some," she said leaning on his shoulder.

"We are beasts and men. Our animals see things in black and white, there's very little gray. The connected dots lead to Hawke. Hawke and Asia understand. He's surprised it's taken someone this long to seek retribution."

She moved to look at him. "This can happen again?"

"No. This challenge will be for Hawke's service in the Liege. I made that clear to Hawke and Storm."

"Storm agreed?"

"Yes. I don't think he cares about anything else Hawke's done. At the appropriate time I will make a declaration so everyone knows not to challenge Hawke over the time spent with the Liege."

She nodded and leaned against his shoulder again. "Good. I wish you were confident Hawke and Asia would win. It'd make me feel a lot better."

He rubbed her arm. "Me too. Storm's agreed to track down the three full-bloods who killed Alpha Ricardo and give Lucian their heads."

"Eww."

Silas chuckled. She really didn't understand how powerful that gesture was. Storm hadn't hesitated when Silas mentioned it. He seemed just as confident in his ability to find the traitors as Romano had been.

"It's been months, and no one has claimed the bounty. Alpha Romano believes Storm will find them. In exchange, I'll fly Storm over and put him up wherever he chooses. Not here in the Compound, of course, but in the hotel in town or a condo since the challenge will be here in the gym."

"That's a deal? He's poor or something?"

"No, I doubt it. He's older than Asia I think. To survive this long he's probably got cash reserves somewhere."

"So, what's the big deal with flying him here? He can get to town by commercial jet and find his own hotel."

"I'm the big deal. La Patron is flying him in for the challenge and offering him lodgings. Optics, Sweet Bitch. It looks good." He leaned down and kissed her on the cheek.

CHAPTER SEVEN

STORM HEFTED THE BAG on his shoulder and walked along the path toward the large house built into the mountainside. He gave the Alpha points for the clever location. No surprise attacks, not even by air. From the distance, the place looked huge, like a mansion. Romano's Pack house wasn't this big.

With steady movements Storm climbed, aware several pairs of eyes watched. He wondered if they were preparing his welcome or if the scent from the bloody bag kept them at bay.

The conversation with La Patron two days ago surprised him. Not that he had any preconceived ideas what the man sounded like or how he would respond to the challenge. But the man listened, asked questions, provided information. In short, he treated Storm's challenge respectfully. The idea of flying on La Patron's plane to terminate Hawke held a certain appeal. It had galvanized Storm into searching for the three, traitorous mongrels guilty of killing their Alpha.

New scars, bullet and a knife wound, littered his body, courtesy of those three, but he took their heads. That made them even. He stopped before the full-blood reached him.

"Who are you? What do you want?" A young full-blood asked.

"I have the heads of the traitors you were seeking." Storm held the bag out for them to take.

The full-blood waved to the men behind him while he watched Storm. One of the men took the bag and opened it.

"Let us all see," the full-blood demanded.

Three heads rolled on the ground with varying expressions on their faces.

"You pulled their heads off?"

Storm shrugged. "Don't have a sword, seemed the easiest thing to do at the time."

The full-blood stared at him for a few moments. "If you can wait a few moments, Alpha Duke is coming to verify the bodies. We've had a lot of hunters show up."

Storm looked at his watch. He'd notified La Patron last night he would be dropping off the heads today and would be ready for transport. The plane would be at the airport in four hours.

"Sure."

"Your name?"

"Storm."

"I'm Solo." He shook his head. "Alpha Solo, it's a new position I won in the Alpha challenge a few months back."

"Congratulations," Storm said looking at the slender Alpha.

"Thanks. If these are the right ones, we really appreciate it. Alpha Lucian hated not being able to go after them, but the Goddess had other things for him to do." Solo stood taller when mentioning the Goddess and his Alpha.

Storm nodded. He didn't have a relationship with the Goddess, wasn't sure he believed the hype, but just in case She was real he wanted to stay off her radar.

"Who's your Alpha?"

"Alpha Adolfo," Storm said without thinking.

Solo frowned. "I don't know him."

"South America." Storm hoped that would stop the questions but doubted it. Solo was probably told to chat him up, and get as much information as he could before the Alpha arrived. Alpha Adolfo had used that tactic many times.

"Columbia?"

"No. A small Pack on the outskirts of the Amazon." He wouldn't say more.

Solo whistled. "The Amazon? How did you know about these three?" Solo pointed to the bag of heads.

"La Patron told me." Storm hadn't wanted to mention the American Alpha, but it might expedite things. La Patron wanted verification of the bounty conditions being met before the flight.

Solo's entire countenance changed. He smiled, stood straighter and seemed friendlier. "La Patron sent you?"

Storm frowned at the hopeful note. "No. He told me about these three traitors. Asked me to find them."

Solo frowned. "When did you speak to him?"

"Two days ago."

"You left South America and found them in less than two days?"

Storm nodded and noticed a heavier, full-blood walking toward them. Using La Patron's name had them moving their asses.

"Hello, I'm Duke. Are the heads in the bag?"

"I had them replaced in the bag," Solo said as he emptied the contents on the ground.

Duke kneeled down and looked at each one. "Crank, Gianni, and Marco. He got the fuckers." He looked up at Storm. "Many thanks, my friend."

Storm glanced at Duke and looked at Solo. "Can you let La Patron know you've verified them?" He needed to buy a few things from the shops before heading to the airport and didn't want to waste any time.

"Si. I will as soon as I return to the house I'll use a phone to communicate so you can hear me." Duke stood. "It's true, he sent you?"

"He told me about them, asked me to find them." Storm didn't want anyone to get the wrong idea about his relationship with La Patron. They weren't friends and probably never would be after he killed Hawke and his mate.

"I understand. He and my Tio Ricky were close. Come with me, I'll give you the reward and contact La Patron."

"Keep the reward for your Pack, they suffered the loss because of those three. Build something in his name." Storm didn't want more blood money; he had enough of his own.

Duke stared at him for several moments and then nodded. "Si. If you say so, I will tell Lucian and he will decide how best to use it. He is not here at the moment otherwise he would thank you himself." They entered the shaded veranda before stepping into a large room with sofas, chairs and tables. Duke called for someone to bring him a phone. Moments later he made the call to La Patron. His gaze lit on Storm a few times during his conversation. When he disconnected he looked at Storm.

"Do you have transportation to the airport?"

"Yes. My vehicle is nearby. I didn't want to drive it up the mountain, it was faster to walk." Storm turned to leave.

"We may see you in the States," Duke said before he reached the door. Solo sat on one of the sofas, watching.

Storm nodded. “Bueno.”

He didn’t care one way or the other and was ready to leave now that La Patron had been notified. His contacts hadn’t come up with any new information, but it didn’t matter since Hawke was the last one. After defeating Hawke, his vendetta would be complete.

Once Storm exited the house, he jumped over the banister and ran toward his car. The challenged was scheduled two days from now. He could’ve waited here, but it’d be interesting to see what La Patron had done in America.

CHAPTER EIGHT

RENEE STEPPED BACK from the canvas and looked at the painting she'd just finished. She tilted her head to the side, eying the shadows and highlights to determine where to adjust. Her siblings had been concerned, she had abandoned art. To do that would be like destroying her beast. Art was an integral part of who she was. She couldn't walk away from it.

Staring at the canvas, she realized things had changed. Her work looked edgy, with a dystopian feel. Lots of gray, black and brown. Violent in an abstract way. She'd been working on this for a few days and couldn't shake the direction it had been going.

From a craft perspective, it was some of her best work. The colors, shading, everything blended and worked well. Theme wise, she had no idea what to call it. "Redemption?" she murmured. "No. Insanity?" she chuckled imagining how Mama would react to that title.

Stretching, she walked to the sink to clean her brushes and put away her supplies for the night. Tomorrow she had back to back meetings at the museum and needed to be on time.

"*Renee?*" her sister Jackie called through their link.

Renee smiled. They hadn't talked in a couple days. *"Hey, what's going on?"* Jackie and her mate, Quinn were overseeing the construction of two medical facilities in Honduras.

"Nothing much, just got in from the mountains. It's really beautiful here. The waterfall is spectacular."

Renee's heart dropped. *"You're canceling on the Art show? Is that it?"*

"Not at all. We're flying over with Lucian and Duke. Pity Raven, that's their sister, can't come, she's in Texas training to work as a teacher and administrator to run the school. Ten of them are there but Lucian wants her in charge. It's perfect for her, she's a nurturer."

"Uh huh." Renee placed the cleaned bowls aside to dry.

Jackie laughed. *"I hear your excitement, what are you doing?"*

Renee told her.

"How's the art show planning coming along? I ordered a new gown, should be there by the time we arrive."

"A few hiccups, nothing major. Crystal and Edmund are working overtime to make sure everything's in place." After insuring her brushes were clean, she stored them in their compartment drawers and locked it.

"There's a rumor you stepped back and are actually allowing your staff to earn their salaries. Tell me it's not true," Jackie mocked.

"I hadn't thought about it in those terms, but I guess it's true."

"What terms did you think about it, then? It's not like you to do things without thinking it through," Jackie said.

"I wanted time off to paint, to clear my head, I guess. They wanted to do it, so things worked out. I still make the final decisions, but I don't have to do the heavy lifting anymore. They can do it." She stretched again and forced back a yawn.

"Yeah, that attitude right there. That's why folks are concerned. You don't hand over the museum to others, especially with a big art show in a few days. Renee doesn't do stuff like that," Jackie said, her voice changing to concern. "*What's going on? Is it the thing with Daddy?"*

Renee looked at her painting. It was violent and desolate and kick ass and life and death, all those things called to her. *"I don't know, I don't think so. I've made peace with the knowledge my Daddy can die. That we can all die. It's not something I ever thought of before; it never touched me until then."* Drawn to the canvas she moved forward and stared at it. "*Something inside changed, I don't know how to explain it.*"

"You don't sound the same."

"I'm not the same. I think my eyes are open for the first time. You changed first. I'm just late to the party."

"Some party. Cain and Abel fight every day to keep the construction on schedule, to do that they have to guard every scrap of building material from the Pack members the clinics will help. We store medical equipment in vaults to keep them safe from vandals. In the States, we have problems, but not like this. The level of poverty and illiteracy is worse than anything I've ever seen. It will take decades to

pull this Pack to a decent standard of living, and that's only if they work together. I'm not sure they can do that."

"*Uh huh.*" Renee turned off the lights in her studio and headed to her bedroom around the corner.

"Okay, okay. Enough of that. What are you wearing to the ball?" Jackie asked.

"My silver gown."

"What?"

"The silver gown I bought last year. I've never worn it."

"You didn't get all new stuff?"

"Didn't need it."

"When has that stopped you before?" Jackie asked.

"I decided on that gown before Daddy went to Honduras. I'm not falling apart. Just growing up." She stepped into her bedroom and started stripping.

"Hmm. You were more advanced than the rest of us. It's only with Daddy you had a blind spot and it colored a lot of other things. I don't want to lose the old Renee. Please don't change too much," Jackie said.

"*Promise,*" Renee said as she walked toward the shower. "*What are you wearing? Sorry, you ordered a new dress.*" She paused as she stepped beneath the spray. "*And you didn't consult me. Who's changing now*?"

"Excuse me, I tried to talk to you about it at least three times. You promised to look at the ones I sent you. They're probably buried under your emails. Quinn picked one."

Renee groaned.

Jackie laughed. "*A purple number that shows a lot of tits and ass.*"

Renee laughed. "*Goddess no. Tell me you're kidding?*"

"Nope, won't say either way. Be prepared to be amazed when we step through the door."

"Amazed I can handle," Renee said.

"I want you to meet Lucian. And Duke," Jackie added. "*Nice guys. Single. Alphas. Strong. Loyal.*"

"Sounds like you're doing a commercial or something," Renee said.

Jackie snorted. "*Lucian is fine. The kind of guy you normally go after.*"

"No thanks."

"What? You haven't met him. He's gorgeous."

"Honduran Alpha? No thanks."

"Because of the distance? The poor country? Or his Alpha status?" Jackie asked after a brief silence.

"I'll take all three," Renee said as she stepped out and dried off. "*I want someone who appreciates art, and sees beauty in the world. Not someone who has to fight all the time to whip a country into shape. Someone who sees fighting as a last resort."*

"A diplomat? Like Papa Jacques?"

Renee smiled thinking of Nana's mate and her father's oldest friend. *"Yes, exactly."*

"Love him, I see the appeal. Quinn can be like that at times." Jackie said. *"Still I think you should meet Lucian, he's delicious looking and level-headed and all about Pack. It won't hurt to talk."*

Jackie had a point. "*I'm sure I'll meet him when he comes, we'll see what happens.*" Renee wouldn't commit to anything else.

"*Perfect,*" Jackie said. "*I'm headed back to the clinic, see you soon.*"

CHAPTER NINE

THE MORNING OF THE challenge, Angus met Storm in the lobby of the hotel. Silas had sent his brother to bring Storm to the gym in the Compound. Few people were aware of the challenge and Silas wanted to keep it that way. Angus removed his sunglasses and extended his hand to Storm who stood in the middle of the lobby dressed in black pants and a long sleeved collarless shirt. He held a small bag in his right hand and took Angus' hand with his left.

"I'm Angus, Beta and litter-mate to La Patron as well as your escort into the Compound."

Storm released Angus hand and nodded. "Nice to meet you, Angus. I'm Storm. Niklas Storm." He paused. "I understand this is difficult for your Alpha, he's made it clear Hawke is a valued Pack member who was a victim in all of this."

Angus nodded.

"I pledged my life to protect my Alpha's pups and his den. If he hadn't been shot with the poison Hawke created, he could've fought his attackers and saved his den. Instead, there is nothing left of my Alpha's line. As his Beta, and one pledged to protect his den, I must avenge this wrong."

Before Alpha Adolfo found him, Storm had been more beast than man, each day he struggled not to return to that state. When Alpha Adolfo died, he took a huge part of Storm's future with him. Each day it became harder and harder to recall Alpha's teachings on justice, humility, and fairness.

Angus nodded. "A long time ago, I lost my Alpha as well. I understand what you're saying. I just don't think Hawke should be prosecuted for doing something he had no control over. If you knew about the Liege you'd know they used all kinds of shit that stripped our people of their will. Cameras embedded in their eyes, chips in their brains, steel in their legs and arms, serums that changed their bodies… I could go on and on. Hawke was taken as a pup and raised in their labs. Believe me he had no choice."

Storm heard the truth of his words. "And his mate? She was a victim of the Liege?"

Angus nodded. "La Patron explained you may be fighting them both?"

"Si. It doesn't matter. I must avenge my Alpha, if it costs my life, so be it."

Angus turned. "This way." He walked out the door.

Storm followed.

Neither spoke during the drive to the Compound. Angus' comments regarding the Liege remained in the forefront of Storm's mind. He knew firsthand how bad those old men were and had a scar on his thigh to prove it. As a pup, Hawke wouldn't have had a chance of surviving if he rebelled. They would've killed him as they had others.

Chips in the brains? Eye cameras? Those evil bastards had evolved since Storm escaped their domain. He rubbed the raised welt on his thigh, a reminder of his time with the Liege.

What would Alpha say? His Alpha would agree with Angus and La Patron. Hawke was a victim of the Liege, just as Storm had been. Had his Alpha not found him in the Amazon jungle dying from the Liege's botched surgery, he would be dead. But Alpha was not here to offer words of wisdom, and for that Hawke would pay a price.

After going through a series of security protocols, Storm walked into a large three-story gymnasium with Angus. Five men, and two women stood in the middle of the floor, watching them approach.

"Hello Storm, I'm Silas Knight, La Patron." He extended his hand, they shook. La Patron turned to a beautiful woman standing beside him. "My mate, Jasmine."

Storm nodded. "Ma'am."

"Hello," she said her tone cool.

"Hawke and his mate Asia." He pointed to a man standing over six and a half feet and another beautiful woman, this one with an athletic build.

Storm nodded. He and Hawke sized each other briefly.

"My sons, Tyrese and Tyrone." They nodded but didn't speak.

"My Administrator, Jacques. He spoke with Alpha Romano the other day."

"Hello," Jacques said.

"Hello," Storm said and then looked at La Patron for further instructions.

"Everyone in this room is aware of your challenge to Hawke, so I will not go into the details again. On behalf of our Pack, we sympathize with the death of your Alpha and his den."

The heartfelt condolence surprised Storm and made him think better of La Patron. "Thank you."

"Security is in place outside to prevent anyone from entering, I don't want this challenge to be public knowledge."

Storm nodded. He didn't care what La Patron's reasons were.

"The challenge will last one hour and no longer."

That hadn't been agreed on before. Storm didn't think it would take longer than an hour, but he'd be fighting two seasoned warriors. It had been a while since he'd faced a real challenge.

"Shifting will be allowed, just do not tear up my gym."

Hawke smiled and nodded.

Storm looked around. Most things had been removed and the floor was clear. He appreciated the high ceilings.

"Storm, are you ready?" La Patron asked.

"Is there a place I can put my bag?" he asked.

"Yes. Anywhere you'd like. No one will touch it," La Patron said.

Storm nodded, turned and walked a few feet away. Opening his bag, he pulled out a black tee shirt, pulled off his dress shirt and changed. He took off his dress shoes, stuffed his clothes in the bag and left it on the floor.

"I'm ready," Storm said walking toward Hawke.

La Patron, his mate and the others had moved to the second-floor balcony, leaving Hawke and Storm on the first floor.

For several seconds, neither man moved. Storm inhaled, called his beast and flew forward, extending his claws as he did. He ran around Hawke so fast, slicing and cutting him with razor sharp claws.

Hawke bulked to his two-footed beast and lashed out at him.

Storm jumped high in the air, flipped twice coming down behind Hawke so fast, slicing him across his arm and back before he could turn. Storm moved out of range as Hawke swung and missed. Ducking beneath Hawke's arm, Storm used his claws, drawing more blood. He flipped high.

Hawke jumped high, swinging.

Storm pulled up his legs, missing Hawke's fist. They both landed hard. Storm jumped and kicked Hawke beneath the chin, sending him sliding across the gym floor. Before Hawke could stand or shake it off, Storm was on him, delivering powerful blow after blow to his face.

Sensing Asia, Storm jumped and did a back flip over her and landed a few feet behind her. She jumped toward him, but missed and slid across the floor.

Hawke slammed into Storm's back, hitting him in the head several times.

Storm jumped forward and then backward as if being shot from a cannon and hit Hawke so hard, he flew into the wall making an impression in the concrete. Storm ran forward, grabbed Hawke's arm and threw him toward Asia who was running toward them.

She tried to grab Hawke, but his momentum took her and they both hit the opposite wall.

Storm shifted into his two-footed beast and ignored the surprised gasped as he stalked toward Hawke and Asia who were standing slowly. Asia walked in one direction and shifted. Hawke, walked the other.

Storm inhaled and closed his eyes. It had been a long time since he allowed his beast free reign. Do not kill them, he instructed his beast as he waited for one of them to attack.

Asia leapt forward, kicking him in the side, sending him back a couple feet. Hawke's similar attack from the other side came seconds later. Then his beast flew forward, with blurring speed, making him hard to track as he attacked Hawke.

Asia tried to draw his beast's attention, but he would not be denied the opportunity to kick Hawke's ass, and tossed her aside time after time.

"Stop."

Storm's beast obeyed the command immediately. He stepped away from Hawke and morphed to human while looking up toward La Patron, ready to argue over his interference.

"Enough," a deep, booming voice from behind him called out. The authority in the voice grabbed Storm's beast and held him fast.

Storm turned and watched as an old man, with long white hair move toward him. Something about the full-blood looked familiar but Storm couldn't place him.

"You stopped my beast?" How could this stranger do that? Why had he interfered?

"Yes. You made your point. This challenge is over." The old man waved his hand dismissively.

"What? No! Who the fuck are you?" Storm moved to stand in front of the man, prepared to fight in his human form. La Patron and the others came down, and dealt with Hawke and his mate.

"I'm called many things. Black Wolf, Grandfather, and other names not very complimentary." Grandfather looked at Hawke and Asia who were sitting against the wall, healing. "Are you alright?"

La Patron and his mate walked to Storm. "What the hell are you?" La Patron asked.

Storm frowned at them.

"We watched, tried to watch more like it. You were like a hazy ball of blackness moving so fast we couldn't keep up. None of us are that fast."

"My beast is fast," Storm said growing uncomfortable with the discussion. He rarely unleashed his beast to battle because of how deadly he became with it. Alpha Adolfo had encouraged him to embrace that part of himself, he had been working on it for decades, but disliked the destruction his beast left behind.

"Again, what kind of beast?" La Patron stressed.

Storm shifted into his wolf and met La Patron's stunned gaze. He morphed to human.

"A black wolf, but that's not what attacked Hawke," La Patron said.

The others gathered around loosely watching Storm. "Where's my bag?" he asked to break the silence.

"Where you left it," Angus said.

Storm turned and walked off.

"Who is he?" La Patron asked again. Storm looked over his shoulder and met the old man's gaze.

"Grandson of the Black Wolf Alpha."

Storm stopped and then picked up his bag. He'd change at the hotel.

"Wait, that story is real?" Jasmine asked.

"Yes, it is." The old man walked to Hawke and placed his hand on his shoulder. "You're a fine warrior, never doubt it. There are few who could win against one like him."

"One like him?" La Patron asked, staring at Storm. "What do you mean?"

Grandfather turned and met Storm's gaze. "Do you have any memory of your beginnings?"

Storm didn't respond. His memories were fuzzy before the Liege and he hated thinking about those days.

"Black wolf impregnated many humans. With Storm, he lay with a human breeder, she bore a litter of two. One died, the other she tossed aside into the woods."

Storm's eyes widened. He had no memory of any of that.

"The babe was found by a servant who took him to her Mistress. He remained there for ten summers until her niece fell in love with him. The Mistress released him, he wandered a bit until pressed onto a ship that traveled the world robbing and pillaging."

Grandfather took two steps toward Storm and stopped. "The first ship you were on capsized, most of the crew was lost but you survived and were picked up by another ship. You remained with that captain for 22 years until he died. You had just left his funeral when you met Roderick at a pub. He took you to his home and kept you prisoner for years."

Storm's fist curled into a ball as he remembered Roderick. The man had seemed nice, and caring of Storm's misery. He invited Storm to sleep off his drink at his place and leave on his ship tomorrow. Storm woke chained to a bed, drugged while being poked and prodded repeatedly. He hadn't understood what was happening until he overheard Roderick and his friends call him a specimen.

"They operated on you, just like Asia and Hawke, only they lacked skill and understanding in the beginning. Bones didn't mesh with metal, their tools weren't as sharp as they needed, and they used the wrong metals," Grandfather continued.

A low growl rose from Storm's throat.

Grandfather raised his hand. "Adolfo, a kind, wonderful friend. He waited for you."

"What?" Storm hadn't expected that.

"We could not allow them to keep you. If they ever discovered who you were..." Grandfather shook his head. "We sent him to get you, to help you heal and grow."

"Who's we?" Storm asked, growing more confused.

"He took you to South America, near the Amazon. The Liege looked for you, but everyone they sent never returned. You destroyed them all," Grandfather said.

"Did you know Alpha was going to be murdered?" Storm asked taking a step forward.

"No, I did not know. The Goddess shares some things with me, not all."

"The Goddess?" Storm frowned. Why mention Her? He had no dealings with the deity.

"She is not pleased with the way things are unfolding." He looked at La Patron. "We have a problem."

Storm turned to leave.

"Wait, I need to speak with you as well. It's imperative that we talk," Grandfather said.

"Is the challenge over?" Storm asked, his gaze flicked to Asia and then Hawke.

"I cannot allow you to kill them if that's what you want," Grandfather said. "The Goddess would be very angry."

"Why? What does She have to do with any of this?" Storm asked growing more and more frustrated with half-answers and innuendo.

"If you tried to kill Hawke, it would destroy his mate, which would unleash Jasmine's anger and she would attack you," Grandfather said plainly.

"Which would cause her mate to attack as well?" Storm asked as he looked at La Patron's mate who never disputed the old man. Her eyes lightened a bit and he sensed her energy spike.

The old man shook his head. "The Goddess' seal is on her Alpha, which means he cannot be killed. But you would still face his wrath, and that of the entire National Pack. Understand the Goddess set this Nation in motion, it is Her signature jewel and She guards it tenaciously."

Storm didn't fully understand the driving need to fight Hawke, who had been a victim like himself. His heart hadn't been in the battle. Alpha Adolfo would be appalled over Storm's actions, which shamed him. Now that it was over, he felt dirty.

"You have avenged Adolfo against all, but one involved in his murder. We will discuss this in depth," Grandfather said. He looked at La Patron. "I want you to hear this as well, it will impact you."

"Why am I not surprised?" La Patron said as he stuffed his hands into his pocket.

One more? Had Romano lied to him? Storm stared at Grandfather, read the sincerity in his gaze and it sickened him. Was everyone determined to jerk him around like a puppet on a string?

Keeping his face neutral, he glanced at the tightly knit group in the room. La Patron, his mate, his brother, his sons, Hawke, and Asia. It was obvious they all cared and looked out for each other. The only person who ever cared about him, treated him with dignity and respect had been brutally murdered.

Pissed with everyone's interference and the direction of his thoughts, Storm turned and left the gym. In the hall he stopped, inhaled and tackled his beast. Listening to the old man gloss over his nightmarish time with Roderick and the Liege unlocked old emotions that needed to be dealt with immediately.

He took several cleansing breaths and visualized a waterfall. Focused on a mental waterfall, he coaxed his beast down into a cage that appeared in the corner of his mind. He stood opposite his wolf, dragging him forward by sheer will. The beast howled and fought to remain free. Storm expended tremendous energy until the door closed and his beast rested deep in the recesses of his being. He released a long stream of air and opened his eyes.

"Are you alright?"

Across the walkway he stared into an amazing pair of blue eyes. She took a step forward. The overhead light bathed her creamy skin, making her appear other-worldly. His cock jumped.

Tall, busty beneath her tight-fitting tee-shirt, and jacket. She exuded calm, confidence as she approached.

Storm tamped down his base instincts. He itched to grab her close and inhale her tantalizing scent that played havoc with his beast. It had been weeks since he'd taken a woman, none affected him like this. Heat burned in his loins as he continued staring and wrapping her unique scent around him. He stuffed his hands in his pockets to keep from reaching out and watched her.

"Lost? Do you need help? Are you training with KnightForce?" she asked with a slight frown.

KnightForce? That shook him out of his stupor. "No." He took in her long, black ponytail, long neck, and high cheek bones. She looked familiar, but he couldn't place it.

"What are you doing standing out here with your eyes closed?"

"Eyes closed?" What was she talking about?

"When I walked in just now, your eyes were closed. Are you sure you're okay?"

She carried a large red and yellow purse, and wore snug fitting jeans with brown boots. Separate, it wasn't fancy but on her it looked like something one of those models he'd seen on TV wear.

"I'm fine. I just needed some air."

Her brow rose as security moved closer to them. "Is my father in there?" She asked one of the guards.

"Yes, he is."

"Who's your father?" Storm asked.

"You don't know?" She grinned, and he saw it.

"Now I do." The admission killed his rising passion. No way did he want anything to do with La Patron's pup. He shook his head, turned and re-entered the gym.

CHAPTER TEN

GRANDFATHER STOPPED talking when Storm re-entered the gym. "How long will this take?" Storm asked, his gaze on La Patron. The resemblance with the beauty in the hall was unmistakable. Pity. She would have made a nice diversion while he was in the States. He shrugged off his disappointment and looked around. Angus stood next to La Patron. The others must have left.

"Not long," Grandfather said. "We'll go upstairs and talk." La Patron nodded, turned and walked off.

Storm followed and fell in line with Grandfather. "*It's good to see you,*" Grandfather said through a new link. No one had spoken to Storm in this manner since his Alpha. It felt good.

"*Why don't I know you?*" he asked as they entered the elevator.

"*You're hard-headed, stubborn and proud, that's why. I've been trying to get your attention for decades.*"

Storm eyed the man as they stepped off the elevator and walked down the corridor into a conference room. Angus closed the door as the rest of them took seats.

"You didn't try that hard. This is the first time you've spoken to me."

"I've tried but you blocked me."

"Why were you able to get through now? I didn't say come in," Storm said.

"Maybe you're more open than you think." Grandfather winked at him.

Storm leaned back in his chair and watched Grandfather. "La Patron, you know this man?"

Grandfather shook his head and looked at La Patron.

"Yes, I believe I do. Angus has known him longer."

"Stubborn," Grandfather growled.

Storm shrugged.

There was a tap on the door. Angus opened it and a woman rolled in a cart with two shelves of food. Storm straightened in his seat. He hadn't eaten since breakfast, suddenly starving he watched steam rise from several covered dishes.

"Thanks," Angus said as the dishes were placed on the side table on the other side of the room. "What do you want to drink, Storm?"

Unsure how long this would take, he glanced at the food before answering. "Water is fine."

Angus tossed him a cold plastic bottle.

"Thanks," Storm said, opening the bottle while eying the food.

The moment the female left, and the door closed, Storm stood.

"Help yourself," La Patron said.

Hungry, Storm walked to the side table and stopped. Roderick offered him food and beer at the pub that night. Where had that come from? The problem with stirring up the past was you had no control over unleashed memories.

Storm filled a plate and returned to his seat. If they meant to kill or enslave him, he'd deal with it later. His gut said La Patron was an honorable man, he'd go with that.

When La Patron pushed his plate away, he looked at Grandfather who had waited quietly while the three of them ate.

"Ready?" Grandfather asked.

La Patron nodded.

"I gave an abbreviated telling of Storm's past." He looked at Storm. "Your sire, sired many pups, most have died, didn't live to 50. Your sire was killed before he turned 200."

None of that information meant anything to Storm. He never knew the people responsible for his birth. Both of them made sure of that. Grandfather needed to speed through the history lesson and get to the part about who killed Alpha Adolfo.

"In the beginning, a deal was struck with the Goddess that half-breeds would come through that line."

"You said they came through your line," Angus said. "When they wanted to strip Silas and Jasmine —"

"Yes, that's true," Grandfather said.

"So, you're the Black Wolf who started half-breeds?" Angus asked.

Grandfather exhaled. "It's more complicated than a yes, but that's what I'll say for now." He raised his hand when La Patron started to ask a question. "I cannot tell you more, Silas. Let that be enough."

La Patron nodded.

"Silas?" Storm asked grandfather.

"That's his name. Now pay attention."

Grandfather looked at Storm. "Your sire was one of my sons, your mam a breeder also came from my line. We suspect that is why you've survived when many others have not." He looked at La Patron. "When dealing with human behavior, it is hard to plan for every contingency. Things did not go as we hoped." His shoulders dropped as he gazed at his clasped hands. He looked as if he carried a terrible, heavy burden. "To date, there are three living male pups from my sons." He looked at Storm. You are one. Another is insane and will be put to sleep before tomorrow's sunrise. And there is one other."

"One other?" La Patron asked.

Grandfather waved down his question. "Later. First, I must ask Storm if he recalls any of his past? The past I spoke of earlier?"

Storm shook his head slowly. "Just the Liege part and then Alpha."

"Remember." Grandfather touched Storm's hand. Energy raced up his arm to his head. Incredible heat scorched his head. He thought it was on fire and stood quickly. His chair hit the floor.

"What have you done?" he yelled at Grandfather.

"Calm down. Give it a minute to settle. Your memories will return."

Silas reached over and touched Storm's finger. Cool air, rolled through him, easing his discomfort. He took a deep breath and returned to his seat. Subtle clicks sounded off in his head. Pinholes of light obscured his vision for split seconds, disorienting him.

Angus was speaking.

Storm tried to focus but the light behind his eyes brightened and then rolled into color frames. Pictures slid quickly through his mind without sound. Curious, he tried to grab hold to one of him on a ship scrubbing the deck, but it floated with no substance like a ghost. Additional images, one behind the other filled his mind, all meaningless without knowing more.

"*Pay attention. Your memories will be with you from now on, you need to understand what I'm saying*," Grandfather told Storm drawing his attention.

"Earlier I mentioned the Goddess protects you," Grandfather said looking at Silas. "Storm is also protected."

Angus straightened in his chair. "Is that why he's so fast?"

"No, that's a gift passed from his father," Grandfather said. "The first generation are protected by the Goddess and given warrior abilities, that gift is from me. Only a few could handle the combination."

"Smaller than Hawke, he kicked his ass all over the gym without morphing to his next size," Angus said. "And Hawke has metal arms and legs."

Storm looked at Angus. "Really?"

Angus nodded.

"They were able to make the transplants work?"

Angus frowned. "Yes. Both Hawke and Asia had cameras and computer chips installed. The chips controlled Hawke's arms and legs."

"Making him a prisoner in his own body," Storm said surprised he hadn't thought of it earlier. Hawke's hits were powerful, as was the man himself. Asia's moves were fast, her jumps high, she was as good as he'd heard.

"Yes. Can you get to the point, please," La Patron asked Grandfather.

"Yes, of course. Another son had a son who lives. For decades I have worked to keep the last of my seed hidden. With Adolfo's death, Storm left the protection of South America. There's a high bounty, 25 million, on your head."

Storm shrugged.

"You should care." Grandfather pointed at him. "It's possible someone destroyed your Alpha's den to flush you out."

Storm stared at Grandfather. Words of denial touched his lips. It couldn't be true. Who wanted him that bad they'd kill innocent pups?

"What?" he whispered as memories with his Alpha flooded his mind. The day his Alpha picked his bleeding, broken body up off the ground and carried him to a place to heal. Back then it was an old shack, barely standing, but it provided shelter from the elements. Another memory of his Alpha explaining honor and loyalty, what those meant in a Pack and how Pack operated. Storm had never heard of those traits and wanted to learn as much as possible to please his Alpha. Memory after memory rushed across his mind. Tiny snapshots frozen in time. Things he had forgotten.

Storm bent forward, holding his head with both hands, wishing it would stop. "I killed him?"

"No." Grandfather grabbed his arm and spun him around. "No. I think Razor sent them."

"Who is Razor?" La Patron asked. "Your other grandson?"

"That would be correct. As I said there are only two left who are sane. Storm and Razor, although some might question that. Razor is mated and extremely strong. Carlotta, his mate, is not like your Jasmine," Grandfather said looking at Silas.

"Is she a breeder?" Angus asked.

"Yes. According to the Goddess they will both mate with either half-breeds or breeders."

Images of Storms' Alpha crystallized and evaporated. Fueled with anger and hate over the death of his Alpha's pups, his beast rose to the surface, snapping, eager for vengeance. "Where can I find him?"

Grandfather grabbed his hand. "Listen to me. Just as I kept you hidden, so was he. Adolfo was an Alpha with a love for Pack. Razor wasn't as lucky and rebuffed the teachers the Goddess sent to assist in his growth. He's cold and calculating. You're not ready to meet him. He's too strong."

Storm shrugged off grandfather's hand. "He killed Alpha? Or ordered it done?"

"I believe so, but I have no proof and the Goddess will not say."

"Why do you think Razor's involved?" Angus asked, his gaze going from Storm to Grandfather and back to Storm.

"He and his mate are twisted and power hungry. They're moving from the Romanian mountains into Russia, creating a Pack." He shook his head. "The only thing I can think is they learned of Storm from Roderick, otherwise... I don't know how they learned of him."

"Roderick? From the Liege?" Angus asked.

Grandfather nodded.

"They're aging and should be dying soon," Angus said.

"Dying is not dead," Grandfather said. "Plus, he was in Lyrill and may have accessed whatever they use to slow their aging process, who knows," he said.

"Does Barticus know Roderick was in Lyrill? He's been rounding up all the Liege and locking them away," La Patron said.

"I don't know. Feel free to share that information with him if you'd like." Grandfather looked at Storm. "I think Razor and his mate wanted to find you, possibly they heard about a half-breed in South America and sent someone to watch you for a while. It's possible one or two spies attacked to test your skills. To make sure you were the one equal to Razor."

"Research before moving forward," Angus said.

"Is this true?" Storm asked.

"It's my feelings. I think they want you out the way before they do whatever it is they're planning. To bring you in the open, they attacked your Alpha's den," Grandfather said with an earnest expression.

"Sounds vague, a lot of speculation," La Patron said frowning.

"Exactly," Storm snapped, aggravated at the delay. "Why bring this Razor up now? Why not verify his role in Adolfo's death before mentioning him to me?" Storm slapped his chest and pointed at Grandfather. "You want something. Something you haven't said yet. What is it? Is there a mission you want accomplished first?" Storm taunted. "Someone pissed you off? What the fuck do you want? Stop playing this fucking game and tell the truth," he yelled.

Silence filled the room.

"Since you don't know me, I'll tell you what I want," Grandfather said. Energy whipped around the room, ruffling papers and rattling dishes. "I want my seed to prosper. This experiment, breeding humans and full-bloods... that's what I want to see succeed. No matter what it takes, that's what I want."

"No matter who gets hurt or is killed in the process?" Storm spat.

"Every war has casualties," Grandfather said after a few moments of silence. "I died in an ambush. Wasn't fair but it happened. I'd served the Goddess for decades and She rewarded me with this deal. My line, Black wolves would save dual natured wolves. We were dying out, almost barren, lots of problems that were solved by breeding with human females."

"Caused a lot of problems, too," Storm said without heat.

"True. Human nature, as I said, unpredictable," Grandfather said. "I'm not holding you hostage. In the past you've ignored my attempts to communicate with you. Either I risk that again and not tell you about Razor or tell you I'm looking into the possibility that he's coming for you."

Storm sat quietly logging memories and setting them aside. He would take them out later, review each one when he had time. First, he needed answers.

"Is there a way to be sure?" Storm asked after a few moments.

"Yes. I promise there is. I won't keep that from you. Adolfo was a great Alpha and my friend. If Razor is responsible I'll help in any way I can," Grandfather said.

Storm's head hurt. He wanted to complete his mission and then what? Return to South America? Alpha's pack was gone, absorbed into other packs for survival. What was once was no more. He had a home in Hawaii, he could lay in the sun while waiting to hear from Grandfather. Or he could travel to Mexico, finish this last job for Romano and be done with it. Regardless, he was done with this meeting. He stood. "Contact me when you know more. I'm out."

Angus stood. "I'll take you back to the hotel."

"Thanks."

"Why don't you stay here for a few days?" Grandfather said. "If Razor is involved, it'll be easier to get a flight from here than Brazil."

Storm looked at La Patron to gauge his response. It was one thing to allow him to come for a challenge, another to let him hang around. He detected nothing from La Patron's neutral expression. "I'll let you know."

Angus opened the door and walked out after Storm. "Can you teach me how you jumped that high and did those spins in the air?"

CHAPTER ELEVEN

"I WANT TO THANK EVERYONE for coming to this year's Art Show entitled, "Forces of Nature." Renee waited for the applause to die down before continuing. "Every floor has incredible submissions from Pack members all over the country in every medium imaginable. Please look in your program book for the flow chart of the displays, as well as the names and contributions of each artist, and a way to contact them. Don't forget to walk out to the sculpture garden, we have a lot of surprises waiting you there as well." Renee paused as guests applauded. "On the second floor we have a special section where our local talent is displayed, I think you'll be pleased with our budding artists." She looked at Cameron, Lilly and their three daughters who blushed at her compliment.

"I want to thank the underwriters for this annual event. La Patron and La Patroness are the primary supporters of the art museum, this year they also underwrote the cost of the ball tomorrow."

The crowd cheered and whistled.

"Thank you to La Patron and La Patroness, Silas and Jasmine Knight," Renee said pointing to her parents who stood to the side of the podium. Her parents smiled and waved but didn't move to the microphone.

"Thanks to the best staff imaginable, Edmund, Crystal and the support team, they were instrumental in pulling this off and I'm eternally grateful." She waved the two on stage and clapped along with the audience. They stood behind her as she finished the opening ceremony.

"Daddy, anything you want to say?" She looked at her father.

"No, everything looks great. We're so proud of you," he said.

Smiling inside and out, Renee searched the audience for her five siblings, winked at them and then spoke. "On behalf of La Patron and his den, Forces of Nature is officially open. Take out those checkbooks and hire an artist."

Several artists applauded her last comment as she left the podium. Edmund hugged her. “I’ll be with the sculptures.”

Renee nodded.

“I’m on the second floor,” Crystal said after hugging Renee.

“Okay.” Renee went to her parents with a wide smile. Her father was dressed in a tailored inky black suit with a white collarless shirt. “*Daddy you clean up nice.*”

Smiling, he tweaked her nose.

“Mama, you look beautiful.” Renee Mom who wore a teal, short sleeved dress that hugged her curves and fell mid-thigh, with matching teal, red and yellow heels. “I like your hair like this with that dress.” She placed a few loose strands of hair behind her Mom’s ear. “Yeah, that up-do definitely works.”

Mama smiled. “Thanks for your approval, that’s high praise from you. That dress is gorgeous, and so are you.” Mama kissed her cheek.

Glancing at the red dress with black piping along the collar, and hem, Renee took her Mom’s arm. “You’ve seen this before. I want you to see my latest piece. Come on, Daddy.”

The walk to the exhibit took longer than Renee would’ve liked but her parents were considered royalty, and everyone wanted to speak or touch or take a picture with them. Next year she would have a private showing the day before, so her family could actually see the art before it was sold.

Almost an hour later, they stood in front of the dark painting Renee had completed a few days ago. Initially she didn’t think she’d want it displayed but changed her mind. Edmund and Crystal agreed the emotion displayed in the piece was brilliant, easily one of Renee’s best works. But they spoke from a technical perspective. She wanted her parent’s opinion of how it looked? Did it speak to them in the same way it spoke to her?

For several seconds, no one said anything. Her parents stared at the art, no doubt speaking to each other, deciding what to say.

With each passing moment, Renee’s heart dropped. They hated it. Had she lost her ability to create pieces that made people happy? Had her world changed to the point everything was muted or drab. How awful.

“It’s unbelievable,” Daddy said softly. “Don’t sell this one. I want it for my office.”

Frowning, Mama looked at her Dad. "I just told you I wanted it for my office."

He pulled Mama close. "But this is more me, wouldn't you agree? It's how I feel after most of the meetings or dealing with problems all day. That speaks to that."

Mama shook her head. "Not at all. It's how I feel when dealing with problems the women face all over the country. The buck stops at my desk, remember? See the shades of light trying to break free from the dark shade. That's me, trying to make a difference." She looked at Renee. "Baby, this is wonderful. Different but realistic in a way it touches my heart. Thank you for painting it for me." She glanced over her shoulder. "Paint another one for your Dad."

He snorted and winked at Renee. *"Do not sell this one. Your Mom wants it and I want her to have it. It's brilliant, just like you."* Her Mom squeezed her shoulder before walking off hand in hand with Daddy.

Renee smiled to cover her confusion. "*Okay*." She didn't know what else to say. Instead, she looked at the painting again, trying to see what her parents saw and didn't.

"*There you are*," Jackie said linking their arms. "*This place is packed, not much room to move around. Another successful show. I've bought a couple pieces already.*" She waved at her parents as they moved away. "*Hey, this is yours?*"

Renee nodded and held her breath. Jackie would tell her the truth. Was this as good as Mom thought or were they pacifying her?

"It's different. Not your normal bright, cheery colors or design." Jackie pulled them closer to stop people from stepping in front of them. *"Was this hard to do?"* She looked at Renee.

"*Hmm*?" Renee met her sister's curious gaze.

"What's going on with you?"

"Nothing, just thinking. Where's Quinn?" Renee looked around to avoid her sister's gaze. *"Do you know this guy?"* Tall, with slightly wavy hair, this guy reminded her of the British actor Jude Law. She'd loved him in the Sherlock Holmes movie.

"What guy?" Jackie turned in the direction Renee faced. "Hi Lucian, Duke." She waved. *"This is the guy I told you about, the Alpha from Honduras. Good looking, sexy, right?"*

"*He's okay.*" Not as sexy as the guy she'd seen in the tunnel a couple days ago. She'd been returning from a day full of meetings and was exhausted. Too exhausted to ask more than basic questions. Her beast had stirred but she'd ignored the attraction and headed to bed. He hadn't told her his name and hadn't realized who she was until getting a good look at her. Was he here? She looked around but the place was too crowded to see much.

"*We're going to talk,*" Jackie promised Renee as Lucian kissed the back of her hand. "Lucian I'm so glad you and your brother could make it. This is Renee, she runs the art museum."

"Your sister?" Duke asked as he took Renee's hand and kissed the back of it.

"Yes. Litter-mates," Renee said looking at him. It wasn't that he or Lucian weren't handsome, they were. They smelled incredibly delicious, like sex on steroids. It had been months since she'd been with a man. She should have been interested. Her beast should be clawing at her to get to either one of them.

Nothing.

"You're very beautiful," Lucian said. She heard the ring of truth in his words and smiled her thanks. "Will you give me a tour of the museum? Your father speaks of this place as the jewel in the Nation."

Renee smiled and nodded. "Sure." She looked at Jackie, who stared at them with a goofy smile as if she'd just landed a major coup. "*Not happening.*"

Jackie's smile dropped a bit. "*Why not?*"

"*My beast isn't interested.*"

"*Shit. Okay, show him around and then we need to catch up, something's going on with you and I don't like not knowing what.*" Jackie moved in the opposite direction with Duke.

"Have you heard anything about Honduras?" Lucian asked as they picked their way through the crowd to arrive at a collection of oil paintings. Renee had submitted two before her father's trip. Both had sold badges on them.

"Yes, my Father told us a bit about it and we researched it while he was there." She reached out to Crystal, told her to place a sold sticker on the painting for her parents.

All around them, people studied each canvas and discussed the beauty of the art, brush strokes and talented depictions of nature. She wondered if Lucian was interested in art or just at this event to score political points with her Father.

"The internet hasn't been kind to my country," Lucian said. "It picks and chooses locations to highlight or demean. You have to see it to recognize it's inherent beauty." He looked at her. "What is it you do?"

Her brow rose as people around them glanced in their direction. She left that area and headed outside to the sculpture garden where fewer people roamed.

Lucian followed.

Anger under control, fake smile in place, Renee faced him. "I'm sorry, what were you saying?"

"Oh, I asked what is it you do? Jackie is an excellent strategist, she's been able to save us a lot of time and money in our reconstruction efforts. Quinn, the man is phenomenal with a heart for helping the sick. Adam is a sports guru. I recall watching the championship game and couldn't believe some of the plays he made." Lucian smiled widely and shaking his head. He stuck his hand into his pant pocket. "So much talent, amazing talent," he said.

Dressed in a tailored navy-blue pinstripe suit, white shirt and red print tie, Lucian looked every bit the part of a powerful, successful businessman. An impressive piece of spit and polished eye candy who didn't see any of the beauty surrounding him. Not once had he mentioned anything in the museum. Nothing here caught his eye. That alone disqualified him from being a close friend.

"He is talented, so is his mate. She's performing tomorrow at the ball," Renee said disappointed in his tunnel vision.

"I've heard how good she is," Lucian said smiling. He leaned forward. "Will Adam return to play ball?"

"Ask him," Renee said, determined to be nice.

Lucian looked around. "Is he here? I haven't seen him."

Renee held back a long sigh. There were so many art enthusiasts here today and she was stuck with him. She'd fix that. "*David?*"

"Yeah?"

"Save me or I'll say something rude."

David chuckled. "*On my way.*"

"Sports has a way of unifying people, don't you think?" he asked.

She nodded and looked at the group of people around Edmund's sculpture. He saw her and smiled.

"I've sold three pieces already, so have most of the other artists. Jamison has a commission for Alpha Greg and I'm working out the details for my second commission. This has been the most successful show yet."

"I'm happy for you," Renee said, half listening to Lucian talk about Honduras and their problems.

"*Who's the guy?"* Edmund asked.

"*Honduras Alpha,*" Renee said smiling at Lucian when he paused from talking.

"You agree?" Lucian asked.

Renee looked over his shoulder at David. Dressed in a dark brown tailored suit and collarless shirt, he looked fabulous. "I don't know, ask my brother, David." She smiled at her litter-mate. "David, this is Lucian, Lucian my brother, David."

David extended his hand, the two shook and Lucian started talking again. "I think I'm boring Renee with all my talk of Honduras," Lucian said smiling at her. "You never told me what it is you do."

David's nostril's narrowed as he looked at Lucian.

"I'm an artist. I manage this museum for the Nation," she said striving for a neutral tone.

Lucian frowned. "Artist?"

"Yes, I create art," Renee said watching him intently. "Jackie didn't' tell you?"

David looked at her. "*Jackie introduced him to you?"*

"Yep, thought we'd hit it off."

"You look like you want to hit him," David said.

"*He doesn't think much of art or what I do,*" she said, unsure how she felt about that.

"His thoughts don't matter, you're our crown jewel, the best of the best and that's a fact," David said.

"Is any of your art here?" Lucian asked looking around.

"Not out here, I'm not a sculptor. Inside, where we were standing a few minutes ago. I had a few pieces there." She continued to watch him.

"I see." He stared at her. "You didn't point them out while we were there?"

"No, we were discussing something else," she said softening her response.

"I would like to see what you can do," he said. "Will you show me your work?"

He extended his hand.

Renee took it and glanced at David. "*Why me, Goddess? Why me?*"

David smiled. "*Last single daughter of La Patron, quite the catch.*"

"*Ugh... remind me to strangle you later*," she said turning to head back inside.

"*Of course.*" David headed toward an iron sculpture of a wolf and a woman.

A side door opened. A low growl brushed against Renee's arm and raced across her body. Her beast stood, scenting the air. Someone smelled utterly fantastic.

Lucian's grip tightened on her arm.

The growl rolled across her again. She turned to discover the source of the scent and stopped.

Standing in the exit leading into another area of the museum stood the guy she had seen in the tunnel a couple days ago. Dressed in a tailored black suit, white shirt and burgundy tie, he looked like he'd just stepped off the runway. Her beast certainly approved. Her nipples strained against the fabric of her dress as her gaze met his.

Lucian wrapped his arms around her as if she were some human damsel in distress. The guy's eyes lightened as he stepped further into the garden. Renee had the distinct impression he was upset about something or someone. She looked around.

Several guards entered the area behind him. Daddy, Mama, and Uncle Angus entered from another entrance and stopped. That was strange.

"Lucian, move away from Renee," David ordered in a no-nonsense voice.

"What?" Lucian looked at David.

"Step away from Renee, now," David snapped.

Slowly, Lucian removed his hand and took two steps back.

Renee stared at David and then glanced at Lucian. "*Thanks, I think,*" Renee told David. "*I didn't like him, but you called him out in front of everyone, why not let Daddy handle it?*"

"*Because that guy was going to attack Lucian.*"

"Really? Why? Because of what happened in Honduras? Did he follow Lucian here? Is Daddy safe?" Fighting back fear that her father was in danger, she looked at her brother.

David laughed. *"He didn't like Lucian touching you. Look at him now, his eyes and body have normalized. I think —"*

Shock ricocheted through her as she looked at the guy. His stance screamed bad ass. The thousand dollar suit he wore didn't hide the cold, merciless gleam in his eyes or his apparent disdain for everyone in the garden. He was everything she didn't want. *"Don't say it, don't you dare say it,"* Renee yelled through their link.

"He's your mate." David winked and walked toward their Father who remained on the other side of the garden.

STORM HADN'T MEANT to remain in West Virginia. In fact, he told Alpha Romano he would be heading to Mexico City yesterday. Yet, he hadn't left as planned. Instead, he created excuses to remain another day. And then another.

This morning, he purchased this suit, which wasn't in his plans and took a cab to the Art Museum. Something else not on his itinerary. The place was huge and the artwork amazing. He'd purchased a gorgeous painting of a dark-haired woman and a wolf having a picnic.

Looking at the art, moving among people like himself, he almost convinced himself that he wasn't looking for anyone or anything. Until he stepped into the sculpture garden and lost control of his beast, possibly his mind. Seeing her. Renee, La Patron's daughter, all cozy with the Honduran Alpha sent his beast reeling. Logically, it made no sense, he and Renee hadn't even been introduced. She probably didn't know he existed, but his beast didn't care.

No one should touch her.

His beast took exception to the way Lucian sought to protect Renee from him. As if he would keep them apart. He'd been about to attack, to tear the man apart when he released her. The man was too close for Storm's comfort, but he could breathe better now. He released a pent-up breath when the Alpha walked away. His beast strained to attack but it wasn't as visceral. He could deal rationally with his wolf. Once he got himself under control, Storm realized La Patron, Angus, and a few others watched him.

Shit.

He'd lost control again and would have created havoc at this event if Lucian hadn't moved. Renee had to be repulsed by his actions, the look on her face said as much. He pulled the lapels on his coat to straighten it, turned and walked out.

"What was that about?" Duke asked as he passed him. They were staying at the same hotel and had spoken at length last night in the bar.

"Nothing." Storm refused to look closely at his behavior, he wasn't ready for a mate, especially La Patron's daughter.

"You were growling and throwing off energy so strong it drew me from the second floor," Duke said catching up with him.

Storm stopped. "I don't know what that was about."

"You sure about that?" David asked walking toward them.

Just what he needed, Renee's brother, La Patron's son, scolding him on his actions. "Pretty much," he said.

David stared at him for a few seconds and nodded. "Can I talk to you for a minute?"

Storm sensed no guile or disgust or anger. "Yeah." They moved through the crowd and entered a side door with a "No Admittance" sign. Inside it was quiet and clearly the management side of the museum. He noticed several tagged paintings, stacked and locked in metal storage containers. The air smelled of paint and spirits.

David passed a few closed doors and stepped inside a staff lunch room. "Want something to drink?"

"No, I'm good," Storm said looking around. Everything was neat and clean. He pulled out a chair and sat. Eventually, David would say whatever was on his mind.

"A few days ago, you challenged and from what I've been told, defeated two people I see as godparents. Grandfather explained your origins and quite frankly I'm happy to meet you. We were surprised you didn't leave immediately. You mentioned, Mexico." He paused.

Storm didn't add anything.

"Until you stepped into the sculpture garden, no one knew why you hadn't left, did you know?" David pulled out a chair and sat facing Storm.

He didn't have to answer. His reasons were his own. He could come or go at will without explanation. "No. At least I didn't admit it to myself until a few minutes ago."

"When you saw her with Alpha Lucian?" David asked.

Storm's hands curled into fist as the image of her standing close to Lucian flashed through his mind. "Yes," he said in a low guttural voice.

"She doesn't like him."

It took Storm a moment to digest that comment. "No?"

David shook his head.

Tension rolled off Storm. The tightness in his chest eased and his beast relented. "Good."

David chuckled.

"Not that he's a bad guy or anything," Storm said.

"No, he's a good dude, just not for Renee. What do you think of the exhibit?" David asked.

Storm smiled. He'd always been in awe of people who could see something in their minds and bring that vision into reality in such a way it touched people. Alpha Adolfo's mate had a good eye for color and dabbled in sketching. He considered the portrait she'd done of him one of his prized possessions.

"Awesome, I purchased a painting."

David smiled. "There's a lot of talent in our Pack."

"It's true? All the work on display is from full-bloods or half-breeds?" Storm had never heard of such a thing.

"Yes, it's true." He paused. "Have you seen our communities? Schools? Anything since you've been here?"

Storm hadn't left the hotel until today. "No, I haven't."

David's smile widened. "We'll need to change that." He stood.

Storm stiffened as her scent crawled up his leg and wrapped around him. His breath caught in his throat as the door opened. He didn't have to look to know Renee was there, his heart leapt in his chest as his beast demanded they bond.

Storm stood and looked at her. "Hello, Renee," he said.

Her brow rose in perfect imitation of her father's. "Hello, you know my name, but no one's told me yours." She looked pointedly at David who shrugged and inched sideways to the door.

"Storm. Niklas Storm." He watched as she scowled at her brother's back before looking at him with those stormy dark blue eyes. "Are you angry?" He wasn't sure why he asked her that, but it seemed appropriate.

"Yes," she snapped and then released a breath. "No. I hate playing games. No one will tell me anything." She looked at him. "Who are you?"

He frowned. "I told you —"

She waved a hand. "Not your name, I got that. Why are you here? Why won't anyone tell me anything about you? What were you doing in the tunnel and the gym?"

"I came here to challenge Hawke for the role he played in the death of my Alpha."

Her eyes widened as she reached for the chair her brother abandoned. "What? Hawke did what? When?" She shook her head. "Challenge how?"

Retaking his seat, he explained the death of his alpha's den. His vow of vengeance and the path he took to arrive at the Compound. She listened intently without interrupting.

"You're.... you're an assassin? Mercenary?" She frowned while looking at him.

Storm hadn't ever labeled himself but given what he'd done most of his life, he nodded in agreement.

She released a long breath, shook her head and looked at him. "How could you fight him after learning he was a victim himself? He and Asia were both taken as pups to the Liege," she said.

Glad they moved past his occupation, he wasn't sure how to answer something as visceral as the need to avenge his Alpha. In the spirit of wanting to know her better, he tried to explain. "I could not let it go. The pups are dead, I had to honor my pledge."

"Grandfather stopped it?"

Storm nodded.

"This is where you work?" He looked around needing to change the subject rather than talk about himself. He'd disclosed more than enough information for the night.

"What?"

"This place? You work here? You're an artist, right?"

"How'd you know that?" She watched him.

"I asked about La Patron's pups. Everyone talks about the six of you. Wasn't hard."

"Which painting did you buy?" she asked.

Smiling, he described the piece.

"I remember that one, it's extremely well done. Where will you put it?" she asked.

"I'm thinking in the condo, in the dining room. It'll fit perfectly there." He tapped the program book on the table. "I looked at your pieces, you're really gifted. Pity they're all sold. I would've liked to take one with me."

"Thank you." She paused. "You must be really old if your sire was sired by Grandfather."

He shrugged. "I don't know my exact age, but I'm sure your sire is older. I would place my age between his and Asia's since I remember hearing about her."

"That's because she's awesome," Renee said.

He nodded in agreement. Age wasn't something he thought much about, perhaps grandfather could tell him his date of birth if Renee wanted to know more.

"How long will you be here?" She stood.

Storm stood. "I have a job in Mexico and then where Grandfather sends me."

"One day, two... how long?" she pressed.

"I will probably leave tomorrow," he said realizing he didn't want their conversation to end. But she had other obligations as the manager of the museum.

"The ball is tomorrow night, maybe you could leave after that," she said walking to the door. "I have to deal with a few issues out there, it was nice meeting you, Niklas."

He didn't correct her on his name.

"Nice meeting you, Renee."

She smiled and left the room. Her scent wrapped around him like a cocoon, filling him until he knew he could find her anywhere on this planet.

He stared at the table for a few seconds and then straightened. "*What do you want?*"

"I have information," Grandfather entered the room and stood by the door.

Storm looked over his shoulder, and turned to face the man. *"What's wrong? Razor?"*

Grandfather shook his head. *"He's on the move and will be a threat for sure. I've warned La Patron to watch for him."*

Storm frowned. "*You said you had information?*"

"Yes. Razor was involved, in a way. I don't think he's aware of what he's done or that he was used." Grandfather pursed his lips as if he tasted something sour. *"I didn't know."*

"What?" Storm had no idea what the old man was talking about.

"You. Renee. I didn't know. I should have but I was concerned about the fallout from Hawke I didn't question the timing."

"Timing?" Storm crossed his arms over his chest and stared at Grandfather. Also dressed in a black suit, the old man looked like most of the other men at the event.

"Razor is free, on the move. You're here in this country, a first. He's mated."

Mated.

Storm's gaze narrowed. He wouldn't be a pawn for anyone.

Grandfather continued. *"Razor has the ability to wreak havoc on every Pack from here to the continent. When I say he's strong, I mean it. Just like you, the Goddess gave him protection and cannot withdraw or change Her will. When we struck that bargain, I was supposed to oversee the training of those under Her protection."* He shook his head and looked over Storm's shoulder at the wall.

"Razor's mam refused to have anything to do with his sire and foisted him onto a brutal Alpha to raise as his own. Being a half-breed, Razor spent years as the Omega of his Pack until he outlived most of them. He started training with Nells, an older member of the Pack, someone no one paid attention to. The man's heart was filled with anger, hatred and self-pity. Narcissistic asshole moved into the mountains, used Razor as a slave for decades."

"I thought you hid him?" Storm asked recalling their earlier conversation.

"I had the place warded so it couldn't be stumbled upon. No matter how hard I tried, I couldn't get Razor to leave that old fool. It didn't take long for Razor to take up Nells' bitterness toward Pack or desire to repay those who wronged him. I think the old wolf paid someone to find Razor's mate and corrupted her the same way."

Storm frowned. The odds of that were slim but he didn't say anything.

"*No matter. We are at an impasse and once again I find myself at the center of the Goddess' displeasure. She does not want Razor to wreak havoc here.*"

Storm could understand why, but failed to see the reason he was being told all of this. He didn't care about Razor's history, or his sad upbringing. Storm had survived the school of hard knocks and lived to tell the tale. "*Did Razor have anything to do with Alpha Adolfo's death?*"

"*From what I was told, and this hasn't been verified. He was told about you and made an offhand statement to the effect that he would destroy you if you stood in his way. One of his loyal followers sought you out and ambushed you. When they realized how good you were, they took it out on your Alpha.*"

"*The men who ambushed Alpha?*"

"*You killed them.*"

Storm nodded and looked toward the door. "*It is over then?*"

"*Yes. It's over.*"

"*One question,*" Storm said watching him.

Grandfather's brow rose.

"*Are you dead or what?*"

"*I fall under the "or what" category,*" Grandfather said and disappeared.

CHAPTER TWELVE

RENEE MOVED AROUND the ballroom smiling and greeting guests. Crystal and Edmund had turned the large room into an elegant, sparkling fairy tale affair with several food and drink stations, extra-large photo booths, a large dance floor and great music. Everyone seemed to be having a great time.

"Will you dance with me?" Lucian asked as the band played a slower song. Dressed in a black tuxedo, he looked very handsome. Several females watched him with longing. Renee wasn't one of them.

She nodded, and they headed to the dance floor. He held her lightly in his arms, still it felt wrong.

"I must apologize for yesterday. Jackie reminded me of a conversation she and I had when we first met. She told me of your great contribution to this Nation," he said.

Renee had forgotten about that. From the moment she left Storm in the break room, he'd filled her thoughts. She hoped he would follow her last night.

He hadn't.

She thought he would return to the museum today, begging for a conversation.

He hadn't.

This afternoon, she bugged David into learning if Storm had left for Mexico.

He hadn't.

Which was why she continued looking across the sea of people, hoping to see him. They needed to talk. He should be here with her, discussing what was going on with them. If he was her mate, why hadn't he sought her out? It made no sense. Once Quinn realized Jackie was his mate, he wouldn't leave her side. Adam hinted the same happened with Bella.

"Is it possible you and Storm are mates?" Lucian asked.

"What?" Had he been reading her thoughts? How did he know she was thinking about Storm?

"David seems to think the two of you are mated, but as half-breeds, neither have to act on it. Or you can take your time, separate, that kind of thing." He paused. "It's fascinating really. I wonder if we have half-breeds in my country. Tomorrow I will spend time with your brother Tyrone, learning of his department that integrates half-breeds into the Pack."

"Un huh," she said while searching the room.

"When this dance is over, go outside to the veranda," David said in a serious tone.

"Okay, thanks."

"Don't play with him, Renee. You shouldn't be dancing with Lucian," David said.

"He should've been here to ask me to dance," she snapped.

"There she is, welcome back, Sis," David said.

Renee rolled her eyes. As soon as the music stopped, she backed up, thanked Lucian for the dance and headed toward the open doors that led outside.

Cool air brushed against her skin, followed by rolling heat. She turned and looked into Storm's dark gaze.

"Every time I see you, you are in his arms. Should I kill him for that?" Storm's spoke in a low gritty tone that scraped her skin.

"Hello to you, too. I'm doing well, thank you. Yes, I've had a long day and the ball is going fine. It's good to see you as well," she said crossing her arms, meeting his gaze.

For several seconds neither spoke.

He rubbed the back of his neck. "I'm not good at this."

"With what? Manners? Being polite? Please tell me what it is you're not good at." She took a step forward.

He moved forward. "All of that. I don't know... I didn't think beyond what I saw. Your day was long?"

The change in conversation threw her. "Yes. Wait. Why aren't you good at any of this?" A man as sexy and hot as Storm had experience with plenty of women.

He moved closer. They stood almost touching. She looked up at his lips.

"I don't talk to a lot of people. Don't have much experience with how to interact in society," he said in a low voice. The dark cadence brushed against her nipples, causing them to pebble, begging for attention.

Her core throbbed as his scent wrapped around her. "Where have you been all day?"

Did she ask him that? What was she thinking? That was the problem, she couldn't think. Not with him this close. She stepped back.

He grabbed her arm, holding her in place. Heat from his touch seared her skin and spread through her body.

"I was at the hotel, preparing to go on another job tomorrow. Mexico," he added.

"What kind of job?" Keep talking she thought. Don't pay attention to what you're feeling. Focus on his words.

"Picking up a package for an Alpha and taking it to him." His hand rubbed up and down her arm. Her skin prickled from the contact. "You look amazing in that dress, like a star. So very beautiful."

The silver gown sparkled beneath the light. She moved her leg, revealing the high slit along the side. He glanced at her thigh and then the low-vee displaying the tops of her breasts. "Beautiful."

Her heart raced. Over the course of her life, she'd been called beautiful too many times to count. Never had the words touched her body the way his did. Is this what Jackie meant? This connection that made no sense. Storm wasn't the kind of man she wanted in her life. Yet, standing here with him right now, it felt right.

"Thank you." She smiled and looked him over. "You look good too."

He laughed. "Thanks." He looked over his shoulder. "Is the museum closed?"

She thought he was kidding until she looked up into his eyes. "Yes, it's closed."

"Good, I never saw the second-floor exhibits, can you give me a personal tour?"

He couldn't be serious. They were at a ball with over 500 people and she was in charge. "What?"

"Yeah, I'm leaving in the morning and I'd like to finish seeing the exhibits. As the manager, I'm sure you have a key..."

She didn't need a key but that wasn't the point. Did he really enjoy art? Had someone told him to pretend to be interested to gain her interest. That was wasted advice because she and her beast liked him just fine. There was only one way to determine if he was serious. She reached down and grabbed his hand.

"Come on."

They re-entered the ballroom and walked slowly through the crowd.

"Everything alright?" her Daddy asked from the other side of the room. Renee had forgotten she held Storm's hand and how they looked.

"Yeah, we're going to the museum. Be back in a bit." She tried to add a mental shrug into her tone.

"Don't play with him, Renee. If he's your mate, you can't play with him," her Dad warned.

"I must've been really bad with guys in the past for you and David to say the same thing," Renee said as she and Storm reached the exit.

"*You've dated several guys, but only cared about one before. And you dropped him when he wasn't your mate. You won't be able to walk away from Storm if you start the mating process. It'll impact you and your beast. If you don't want him, don't start anything with him. Half-breeds can walk away, but only if your beast don't bond. Once mated, it's a different matter. So, don't rush into anything, get to know him. Wait if you can,*" her Dad said.

"He's leaving tomorrow," she said as they walked slowly down the corridor leading to the museum.

"*He's been leaving for several days,*" her Dad said. "*He stayed because of you, probably didn't realize it at the time.*"

She glanced at Storm. Their gazes met. Her beast strained against her belly wanting to get closer.

He smiled.

Her stomach clenched with need.

"It's hard, Daddy. My beast, wants him bad," she admitted.

"*I'm sure his beast is kicking his ass to get to you too,*" her father said. "*The attraction is to ensure you mate. I just wanted you to understand what that would mean to you.*"

"You like him?" Renee asked as she placed her palm on a scanner and then typed in the security code.

"*I don't know him well enough to have an opinion. If he's your mate, we will accept him as the Goddess' choice for you.*" He sounded resigned.

Storm pushed the door open and walked in first, glanced around and then extended his much larger hand to her. Renee took it and closed the door behind her.

"It's quiet in here," he said staring down at her.

His voice rolled over her like warm syrup. She cleared her voice and hopefully her mind. "This way, we can take the stairs over here." She tugged on his hand to get him moving.

He chuckled but didn't say anything. The walk to the second floor was in silence, a comfortable silence. She liked he didn't talk for the sake of talking. She placed her palm on another security scanner to enter the second floor. This time she walked in first, she wasn't helpless, and he needed to understand that upfront.

"We'll start here and work our way around," she said, expecting him to change his mind now that they were there.

"Sounds good. I saw a few photos from the ground floor and wanted to see them up close." His gaze scanned the walls as he stepped toward an alcove filled with pottery. "Tell me about these." He pointed to the pieces.

Surprised, Renee picked up a few pieces, remembered the entries and told him what she knew. Tomorrow all the sold pieces would be packed and shipped to their new owners. Later in the day, the artists would return for their unsold pieces and some would receive checks. They moved slowly through the exhibit, Storm asked pertinent questions, displaying a limited knowledge but a real appreciation for the art. She had run to her office for sold tags and her tablet when he purchased a tapestry, two large photos and a basket with an image of a wolf woven into the design.

"This is from the state Alpha's den." She pointed to the drawings from Cameron's teenagers.

"No one purchased them?" He looked at the drawing for a few seconds.

"Someone will." She smiled. "Either my parents or someone in the local Pack."

"Sell it to me. Have them autographed and framed in three identical frames. Send them to the same address as the other painting I bought."

"You don't have to do that, as I said someone will purchase these. We should've placed a sold sign on them already." She stepped away.

Storm grabbed her hand, stopping her. "Seriously, I want to buy it. To have the courage to create something knowing it will be displayed among the best... that's heart. I want these."

For several seconds their gazes clashed. "If you're sure..."

He released her hand, turned and looked at the pictures. "Very sure."

Renee placed a sold tag on all three. "Okay. I'll make sure to have it shipped with your other things."

"Thanks, don't forget to have them autographed." He took her free hand and pulled her forward to the next exhibit. Inwardly she smiled at how comfortable they had gotten talking about art history, the motivations of the artist for several pieces. He stared at a photo of a large black wolf for several seconds before asking what she thought of the picture. It had been one of the first sold items displayed.

"Looks hungry, maybe he's wondering what's for dinner," she said, not giving it much thought.

"Possibly." He continued staring at the photo. "Or he's wondering where's everyone else, why is he the lone black wolf?" He looked at her and pointed to the picture. "See the other wolves in the distance, they're not like him. He's the odd one."

Renee stared at the photo and realized he was right, she hadn't noticed it before. "Why would he consider himself odd? There aren't that many black wolves in the States, should be something he's used to by now." She wasn't sure if they were talking about the photo or him.

He shrugged. "Is that something you ever get used to? Or just go into survival mode, accepting what is?" He looked down at her. "He looks lonely to me."

His words chilled her, and she didn't know why. "Would you have bought that photo?"

"No." He glanced at it again and stepped away. "Great photo, though."

They moved steadily through the floor, stopping a few more times, but she grew tired. The day had been long. Jackie and Adam both had reached out, checking on her. Offering to interfere if she wanted. They were surprised she and Storm were really looking at art.

When they finished, Storm wrapped his arms around her waist and pulled her close. His hard cock pressed against her. Smiling, Renee leaned against his chest, listening to the steady beat of his heart, and inhaling his scent. She wished she could bottle it.

He placed a kiss on the top of her head. "Thank you for this, I enjoyed it. Time spent alone with you, getting to know you better, I cannot imagine anything better." He laughed as he moved back and forth. "Maybe one thing better."

She grinned and held onto him. "You know you're not my type."

He rubbed her back before resting his hand on her hip. "No? What's your type?"

"Non-violent."

"I can be non-violent," he said after laughing.

She hit his chest and then rubbed it. "You were built to fight. Asia and Hawke are really tough to win against."

"No one won in that fight, it wasn't fair," he said turning so that she leaned against the wall. He placed a hand above her head and kept the other on her waist, boxing her in.

Renee wondered what his lips felt like. How different would it be with him? Would she lose herself? Jackie hadn't, not really. Neither had her Mom or Aunt Renee. They were still the same, maybe more.

"What's got you thinking so hard?" He squeezed her waist lightly.

"This." She pulled his lapel, bringing him closer until their lips touched. "I've been thinking about this."

"Are you sure? Half-breed or not, I don't think I'll be able to turn back if we start down this path and I'm leaving tomorrow to finish a job."

She brushed her lips across his. "But you'll be back."

He nodded and placed a chaste kiss on her lips. "I'll be back, but —"

"But what?" she asked not caring much at this point. Her nipples ached. Her womb throbbed, and her beast tried to break free.

"I don't think I can live here."

Live here? Those two words bounced around her mind, demanding she pay attention. If he wasn't here, where would he be? Did that mean she had to move? Follow him? What about the museum? Her family?

Questions flew on the winds of uncertainty in her mind. She pushed back and took a deep breath. "Where will you live?"

He moved back and ran a hand through his thick, dark hair. "I have a place in Hawaii, another in Brazil." He shrugged. "Lots of uncertainty right now, I'm not sure where I'll be." His gaze never left hers.

She moved from the wall, took a deep breath while fanning her face with her hand. "We should wait." The words were pulled from the pit of her belly. Her beast objected, so did her body. Her mind fought this battle alone.

"Until after Mexico... or when?" Disappointment coated his words.

Could she be strong enough to wait a few more days? She had to be. They needed to talk more, she needed some kind of direction. Smiling brightly, she turned to face him. "We'll decide what to do then."

"I want to mate with you, that's not going to change." He remained rooted where he stood, which helped her remain strong.

"But you're on stand-by to go to different parts of the world to fight. Where does that leave me if we're mated?"

Storm frowned. He understood her point of view, but his beast didn't care. This past couple hours had been a constant battle to keep his hands off every part of her. Walking through the museum helped but also made his feelings for her change from lust to something more. Sexy, smart, creative with an interesting perspective on life. Renee saw the world through the eye of what life could also be, something unique and refreshing. He liked that. He liked her.

"Honestly Renee... I don't know where that leaves either of us, but it doesn't change how I feel. Doesn't change this gnawing need inside to hold onto you and never let go. To make you mine in every sense of the word. To bind you so tight there's no space between us." He paused to pull his thoughts together. "I can't answer with any degree of certainty as to where we'll be next week, next year or 50 years from now, other than we'll be together." He inhaled, filling his body with her luscious scent. "That's the one thing I'm certain." He waited for her to tell him he'd lost his mind, as a breed she could survive without him. It'd be bumpy but not impossible.

"I don't want to be left behind and alone while you go off doing whatever you do. That's not a life I want to live. I want to share the day with you, see the world through your eyes, share my vision of the world with you. That's not possible if we're together now and then. I need a man to love me in real time, every day."

He'd never thought of a relationship like that.

"One day I want kids. I refuse to raise them by myself. I want it all, Niklas. A home, a husband, father, kids... a place to paint, to create." She stepped closer to him. "Can you give me that? Is there a way to make that work?"

Pups. Home. Husband. Father. Those words hit him like bullets and penetrated his mind with critical precision. Why hadn't he equated being mated with any of those things? Why hadn't he thought of pups? He hadn't thought further than making love to her all night and keeping her by his side. For what? Sex? That wasn't fair to her. Renee was so much more than a piece of delectable ass.

Mother of his pups? Yes.

Pups? There were times he played with the Alpha's pups when he wondered what it would be like to have them full time. But he'd never thought to sire his own. Over the years, it never happened, at least not to his knowledge. He assumed it wasn't meant to be. Being mated changed that. He pulled Renee close and held her gently, revising his opinion of her and this whole mating thing.

"I'll give you whatever you need to make it work. I promise you that. This last job closes the book on my past, when I return we'll begin a new chapter. A new book if necessary." He kissed the top of her head, desperately wishing he could have more.

She leaned back and stared at him. Reflected in her eyes, he saw the same need he felt. It took no coaxing at all for him to lean down and kiss her.

CHAPTER THIRTEEN

RENEE LAY IN HER BED, on her side in the dark. Three hours and nine minutes had passed since Niklas Storm kissed her goodnight and left the museum. She turned over searching for a cool spot to ease the burning heat racing through her body. "Cut it out," she muttered to her beast, certain this was some sort of repayment for not having sex with Storm earlier.

Unable to rest or get comfortable, she flopped onto her back and released a long stream of air. "*Jackie?*" She waited a moment. "*Jackie? Are you sleep?*" She paused. Biting her lip, she closed her eyes. "*Jackie? Are you up?*"

"*I am now.*"

"*Good, come to my room. I need to talk.*"

"*Why do I have to leave my bed to talk?*"

Renee had no real reason other than she didn't want to be alone. "*I want to see your face when I tell you about Niklas.*"

"*Niklas? Is that the guy you left with?*"

"*Yes.*" She wasn't surprised Jackie knew about that.

"*Did something happen?*"

"*Are you coming or not?*" Renee snapped and then felt bad. Jackie was in bed with her mate, Renee needed to learn to handle her own problems. "*Never mind.*"

"*You okay?*"

"*Just got stuff on my mind.*"

"*Open the door.*"

Renee rolled out of bed, inhaled and opened the door.

Jackie walked in yawning, grabbed the extra blanket from the foot of the bed and wrapped it around her shoulders. Once she tucked it around her legs she looked at Renee. "What's going on?"

Renee joined her sister in bed and told her everything since she met Storm in the tunnel. When she was done Jackie released a breath. "Wish you'd told me about him before I got Duke and Raven's hopes up about you and Lucian."

"He doesn't have any interest in art," Renee said.

"He's rebuilding a poor country, they'll get around to art after food, housing and health needs are met. Not that it matters, Storm's your mate." Jackie paused and then smiled. It grew bigger and bigger. "Your mate. You're mated. Renee you're mated."

Forcing a smile, Renee nodded. "Yeah, I just told you that."

"Didn't register until now." Jackie frowned. "He's really leaving tomorrow? How're you going to handle that?"

"Fine I hope. We only kissed once. Thought I'd crawl into his skin, but we stopped short of... well sex." She looked at Jackie. "I'm scared that's not enough. I can't sleep. I keep thinking about him. Keep seeing him, hearing the disappointment in his voice and then the total resolve to make this work." She shook her head. "Make us work. He's really intense."

"Again, I ask, is he really leaving tomorrow?"

"This is the last job from his past. We start together when he comes back," Renee said.

"Hmm, okay. Let's hope nothing goes wrong and he makes it back soon. I don't want you to suffer."

"I don't want to suffer. I also don't want a mercenary for a mate. Seems like I got the daily double," Renee said.

"Come here." Jackie wrapped her arm around Renee and stroked her hair. They laid in comfortable silence for several minutes. "I think Adam is going to quit playing ball for Bella."

Renee jerked and sat up, brushing her hair from her face. "What? Why?"

"You missed her performance tonight, Bella had Mama and Nana crying. She was that good. Several Alphas asked her to perform at various events around the Nation. Higley told Adam to hire Bella an assistant since it was obvious she loved performing."

Renee's hand covered her mouth. How could she have missed Bella's performance after working so hard to reassure her sister-in-law to sing in front of the crowd. "No. What did Adam do?"

Jackie shrugged. "He said if that's what Bella wanted to do, they'd do it."

"What about playing ball? Will she perform during the off season? Wait, do they have an off season?" Renee asked.

"I don't know. She's brilliant, and would take the world by storm if she wasn't a breeder. Pictures, recordings, technology..." Jackie shook her head. "Too easy to tell she wasn't aging like other humans, that something was different about her. Exposure would happen eventually."

"True. But Adam plays sports. That's the definition next to his name, like art is next to mine. It's hard to believe he'd give it up," Renee said thinking of Storm.

"Maybe he won't give it up, just make changes so they can both do what they need to be whole, happy. Loving someone is about compromise. Quinn and I both gave up things we thought we needed to make our life work better. When I look back, I realize I don't miss anything, I'm complete."

"He completes you, I get it. I'm not there yet." She looked at Jackie. "I don't want to give up my studio, or live in tents or travel to dangerous places. That's not me. I'm not an outdoorsy kind of chick. I want, need, air condition, dry cleaners, a bed and a room with no bugs."

Jackie laughed. "I want those things too. It's just... when we're helping people who've never had AC, or a bed and bugs are a way of life, I don't think about my discomfort. I know it's temporary. For them, it's an everyday reality."

Renee sighed. "To be a doctor's mate and not a mercenary's."

"I agree there is a big difference. But he's going to change his ways, just for you. That means something, right?"

"What if he can't change? Do I have the right to ask him to change who he is?"

"That's what he does, I doubt it's who he is. And yes, as his mate, you have every right to ask him to change jobs," Jackie said. "Not only ask, but expect him to do so. There's a bounty on his head, which puts his den at risk. Does the Goddess' protection extend to his den?"

"Good question," Renee said. "Who knows the answer?"

"He's handsome in a rugged, James Bond kind of way," Jackie a few moments later. "Can't wait to see your pups."

Renee snorted and hit her sister with a pillow. "I want to see yours first."

Jackie laughed. "Not for a while. Quinn's going back to do his residency. He's been accepted a few places, we haven't decided where yet. So... that means you first."

Renee snorted. "Or Bella."

Jackie laughed. "I can see that."

"Can't believe my mate gets paid to kill people," Renee muttered. "The Goddess must be mad at somebody." She looked up at the ceiling. "Why take it out on me?"

Jackie rubbed her arm. "Call him. You should be talking to him."

"It's late," Renee said even though her heart jumped at the idea of talking to Storm. She ached to hear his voice.

"You think he's sleeping?" Jackie yawned and scooted off the bed. "Doubtful." Standing, she looked down at Renee. "Why are you here and not with him anyway?" She held up her hand when Renee started to speak. "Rhetorical question to get you thinking. I'm going back to bed." She waved and sauntered toward the door. "Call him, you know you want to."

Renee stared at the closed door and exhaled. What was she doing? She hated games. Jackie was right, she wanted to talk to him. Leaning toward her nightstand, she picked up her phone, called the hotel and asked for his room. Storm picked up on the second ring.

"Yeah?"

"Hey." She closed her eyes and lay back. His voice sent a needy chill through her.

"Renee. I can't sleep thinking about you."

Her heart melted at his words. "Same here. I figured if I couldn't sleep —" How much should she tell him? They weren't mated yet, they had no mental links.

"Yeah, I know. If I had a way to contact you, believe me, I would've called. This burning need inside, I can't believe how intense it is. Wonder if it's normal or because of my connection to Grandfather."

She hadn't thought of that. "I don't know. I can ask my sister or brother, they're mated."

"Doesn't matter. Won't change anything." He paused. Took a breath and released it. "Do you cook? What do you like to cook?"

Smiling at his attempts to calm down, she said. "All of us cook. Mama taught us. I enjoy baking. But I can prepare almost anything. What do you like to eat?"

"Meat, not a lot of green leafy stuff, don't have much of a sweet tooth. Although I'm sure it's because I never had much growing up." He paused. "I eat a lot but not often."

"My brothers are like that," she said. "They miss meals all the time but when they sit down to eat, they make up for it."

"Exactly. Bake something for me when I come back." His voice dropped an octave, rolling over her like warm honey. Her pussy throbbed. Nipples hardened. Chill bumps rose across her arms in anticipation.

"Okay." She took a deep breath to focus. "Do you cook?"

"Not at all." He laughed. "I've tried but haven't had much success. Will you teach me?"

Goddess, he was killing her. She squirmed, trying to put a damper on the fiery need building in her belly. "Sure. I'll start a list of things to teach you."

He groaned. "What's your favorite color?"

"Blue. Yours?" She turned over trying to find a cool spot on the bed.

"Gray." He laughed. "That's a shitty color. What about red?"

"Only if it's your favorite," she said enjoying the light banter.

"I never thought about a favorite color, red is as good as any. I can still smell your incredible scent, must've taken found a spot inside and settled. Every time I move, even an inch, I smell you." He paused. "This isn't working."

Renee bit her lip and placed a pillow between her legs. "What's not working?" Her beast clawed and snapped, demanding she go find their mate.

"I need you, so bad." The words sounded as if they were ripped from his throat. "Never experienced anything like this before."

The more they talked, the more the need grew. Their words were fertilizer, or gas fueling the flames of need. It was more than sex, Renee knew the difference. On some level, she craved Storm in a way she never wanted anyone else, not even Tomas and they were in love. If she could step outside herself, the way she did when creating art, she could see how remarkable this attraction was. Driven by gut-wrenching need, she was handicapped, lost her focus and objectivity. Rolling out of bed, she grabbed her purse and keys.

"Me neither," she murmured, looking at her boy shorts and tee shirt. She grabbed a long jacket from the closet, slipped it on and left her room. Fuck this, she was going to get what she needed. When she reached the lower level, and was in her car, she interrupted Storm.

"I'm going to my condo in town. Meet me there."

STORM LEFT THE HOTEL minutes after Renee told him she was on her way. He ran the five miles to the edge of town and paced in front of the condo building. She was coming. She was on her way. Need for her became a living, breathing thing. He leashed his beast, promising him they'd be with their mate soon.

Skin tight, heart racing, he sought a cool breeze to ease the fire burning in his loins. How did mates handle this? It seemed extreme. How would he leave her tomorrow? Could he?

Romano had been understanding once Storm told him he'd met his mate. The Alpha pushed for more information, but Storm refused. As La Patron's daughter, Renee could be targeted for kidnapping or used as leverage against Storm or her father. Romano offered to release him from this promise in exchange for another one in the future. Storm said no. He wanted this over, so he could focus on his mate.

Noise from a car turning the corner and moving fast down the road caught his attention. The silver car stopped in front of him. He picked up her scent and slid in the front seat. She took off and they entered the secured parking lot after she passed through security.

Storm didn't look at her.

He sat still with his hands clasped tightly in his lap. He ached to fill her, to merge with her. But if he touched her now, they wouldn't make it to her place. He sensed she felt the same. She zipped into a numbered parking space, got out the car while grabbing her purse. He slid out the passenger side, closed his door and ran to the driver side to close it as well. He caught up with her in the elevator.

Inside that small cage her scent amplified. Mindful of the security cameras, he edged away from her. She took several deep breaths as if she had just run a marathon. He understood, they were both on the edge. The doors opened on the third floor. She strode out without a backward glance; her coat hid what was indelibly printed in his mind. The sway of her hips mesmerized him. She stopped in front of a door at the end of the hall, unlocked it and walked inside.

"Easy," he said to calm down before following and closing the door.

"Lock it." She had removed her coat and stood in the middle of the living room in a pair of short shorts and tee shirt.

Storm's mouth went dry at the delectable, sultry manner she watched as he fumbled with the lock. The moment the lock hit, she wrapped her arms around him and bit his arm.

His beast howled as he turned, held her tight and kissed her deeply. Goddess she tasted good. Her arms moved from his waist to around his neck, pulling him closer. He couldn't think. Her scent filled his nostrils, and fueled his blood to boiling. He grabbed her hair, pulled her head back and kissed her face, neck and anywhere he could taste her.

She pulled him back to his mouth and kissed him, her tongue played havoc with his, demanding more. More than pleased she could lead as well as follow, he gave in to what she wanted. When she placed her hand on his cock, it throbbed in the introduction. She took her time kissing him, deepening the kiss slowly with her probing tongue, his cock ached to be inside her.

Mindless with need, his hand ventured lower, felt her heat. "You're so hot. So fucking wet for me," he murmured as his fingers slipped between her slick folds. Fascinated by her desire, he slid a finger into her pussy. Her head dropped to his chest as she widened her legs, moaning.

Male pride surged through him. He added another finger, scissored and stroked her, as sweet juices flowed down his hand. Doing this for her turned him on to the highest degree. "You want me?" He stroked faster, feeling her walls contract around his fingers, he ached to be inside her tight warmth.

"Your pussy says you want me. Tell me," he demanded as she bucked against his hand, inching closer to eruption.

Her moans grew louder. That wasn't good enough. She could get this from anyone.

Leaning down, he bit the tip of her nipple.

She screamed. Her walls clamped down and then pulsed around his fingers. Renee hit his chest over and over while shaking her head.

"Yes, damn it, I want you. Only you, Niklas."

His name on her lips sealed their fate. He picked her up and walked to the sofa.

"No, the bedroom is down there." She pointed.

With single-minded determination, he strode in the direction of her finger and saw a bed. Inside, he tossed her on the bed and pulled off his clothes. "Strip."

She looked at him and pulled her shirt over her head and shed her boxers. He lost the battle for smooth lover, this would be hard and fast. She rolled to her back and opened her legs wide. Her scent teased his nostrils, grabbed them and pulled him forward until he covered her. She grabbed his cock, placed it at her entrance and moved, sinking the tip inside.

Groaning, he slid all the way in. His body tingled as he hovered above her. They remained in that position for a few seconds, allowing her to adjust. He hadn't missed the spasm of discomfort on her face.

When she wrapped her legs around him, he looked at her. "You okay?"

"Better now, you're bigger than I expected. But you feel so good, Goddess this is good," she said watching him.

"I want you," he said. Uncertain what he was asking but something deep inside prodded him to say those words.

"I want you too," she said, a smile on her lips.

He shook his head, that wasn't right. He fisted her hair, forced her to look at him. "No. I mean I want you, as my mate, as my world, Mam of my pups. I want you." He stressed the last word as his mind spun, ran wild at the implication.

A flicker of fear slid through her eyes as she watched him for several moments. "I'm not sure we should mate right now, you're leaving, and I might not..." She closed her eyes. "I couldn't sleep tonight, and we hadn't mated. What makes me think if we don't mate it'll be anything different?"

When he didn't respond, she opened her eyes. "We have to do this, don't we?"

"I think so. This is different than anything I've ever experienced before. Like I said, it's more than wanting to fuck, which I plan to do, it's... it's deep inside." He shook his head. "Can't explain it but it's real."

She nodded slowly. "Yeah, I know. I left one bed to come to another. You're right, it's not just the sex, I wish it was that easy."

"Renee Knight, I want you."

"Niklas Storm, I want you."

"Argh," he moaned when she moved her hips up and down, clenching her pussy tight around his cock. He pulled her legs from his waist and placed them high on his shoulders, watching her eyes widen as his cock moved even deeper inside her, hitting on her pussy walls from another angle. He pressed down onto her, moving his hips rapidly, matching her moan for moan. He was fucking flying, nothing, nothing compared to this. Hot, tight, pleasure raced up his balls, down his back, his fucking toes curled as they flew higher and higher.

Renee screamed, her fingers leaving impressions in his arms as she held on, taking what he gave. Bodies slapping, grunts, moans, their mixed scents, just perfect.

Her legs shook. Her walls tightened. She arched her back, opened her mouth and yelled her release. Pride and need tipped him over the edge as he joined her in ecstasy. Taking several deep breaths, he rested on his arms above her crushing her breasts. Once he could think, he lifted on his arms and looked at her firm breasts.

"Nice." He licked a nipple and then suckled it.

"Niklas," Renee moaned, holding the back of his head in place.

He took the other nipple in between his fingertips, squeezing and rolling it around while suckling the other. She squirmed beneath his attention. "One day my pup will do this," he said, amazed by how much that idea pleased him.

"One day," she said. The tone of her voice clearly meant not soon. Which was fine with him, he wanted to spend a lot of time with just her.

He moved to the other nipple, laving attention on it while his hand splayed across her flat belly. Now that he'd sated his initial craving he would take his time to become acquainted with her body. Moving downward, he blazed a trail of fire from her chest to her belly as he licked and placed kisses beneath her breasts, on her stomach, thighs and finally reached her honey pot. Her pussy was almost bare except for a thin layer of dark soft curls resting over the small apex between her legs. Her folds were wet from copious juice. She smelled incredible.

An overwhelming desire to taste her enveloped him. He licked her tender folds.

She gasped and held the back of his head in place.

Pleased by her reaction, he placed both hands beneath her hips so he could feast. He continued licking her, drawing out more of her juices and then twirled his tongue on her clit. Moaning, her hand fisted his hair as she moved against his face. His lips latched onto her clit, alternating between hard and sucks and licks. His teeth grazed the tiny bundle of nerves lightly and then his tongue danced across the nub in a hard, fast rhythm.

She bucked against his face.

Moving slightly, he stuck his thumb into her pussy while playing with her clit. Her movements became erratic, as if she wasn't sure which sensation to focus on. He released her ass just as she climaxed and slid into her sweet pussy. Tight and hot, he waited until her walls slowed down and pumped into her again and again. He stopped and looked down at her.

"On your hands and knees." He pulled out and watched as she complied. His gaze feasted on her round ass. He placed kisses on both globes while fingering her quivering pussy. His bitch was sexy, hot. After lining up, he buried deep between her thighs, in that slick, hot velvet sheath.

"Yesss," she yelled.

Holding onto her hips, he shuddered as his thrusts quickened. He slammed into her, their thighs connected with a slap. Mindless with pleasure, he was hit with wave after wave of almost unbearable ecstasy, yet he continued driving into her, pounding her sweet pussy.

"Mine," he ground out as he reached his peak. His beast echoed his claim. Storm increased his pace, slamming into her hard.

Renee's body stiffened. "Niklas," she screamed as she shattered on his cock, releasing loud breathy moans from her throat.

Her silken sheath rippled around his cock and sent him spiraling over the edge. He jerked hard into her, his hot cum bathed her insides over and over again as his world exploded with her name on his lips.

CHAPTER FOURTEEN

THE NEXT DAY, RENEE leaned up on her elbow and looked at the window on the far side of the room. Time played havoc on their sex-life. She wanted to ride Storm one more time but had to make sure the artwork was shipped out and the artist picked up their checks.

She smiled as sounds from his sleep broke the quiet. He should be exhausted, the man refused to let her sleep, taking her over and over again until she made him stop so she could rest. Easing out of bed, she went to the bathroom to handle her business, brushed her teeth and took a quick shower. Her hair looked like a black bird nest, but she didn't have time to wash and dry the thick mass. She combed out the tangles and pulled it into a pony tail. Fortunately, her closet was in the large bathroom, so she dressed quietly while planning her day. Cutting checks was the most important thing, Crystal and her staff could handle shipments. She'd pop into the office, handle finances, delegate and be back here for round two. Made sense to her.

Leaving the bathroom, she looked at Storm tangled in sheets. Goddess he was sexy and potent. She would hurry back so they could get busy. During the ride to work she missed his scent. When she entered her office, thoughts of Storm filled her mind. She pulled up the records, entered the financial information and printed checks, the entire time her body ached for Storm. Twenty minutes later, checks printed, signed and in envelopes, sweat beaded on her forehead. What the hell?

"*Jackie?*"

A few seconds later her sister responded. "*You okay? I thought you'd be sleep.*"

Renee told her sister what happened after they talked last night, leaving out the marathon sex-capades, and asked what was wrong with her.

"Mating heat," Jackie said with authority. *"Everybody's different, some last longer than others. It's the best and the worst because it holds you tight. Storm's feeling it too."*

"He's sleep."

"Don't bet on it," Jackie said. *"You guys are linked and if you're feeling off, he is too."*

"I'm just waiting for Crystal or Edmund to come in to give them instructions, then I'm heading back to the condo."

"Good idea, and congratulations. I'm so happy for you. Can't wait for the wedding."

"Wedding?" Renee hadn't thought of that, but now that Jackie mentioned it, she smiled. Her own wedding.

"Bet you have lots of ideas, huh?"

"Yes indeed, I have to get with Mom. When are you leaving?"

"I want to stay home for a bit, sleep in a good bed, no tent or bugs." She laughed. *"Quinn might leave tomorrow with Lucian and Duke to help with the medical center."*

Renee's smile brightened at the idea of Jackie hanging around. *"I'mma be selfish and say I hope you stay, I'd love to spend more time with you planning the weddings."*

"Weddings? Is Adam and Bella having a ceremony again?"

"Not that that's a bad idea, but I was thinking of you and Quinn, me and Storm."

"If I do it, I want my own day," Jackie said.

Deep down, Renee felt the same. "*Okay. No problem.*

Her office door opened. Her skin prickled before she looked up. Storm stood on the doorway, looking at her as if she were a prime rib. Her beast demurred, no doubt sticking her ass in the air, ready to be taken. Renee licked her lips and stopped, she was no better than her wolf in wanting this man.

"*Gotta go*," she disconnected from Jackie.

"I had to get the checks for the artists, I planned to be back before you woke up." She spoke fast and frowned. Why was she explaining? He hadn't said anything.

He closed and locked the door. "I need you." He zipped down his jeans, exposing his pubic area and cock, leaving it open while watching her. Her stomach clenched. Everyone would know what happened in her office. She always kept her personal life separate from her professional life. The pull to take care of him was so strong. Standing, she moved to the side of the desk.

Crystal knocked on the door.

Renee took a deep breath, zipped up his pants, took his hand and pulled him behind her. "Come in, Crystal."

Crystal stopped when she saw Storm. Her gaze flew between the two as she inhaled. "You're mated?" Her hand flew to her mouth as she squealed. Eyes sparkling, she took a step back. "I'm so happy for you, for both of you. But you shouldn't be here."

"I just came to do the checks for the artists, somehow I don't think they would care about my changed status." Renee's wolf bristled at Crystal's close proximity, in the small room, to Storm. She handed Crystal the envelopes. "Take care of these and ship out the orders as well as overseeing the artist picking up their artwork. You're right, we shouldn't be here, we're out."

Crystal nodded. "Let me go first, I'll clear the area, make sure no one stops either of you. Stop looking like you're going to kick my ass." She ran out the door, closing it behind her.

Renee turned into Storm's arms. "I'm a terrible person."

"No, you're a wonderful person." He rubbed her back.

"If you knew what I wanted to do to her for being close to you, you'd agree with me."

He paused and then resumed rubbing her back. "Remember, I threatened to kill Lucian for touching you and that was before we mated. No judgment here."

She smiled. "Let's go. We need to be alone."

"Definitely." He placed his fingers beneath her chin, tipped up her face and kissed her.

She melted against him. He squeezed her ass and rubbed her against his hardness. They broke apart on a gasp. "Let's go." She looked at him. "How'd you get here?"

"I ran."

"Oh." She pushed down the giddy feeling his words evoked. He took her hand, and they left the office. Crystal had been effective, they didn't come in contact with anyone, not even after reaching the condo. Once back inside, Renee undressed Storm. She hadn't gotten a good look at him last night and all through the wee morning hours. He remained pliable beneath her hands, allowing her to touch, caress, and kiss wherever she wanted.

"What happened here?" Her fingertip stroked the long, welt on his thigh.

"Surgery from the Liege." There wasn't much else to say. Those butchers had limited experience back then and almost killed him.

"And this." She touched one of his bullet wounds, then where he'd been sliced open by a knife in a fight. His body told the history of his brutal life. "I didn't know half-breeds scarred." She looked up at him.

Since her hand was wrapped around his cock, it took him a moment to respond. "Must be my unusual make-up." He didn't know why and at the moment didn't care why his body was riddled with reminders of his battles. Her mouth was too close to his cock for a prolonged discussion.

She sucked the tip, pulling it into her warm mouth. Her tongue slid beneath the crown spending a moment on the sensitive part just underneath the head, lipping it and tonguing the crease of the glans. Slowly, she ran the flat of her tongue from the base to the tip.

"Ahhh," he moaned as she went to work, with her hand and mouth.

"Your dick is magnificent, thick, veined. Smooth against my lips, wet under my tongue, hard, in my hand."

Her words scraped his skin, burrowed beneath it and stoked his beast.

"I love how you taste," she said.

"Fuck," he said.

She continued his torture nuzzling his balls, rolling one around in her mouth, while working his shaft with her hand.

"Oh, fuck that's good," he said moaning.

She scraped over his balls with her teeth.

He shuddered. His cock twitched. He widened his legs, to give her more access.

Her teeth scraped over him again, this time she pinched the skin between her teeth. The pain mixed with stroking his cock sent a thrill through him.

His legs shook. He wanted to cum but also wanted more of her special brand of torment.

She stroked his thigh, and bit down a little harder.

His cock leaked all over her hand a sure sign of how much pleasure he received from her mouth.

She took the other ball in her mouth and tormented it with soft and hard nips. His beast was ecstatic their mate liked a little pain with her pleasure.

Easing back, she looked at him with a smile and winked as she took his cock in her mouth again. She tongued the slit for a second before taking the entire head, sucking and flicking her tongue against the seam.

Storm's hand shook. He couldn't hold out much longer. His cock throbbed for release.

Her head bobbed up and down his length, squeezing his shaft hard between her lip-sheathed teeth. His back arched, her only warning, before he came so hard his body shook. Surprisingly, she took it all, every drop. Her eyes glowed with satisfaction as their gazes met.

She slayed him and knew it.

Storm belonged irrevocably to this dark haired, sexy minx.

HOW WOULD EITHER OF them survive the two or three-day separation? Renee mentioned planning a wedding. He hadn't understood what she meant until she explained it was like a large mating celebration. Uneasy at the idea of being around so many people, security would be a bitch. He almost said no until he saw her face. She really wanted one of those things. Reluctant, he explained why he would rather have all his teeth pulled than have a wedding. By the time they finished their discussion, the wedding was a go and his role had diminished to just showing up when it was necessary.

He could live with that if it made her happy. But this pending trip to Mexico bothered him. After the close call yesterday in the art museum, he didn't think they could be separated, not yet anyway. He could put the trip off for a few more days but that didn't eradicate the debt, which he hated. Staring at the ceiling, he listened to Renee breathe in her sleep. It centered him having her so close, knowing he belonged to her. That she would be there for him, put him first, and in time...love him. Frustrated, he jammed his hands beneath his head. He wanted them to start their lives together now, but this last favor for Romano hung over his head. What should he do?

"What are you thinking about so hard?" she asked.

Turning, he placed a kiss on her bare shoulder. "This last job. I need to get it over and done with, so we can move forward."

"Forward? You mean the wedding and finding a place to live?"

"Hmm." He smacked her ass. She'd been asking questions like that all night. He still didn't have an answer. "We can live anywhere we want." Alpha Adolfo made sure Storm had sound, solid investments that would amply support him and a family.

"What will you do?" She had made it clear, and he agreed, he would no longer be a mercenary.

"Maybe I'll work with you," he said, testing the waters. He wasn't into art as much as her, but he enjoyed her company. They could get along during the day.

"Yeah, no. That won't work for me."

He frowned.

"You need to find something that makes you happy," she said without explaining her previous response.

"Okay, give me time. I'll let you know." He hoped they could discuss something else, like a solution for Mexico.

"Do we need to find another place to live right away?" she asked. "I manage the museum, plus I want to be married here."

"We have time, I just wanted you to know we won't be living here." He held her gaze, so she understood he was serious.

She released a long breath. "Okay. I think you have to take me with you."

"Huh?" He frowned, trying to follow the conversation.

"Mexico. I'm not ready to be apart from you, don't think I can to honest. You don't want to have this hanging over your head." She shrugged. "It's just picking up a package, right?"

"That's what Romano said," Storm said thinking she might be right. For some reason, 48 hours after they first had sex, they were still in the inseparable part of the mating heat. Her sister Jackie hadn't experienced it that long, she could be apart from her mate for an hour or so. He and Renee hadn't been able to do that.

"We take one of the jets, fly down to Mexico, pick it up and head to Brazil. We can be back here tomorrow night." She looked at him. "When we come back, we need to make a formal announcement to my parents. They know, but it's important they see both of us and we tell them we're mates."

His gut tightened. For the most part he had forgotten who her father was. Their private blissful days were ending. Maybe they could put off Mexico until next week?

"Niklas?"

He nodded. "Yeah, okay."

She threw her naked leg over his and gave him a one-armed hug. "Thank you. Let me know when you want to get the jet ready."

"I need to call Romano, get new instructions for the pick-up."

She nodded and rolled out of bed. "Hungry?"

His gaze locked on hers for a few seconds and then roved over her naked curves.

"For food. I want food." She turned, giving him a wonderful view of her ass.

"Food first, then I want that ass." He smiled and looked at the ceiling. Could he take her with him? What about the bounty on his head? What if someone attacked or tried to take her from him? A low growl erupted from his lips at the idea. He and his beast agreed they would destroy anyone who would hurt her.

Still, was it wise? Why not wait, go do the Mexico job next week? It was a thought. He contacted Alpha Romano.

"Hello, Storm. I was just thinking of you and your good fortune. The package has been moved south of Guadalajara, and must be retrieved within the next 24 hours or I could lose it. I know you are busy and will send another. You and I will settle at a later date."

The idea of being pulled away from Renee at any time rankled. He wanted this over. "Send the location, I will retrieve the package and deliver it to you."

"Within the 24-hour window?" Romano asked.

"Si." He didn't want to get into specifics, the less the Alpha knew about Renee the better.

"If you're sure, I will text the location to you and notify the package holder to expect your arrival."

"Bueno. I will see you soon."

CHAPTER FIFTEEN

STORM AND RENEE LEFT the airport in Guadalajara, picked up a SUV and headed south on Highway 80. According to Alpha Romano's directions they had an hour's drive before reaching the small town to pick up the package. He looked at Renee and smiled. His mate had a knack for organizing and getting things done. Once he told her they could leave at any time, she made a few calls, packed a small suitcase and they headed to his hotel to check him out.

Three hours later, they were in the air. The flight took a little over four hours, they were on schedule to meet Romano's deadline. He reached over, took her hand and kissed the back of it. A wide smile lit her eyes. Storm would walk on water to keep that look on her face.

"Thank you for getting us here so quickly. I appreciate it." Very few commercial flights flew from Charleston, the nearest major airport, to Guadalajara. It would have taken hours longer to get here with all the layovers and change of planes.

"No problem." She leaned over and kissed his cheek. "Did you place the address in the map app?"

He hadn't. Three years ago, he'd had a job near the area Romano was sending him and he recalled the directions. Rather than bring up his former life, he pulled out his phone. "I'll do it now."

Once they hit the open road, Renee fell asleep. Not that he blamed her, they joined the mile-high club during their long flight. His woman was phenomenal. Beautiful, smart, warm, funny, graceful... everything he wasn't. Which was a good thing. One oddball in their den was enough.

The silent drive allowed his mind to wander. What did he want to do with his life? Renee thought he should do something he enjoyed, the problem was he hadn't done things in life for enjoyment. For the bulk of his years, he had been in survival mode.

Even with Alpha Adolfo, his main focus was on making sure the Pack's needs were met which meant doing mercenary jobs to help with their finances. Sure, he enjoyed playing with the pups, and watching the others, but he had no hobbies.

What could he do that brought him joy? He glanced at his mate and smiled. Other than being with her all the time, he amended. Renee made it clear she would continue her art and he agreed, she was too gifted to stop. He shrugged, maybe something would come to him sooner or later.

Remnants of his conversation with grandfather emerged. If the old man was correct, and at this point there was no reason to doubt him, Storm would have his hands full dealing with an out of control relative. Razor.

If Razor couldn't be killed, what did Grandfather expect him to do? Whip his ass and send him home to come back another day? Made no sense to him. Hopefully, Razor would remain in his part of the world and not come anywhere near Renee.

He chuckled at his situation.

Nice move, he thought. If it wasn't for his mate, he'd never get involved against Razor, there was no reason to take on that headache. Now that they were mated, he was involved. It would break her heart if something happened to her family, and based on what she told him, her family was huge. They'd need to talk about the Razor thing, come to some sort of compromise regarding mercenary work.

He glanced at her again, his chest tightened. For decades he'd been lost and alone. He thought Alpha Adolfo had been his salvation. He was wrong. Renee saved him. She changed the landscape of his life from grim to bright possibilities. The look in her eyes when she looked past his faults, blood-stained hands, lack of social and professional skills, humbled him. She accepted him as he was, but wanted him to be better, something he wanted but previously lacked focus and drive. During his life, very little made him smile on the inside, eager to start a new day, to appreciate the sands of time as he had the past few days with her. Clearly, they started a new chapter in both of their lives, and for the first time in his life he hadn't bloodied his hands to make it happen. That felt good.

Storm tapped the steering wheel with his fingertips. They should be coming near the turn-off. He glanced at his phone to make sure it was tracking them, it was. According to the app, they had another 23 miles on this road which surprised Storm. He was more surprised when they drove through a residential area while a mile and a half from their target destination. He slowed as he drove down the deserted road. Less than 12 large homes took up three streets. He sensed no one in any of the homes, no vehicles, nothing on porches or yards. Other than well maintained yards, curtained windows and occasional lights, it seemed the area was abandoned.

At the end of a long road, he turned into a long driveway of a large one story, house painted golden yellow. A high fence started at the side of the house and went around back. Several cars and trucks were parked out front. He didn't like the feel of this place.

Why were there so many vehicles? Or so many wolves inside? He should have asked more questions regarding the package before agreeing to bring his mate. *What was I thinking bringing Renee here?*

"I wanted to come, Niklas."

He jerked and looked at her. *"Are you awake?"*

"Not yet." A smile curved her lips. *"Are we there yet?"*

"We're here. And we're mind-speaking."

Her eyes flew open and she looked at him. "*Oh, wow, finally. I wondered why it took so long.*" She leaned over and brushed a kiss against his lips. "*Yum.*" She leaned back and winked. *"Let's get the package and head back to the plane. I want to sleep at your place tonight."*

"Something's off."

She looked at him. *"Like what?"*

He shook his head, allowed his beast to rise and inhaled. *"There's two full-bloods, three half-breeds and a breeder here."* He looked at her. "*Are you familiar with them?*" He hoped she understood the potential danger.

"Yes," she said. "*Good thing I came, she can't affect me or you either now that we're mated. Is she the one with the package?"*

"Doubtful. Our contact is Alpha Cy." He looked at her. "*If things... you may see a side of me...*" he tried to think of a way to explain his beast. "*Don't ever be afraid of me.*"

Laughing, she grabbed his shirt, pulled him close and kissed him. *"My Daddy is La Patron, my Mama, La Patroness and you don't want me to get into my brothers, Uncle Angus or Asia and Hawke. Bottom line, we leave this place togeth-*

er, no matter what it takes." She touched his nose with her fingertip. *"My Mama taught me that. Now, let's do this."*

Once she started talking, his grin started slowly, by the time she finished, it stretched across his face. Phenomenal, phenomenal woman. He slid out the car and headed to her side. She opened the door and met him. Together, they walked to the door which opened before they reached it.

A tall, hulking full-breed filled it. Hands across his chest, he looked down at them. "To prove you can protect the package, you must get through me."

"Seems like I'm going to see you in action sooner than later," Renee said. "*Should I step back?*"

Storm glanced at the man and shrugged. "*No, stay right there. This won't take long.*" He turned his back on the man, inhaled, spun around leaping forward. He kicked the full-blood in the chest so hard he flew backward, hit the wall with a loud boom before paintings fell and crashed on the floor.

Storm stuffed his hands into his pants and glanced at his mate.

"Impressive," she said and winked again.

His back straightened as his chest lifted.

Another full-blood came to the door, this one not as tall or wide. "Greetings, I'm Alpha Cy. Romano was right about you. You'll get the job done." He waved them inside. "Come, let's get this over with so we can all be on our way. Romano's anxious, it's been a few days and we've had to move around."

Inhaling, Storm stepped inside. Immediately he was hit with strong pheromones from the breeder. He reached out to Renee. "*She's releasing —*"

"Bullshit," Renee snapped, sending her energy down their link, coalescing and dissipating the scent.

"*So much better,*" he said and extended his hand to her. She took it and entered the foyer standing beside him.

"Alpha Cy, where is the package?" Storm looked at the man without searching for the breeder. The sooner they got away from here, the better.

The Alpha laughed. The other men in the room laughed as well.

"*What's wrong with them?*" Renee asked.

"*Don't know,*" Storm said, growing irritated. "I won't ask again," he said, fully prepared to leave and call it a day.

"She tried to stop you, but like all of us, you are protected from her charms. Romano is a wily one, he sent a mated courier with his mate. Very smart."

"*What's he talking about*?" Renee demanded.

"The package?" Storm asked Alpha Cy. "Where is it?"

"She's in the room, locked. Please take her off our hands."

"The breeder is the package?" Storm couldn't believe Romano wouldn't have told him, especially knowing he was newly mated. Renee would kill the woman.

Alpha Cy nodded.

Storm glanced at Renee, who stood with her arms crossed, tapping her foot looking at Alpha Cy as if she wanted to slap him. This was not good. Storm called out to Romano through their mental link, for the first time in months there was no response.

Storm glanced at a silent Renee, sensing the storm brewing beneath her narrowed gaze, he faced the Alpha. "There's been a mix-up, misunderstanding, I cannot take a breeder, especially one throwing pheromones, anywhere."

The men stopped grinning. Alpha Cy stood, frowning. "Not my problem. Romano paid a lot of money for her, take her or leave her, I don't care. We're done." Alpha Cy waved to the men, they stood, walked out and drove off in a hurry.

Storm looked at Renee. *"What do you want me to do?"*

"What do you mean?" she snapped, glaring at him.

"I didn't know this, she was, is, the package for Romano. The asshole played me, he knows I just mated and it's not a good idea to have unmated people around either of us. We can leave her or take her, it's your decision."

The woman pounded on the door. "Let me out of here, assholes."

Renee's brow rose.

Storm shrugged. "*Whatever you want is what we'll do."*

Renee's beast liked the idea of being in charge of the breeder problem, her anger inched down a few notches. She'd make a few things crystal clear to the woman.

"Open the door, I'll talk to her." He looked skeptical. *"Just because I'm an artist doesn't mean I can't defend myself. I'm my father's daughter, all of us can protect ourselves. And don't try and act like you weren't thinking along those lines."*

Storm raised his hands and stepped toward the closed door. Before he reached it, he looked over his shoulder at her. *"If I were a betting man, I'd always bet on you. Remember that."*

She nodded, inside her heart fluttered from his praise. Goddess he was great for her ego. He thought she could do anything, which made her want to be better to see that gleam of pride and appreciation in his eyes. Sensing he waited for her, she moved to stand next to him.

"Step away from the door," Storm said. He waited a couple seconds and kicked. Wood holding the deadbolt splintered, wrecking the frame. The door slammed against the wall and hung haphazardly.

Renee stepped inside and looked at the woman standing against the wall.

"Who are you? What are you doing here?" the woman asked, her gaze flit from Renee to Storm to Renee.

"Renee, what's your name?"

"You speak, English, thank God."

"Your name?"

"Trista. Look, I'm not going to fight you over any of these guys. You can have them." Her gaze flew to Storm who hadn't moved.

"Good thinking, why would you think I want to fight for him?" Renee asked.

Trista snorted. "Every female wolf I've met wanted to kick my ass for breathing."

"Could be those pheromones you release that enslave their men," Renee said snidely.

Trista shrugged. "I was told it was the only thing that would save my life." She eyed Renee. "What would you do? Fight them? They'd rip me apart. How can I defend myself?"

What the woman said made sense, even if Renee didn't like it. She and her siblings had been taught to do whatever was necessary to survive. "Do what you feel you need to do, as long as you leave this wolf alone." She tipped her head toward Storm. "I'll rip you a new ass for messing with him. Are we clear?"

Trista nodded and released a long breath. "Where are you taking me?"

"Nowhere. You're free to go and do whatever you want." Renee turned and walked toward the door.

"Wait," Trista yelled.

Renee looked over her shoulder at the woman who resembled the singer Beyoncé, although she was taller, and not as thick. Her long hair was a shade or two darker and she looked as if she rarely smiled. Definitely not the Queen Bee.

"Where am I?"

"An hour or two from the Guadalajara airport." Renee turned again.

"How? What am I supposed to do? I don't know anyone here." Her gaze locked onto Renee's. "I could use some help, please."

Renee stopped and placed her hands on her hips. "That's a problem, you're releasing pheromones, we don't want to be followed by every full-blood in the country trying to get to the airport."

"I turned them off as soon as I saw you and realized the others left." Trista looked at Renee. "Honestly, it's a relief not to attract that kind of attention, I never had to do it before." She wiped her hands on her jeans. "Please, don't leave me here where I'll have to become a whore or worse to survive. I want to go home."

"Where's home?"

"Naples... Italy. I lived there the past 50 years." She looked skeptical but hopeful.

"Will Romano send her to Italy?" Renee asked Storm.

"I've been reaching out to him, he hasn't responded, so fuck him. Whatever you decide is what we'll do."

"Aww, you're afraid to be alone with the breeder. Don't worry, I'll protect you," she said.

Storm snorted. "*Not of her. I won't do anything that could mess up what we're building together. She's a temporary complication, nothing more*."

"*Now I want to kiss you and we have to deal with this. I owe you.*"

"I'll collect."

Renee looked at Trista. "We can't take you to Italy, the best we can do is give you a ride to the States. You can take a flight from there. Do you have a passport?"

"Those assholes took it." She crossed her arms, obviously not happy with the way things were turning out.

"Storm can you look to see if they left a packet for you or something?" she glanced at her mate.

He nodded and walked off.

Renee strode closer to Trista. "Let's get something straight. If anyone comes after you because you're trailing pheromones, they can have you. We are not going to protect you from shit you start. Is that clear?"

Trista nodded.

"If we have any kind of problems leaving, if we come under attack, you do what Storm says immediately, no questions, no comments, if you do, we will leave you. Is that clear?"

Trista nodded again.

"Once we're on the plane, I'll call ahead, to see if we can get you on a flight at the airport, if not today, we'll help you get on a flight tomorrow. Is there someone you want to call?"

"No, not really. I don't know where my sister is. Not that it matters, she's mated."

Renee's brow rose before she spoke. "What does that mean? My sister's mated, so are my brothers. I call on them all the time."

"Carlotta's not like that."

When Trista didn't say anything else, Renee looked around the room. "Is there anything you want to take with you?"

Trista picked up a small leather satchel. "Just this." She held it up.

"I have to look inside before we allow you in the car or on the plane," Renee said.

Trista nodded, opened it and dumped everything onto the bed.

Renee held out her hand, took the bag and sniffed. She felt inside the bag until she located the hidden compartment. Inside was cash and three credit cards with the names "Tristiana Cavil." Renee replaced them, looked at the stuff on the bed and nodded.

"Thank you," Trista said.

Renee smelled and sensed her fear. "We don't rob people."

Trista snorted. "My clothes, shoes, underwear, all stolen. This was too old, beneath their notice." She waved at Renee. "I can tell by the way you dress you have no need of what I've hidden away, but to me it's freedom."

Renee nodded, turned and walked out the room. "*Find anything?*" she asked Storm.

"Yeah, just trying to wrap my head around a couple things." He looked up at her. Trista stood behind her. "Ready?"

"Yes, we are," Renee said glancing at Trista who nodded.

Storm strode to the door, holding a manila folder, he stopped at the exit, looked around and waited for Renee. When she reached him, he kissed her briefly and walked by her side to the vehicle. He opened the door, she slid in the front seat. After he closed her door, he opened the rear door behind her.

Trista nodded and slid inside.

Renee watched as he looked down the long road for a few moments before sliding behind the wheel. "*There's someone watching us. Not dual-natured, a human. Could be working for an Alpha or someone, I'm not sure. I don't smell weapons.*" He glanced at Trista and then at Renee. "*Have her lay down until we reach the highway at least.*"

Renee nodded, turned and gave Trista instructions. Her beast preened beneath Storm's attention to her and not the breeder. He hadn't spoken to the woman yet, which pleased both Renee and her beast.

They pulled out of the long driveway, and drove down the street. Renee picked up the human's scent as they passed and searched the area, but didn't see him. "*He's moved toward the house*," Storm told her.

"*Let's get out of here,*" Renee said, ready to be on the way home.

Storm agreed. A mile down the road, they reached the residential area, there was a street party. Men and women strode from table to table, taking food and drinks, toasting each other in the middle of the road. Men played instruments, a few people swayed to the sounds, they appeared happy and carefree.

Renee looked at Storm when he swore. "*This wasn't here before?*"

He shook his head, grabbed his phone and looked at the map. Turning sharply, he drove down several streets, trying to find a way to the highway. The last road should have allowed them access to the highway. Three rusted trucks blocked the road.

"*This sucks,*" Renee said looking behind them and then at the trucks again.

"*I could move them but...*"

"*We risk exposure. Was there a dirt road behind the house? The one they held Trista?*"

"*I didn't see one.*" Storm turned around, and headed back toward the road with the street celebration. They didn't have a choice, wait or be exposed.

"*Think they'll let us through if they see us waiting?*" she asked.

"*I don't know. Earlier, when we drove through, no one was outside, the area seemed asleep. Strange to see so many people so fast.*" He shrugged. "*Have to wait and see.*"

"*But you don't trust it?*"

"No. The timing, her... I don't trust it at all. Remember, they had to move her before. Someone may be looking for her, who knows?"

"I promised her we'd help her as long as she behaves," Renee said. *"So far she's doing her part."*

"I heard you." He covered her hand and squeezed. *"Like I said, we do this your way."*

They pulled up to the corner, listened to the music and parked.

"What's wrong?" Trista asked.

"There's a lot of people eating and drinking in the street, we're waiting for them to move," Renee said.

"Crap, I'm so sick...they won't move, they're stalling, waiting for the others to arrive."

Renee looked at Storm. "What others?"

"I was on vacation in Puerto Vallarta, saved up for years to come to this hellish place. If only I'd known." Trista paused. "Anyway, they took me from my hotel to someplace, that's where my luggage and stuff was stolen. They showed me my passport and told me if I behaved I'd get it back. I was there for a few days. Then Alpha Cy and his minions took me from that place. Turns out they stole me like a loaf of bread. They've been moving me around every few days." She sighed. "I'm really getting tired of this."

"*She speaks good English for an Italian,*" Storm told Renee.

"For a South American, your English is good too," she told him.

He winked. "*You do what's necessary to survive. Language is the first thing people remember when they have to identify you.*"

Renee couldn't imagine living that way. "*What about what she said, you believe her?*"

"She's leaving out some things but what she said rang true. Not that it matters, as long as she does what you told her, she gets on the plane to the States."

Renee bit her lip and looked out the window. The sun was going down, it'd be dark soon. What if she made a mistake in allowing Trista to come? What choice did she have? If it had been her, she would want someone to help get her out of the country.

"Do you have family you can contact? Other than your sister?" Renee asked Trista.

"No. It's just the two of us."

"*More people just arrived and they're coming toward us,*" Storm told Renee.

"Lay down and cover up," she told Trista who immediately complied.

"Good thing you got insurance on this rental, I don't think we'll be returning to the airport in it," Storm told Renee.

"*I'll have to tell Jacques,*" Renee said as four heavy duty pick-up trucks drove toward them. One drove past and parked behind them, another parked on the side and two maneuvered so they were in front.

"*Wonder if these are the same people we saw in the street a few minutes ago?*" Storm asked. *"It'd explain things. They knew she was down the street. One way in and out. All they had to do was wait until Alpha Cy left."* He looked at Renee. *"Good strategy. Not to mention the bounty on my head."*

"I like your head, they can't have it," she said fighting the fear rising in her chest.

"*My concern is that they may have drugs, I handle those fairly well, doesn't impact me or my beast much but I don't want you to get hit by anything.*" He looked at her. *"I'm going to take one of those trucks, probably the one in front of us. I want you and her to get inside and lock the door. It will protect you better than this SUV."* He stared at her. *"Okay?"*

The idea of him fighting all of these full-bloods alone, didn't sit right with her. But she didn't want to handicap him either. *"What about humans? Are there any?"* She inhaled and didn't sense them.

"Two f*ull-bloods in each truck, no doubt waiting for instructions. I don't sense any humans but that doesn't mean they aren't close enough to come in with guns later.*"

He took her hand. "*This is going to be ugly, brutal. I need you to remain close, in this car and then the truck I clear for you. Under no circumstances will they be allowed to touch you or take you anywhere.*"

Sensing a change in him, she nodded.

He released a breath and opened the door.

THE MOMENT HE STEPPED out the vehicle, his beast growled. A shudder of fury ripped through him. His vision blurred and then sharpened as he merged with his beast. The full-blood in the red truck behind him smoked weed, the black truck had a new car smell and extra metal, probably guns. His throat thickened, and his fingers lengthened in preparation. He moved his head from side to side while inhaling the scent of his enemies.

Storm had no idea who these bastards were, and didn't care. They threatened the safety of his mate and would pay for that. He remained still for a few moments before several doors opened and the eight men stood next to their vehicles, staring at him. Storm decided to deal with the one closest to him first. Moving quickly, he leapt on top of the hood of the rental, used it to give him room to maneuver as he dived downward, and punched the large full blood in the stomach and then beneath his chin, snapping his head back. Storm gripped his head, twisted it and let the dead body hit the ground. Before anyone could react, he leapt to the next full-blood and attacked him, breaking his neck as well.

A collective howl went up as the remaining six full-bloods ran at him.

Storm jumped over the first two, kicking them in the back, sending them flying forward into the ground, before landing in front of the oncoming four. His razor, sharp claws lengthened another inch as he spun around, cutting two across the neck. Blood spurted everywhere, momentarily stopping the other full-bloods who tried to help their friends.

Very few ever healed from ripped arteries when he used his claws. Storm wiped the blood from his face, and attacked the closest full-blood to him, slicing his chest and finally breaking his neck. The last three, surrounded him. Fear and anger rolled off them in waves. The ground was slippery from the blood of their friends.

One of the men pointed at Storm. "Demonio engendro."

Storm shrugged. He'd been called worse than devil's spawn, their words fell on deaf ears. More full-bloods were arriving around the corner.

The full-bloods charged. Storm jumped, came down on the back of one, twisted his head and jumped off. The body fell into a pool of blood, giving it a macabre appearance. Storm didn't stop or allow the last two to retreat, he went at their throats. The men backed away. One slipped and fell. Storm leapt on him, twisted his neck and ran after the last full-blood who tried to get to the red truck. Storm spun the man around.

Cursing, calling Storm all sorts of names, the full-blood swung. His fist connected against Storm's cheek. The next blow was to Storm's stomach and the next beneath his chin. He went flying backward and hit a truck. He sensed Renee's concern rather than heard anything.

Confidence leaked from the full-blood's pores as he wrapped his hand around Storm's neck and tried to break his neck. Storm released his beast and doubled in size. The full-blood lost his grip. Eyes widened with fear he scooted back, while staring at Storm's beast. Storm leapt on him, and severed his head from his body with his claws. Inhaling, he fought the need to howl in victory, there were others. Protect his mate, the thought fueled him. He morphed to human, it took a moment to collect himself and re-energize.

"Storm? I can't see you, are you all right?" Renee asked.

He pulled off the red truck's door, moved quickly so she could see him and opened her car door. "*Come on. Sit in the black truck, there are guns in the back seat if you know how to use them.*"

"*Okay.*" Renee opened her door and then Trista opened hers. Storm used the door to shield Renee from darts, blood and fallen bodies, as she and Trista ran to the black truck, jumped inside and locked the door. The rental had several dents from hits and body slams, it wouldn't be driving anywhere soon. Storm took all of their things from the trunk including the rental paperwork and placed them in the truck with Renee.

"*Have her lay down in the back, you'll need to drive the truck around the corner so I can see it at all times. There are more of them around there waiting.*"

She nodded and moved behind the wheel after giving Trista instructions.

"*Pull up to the corner but don't turn onto the road, I need to clear it first,*" he told her.

"There are a lot of them over there," she said looking at him.

"*Yeah, all adults though,*" he said because that did make a difference.

"When I tell you to drive, that's what I need you to do. I'll meet you on the highway."

"No." She shook her head. "*I'm not leaving without you.*"

"Renee, believe me, I know what I'm doing, —"

"I'm not leaving you. There is no version of this conversation that would make me change my mind. Not happening, come up with something else."

He released a breath, they were running out of time. Soon the others would come to retaliate against the death of their pack mates. *"I think the Pack has assembled, I feel their anger, it's growing. I need—"*

"Come up with something else," she yelled and covered her face with one hand. Lips quivering, she took a breath. *"I can't leave you here. Stop asking me to do something I can't do."* Her eyes filled with tears. She swiped at them and looked away. *"I can't leave you."*

"Okay." He patted her shoulder, awkwardly trying to think of words to calm her and came up blank. "*Okay, don't... don't be upset. I'll fix this.*" He moved to leave.

She touched his shoulder, stopping him. "*I felt Daddy die, he came back alive, just like you would, but I still felt it, that moment when he... when he died.*" She shook her head and her grief slammed into him. *"The thought of anything happening to you... I just can't. We leave together. Okay?"* Teary eyed, she stared at him. "*We're a team, I'll back you up any way I can, but we stay together.*"

Understanding, he nodded. *"Yes, the A team. Grab a weapon, keep them off the car, they'll come for her."*

Renee took a deep breath, nodded and pulled an automatic from the back seat. "*Did any of the other trucks have weapons?*"

He jumped out the truck, ran to each truck and took what they had. Most were still in cases or bags. After three trips, Renee and Trista had a small arsenal.

"*Go.*" Renee waved him off while checking ammunition with Trista and locked the truck behind him.

Storm ran toward the empty trucks, started a silver one, drove around her and onto the road. He floored the truck hitting several full-bloods like bowling balls, sending them flying through the air. When he drove through them the first time, he put the truck in reverse and ran over more. This time he jumped out the truck and tore into three full-bloods who came at him with outstretched claws. He extended his claws and sliced into them.

Their screams filled the air, sending others to join the fight. They piled on top of Storm, his face was on the ground. Inhaling, he called for his beast and released him. His bones popped as he reformed. His face elongated, fangs ripped through his gums and his claws extended another inch. He shook off the bodies and leapt toward two full-bloods coming at him. He ripped off their heads and sliced through the next person, moving fast he thinned the Pack within minutes.

A gun went off.

Storm jumped up and saw three full-bloods at the black truck. He tucked in his knees, did a spin and landed in the middle of the road. Dashing forward, he grabbed one full-blood by the neck and snapped it, before going after the other two. Within minutes he eliminated the threat.

"Get in the truck, Storm," Renee said.

He looked at the full-bloods in the distance standing or crawling. He hadn't eliminated the threat, not fully.

"Return to human and let's go, they aren't going to stop us," she said, her voice soft, alluring. "*I'm ready to go home.*"

His beast reacted without hesitation. He morphed and stared at those he considered his enemies as they tended the injured. They didn't pose an immediate threat. He opened the door, waited for Renee and Trista to move before he slid in the driver's seat.

"Are you okay? They didn't get in, did they?" He glanced at her as he started the truck.

"Yeah, we're good. They'd just run over here. I shot one of them, I think." She looked at him and turned away. "*What about you? They had you on the ground, before you shifted. Are you okay?"*

He reached over and covered her trembling hand. "*I'm fine. Let's get to the plane, I need to take care of you.*" Maybe when they were alone on the plane, she would open up, talk to him about whatever was bothering her. He didn't want anything to come between them.

Driving at regular speed he drove out of the area and onto the highway. Saying very little, she held his hand tight the entire drive. Her thoughts were muted, he wasn't sure what she felt about anything other than she was happy he was okay. That came through loud and clear.

Had his beast scared her? It scared most people because it was so dark, fast and brutal. Now that he knew his origins, his amped up beast was supposedly a gift. For years he had no idea why he was so different, so violent, with a need to demolish his adversaries.

When they arrived at the airport, Renee informed the rental agency about the car and paid the deductible. They boarded their flight with a quiet, but happy, Trista.

"Thank you," Trista told Renee as she took a seat on the jet and buckled up. "You saved my life."

Renee smiled. "Return the favor by not enslaving our men."

Trista agreed. "I had a boyfriend when I left Italy, even though we broke up, I know he's worried. One man is good for me. I don't want or like being around this much testosterone. It's too much." She shuddered and made a distasteful face.

"Chances are she has a full-blood or breed mate," Storm told Renee. He pulled her into a tight embrace, kissing her over and over again until the pilot asked them to take their seats for taxi and take-off.

"Probably." Renee took a seat.

He sat next to her holding her hand, staring into her eyes, being grateful she was his. "*As soon as we're in the air, we're going in the back.*"

Renee smiled. "*Someone has to watch her.*"

"It won't be us," Storm said as they lifted off.

CHAPTER SIXTEEN

ALPHA ROMANO WALKED back and forth in front of his living room sofa, periodically glancing at the large clock on the wall. He sent his mate and their three pups to the countryside with his beta. He prayed to the Goddess he lived to see them later today. A tingle raced up his spine. Straightening, he faced the door as it opened.

"Welcome," he said waving his hand. "Come in, would you like refreshments."

The couple walked inside, looking around. "No thank you, is she here?"

"No. I told you on the phone, she is in the States. From what I've been told, she wants to return home." One moment, Romano stood facing his guest, the next he lay on the floor, head throbbing from the surprise punch as blood trickled from his lip before it stopped to heal.

"Did I ask what she wanted?" Razor growled. His dark eyes held a fanatical gleam. Long, wavy black hair brushed against shoulders as he stood glaring over Romano. Dressed in a black business suit and white shirt, Razor looked like a dark-haired gypsy with a dimple in his right cheek.

Why had he gotten involved with these crazies, Romano wondered? The search for Adolfo's murderers took him places he wished he never went. But he'd been grieving over the loss of his friend just like Storm and hadn't vetted these two.

"No. She's not here." Romano stood slowly, preparing to fight even if it meant his death. And death was all Razor knew.

"Razor, let the man speak. We need to find my sister before harm comes to her." The tall, willowy, dark haired woman moved slowly toward the sofa, sat down and patted the seat next to her.

Razor glared at Romano, straightened his suit and moved to sit next to her.

"Tell us what happened. The last time we spoke your agent was on his way to pick up Trista. Alpha Cy says he delivered her to your man and now she's not here. She's in another country. We never agreed to that."

Romano didn't fall for her reasonable tone, not for one minute. From the beginning it had been clear to him who called the shots, Carlotta was the brains between the two. "To make sure my earlier report to you was not intercepted, I locked everyone else out. During that time, Cy delivered the package to my guy. Ask him, he couldn't reach me either."

"He told us, it's true, we were speaking to you at the time." She looked at Razor. "That was a long conversation, wasn't it?"

Razor shrugged as if the conversation bored him.

"Well then, what happened?" She asked locking her cold gaze onto him.

"He tried to reach me for instructions on what to do with her."

"Why not bring her here?"

"According to Alpha Cy, she released pheromones, they wouldn't have made it around the block, let alone to the airport."

"Yet, she's in the States?" Carlotta's gaze narrowed.

"They were going to leave her, she begged them to take her with them and promised to stop releasing. Once she did that, they took her with them to the States. Do you want me to go and get her?"

"Why can't she be brought here?" Carlotta asked.

"No one will force her on the plane to come here." He waited to get smacked again and released a breath when it didn't happen.

"For the time being, she's safe and out of the way," Carlotta mused. "That trip to Puerto Vallarta had been a gift," she murmured. "If she returns to Italy, it'll be almost impossible to get her without starting a war we aren't ready for. Her boyfriend has friends in high places."

Romano picked up a thread of jealousy in her tone.

"What about the bounty? Is it still on his head?" she asked, cutting her gaze at him.

Most were dead, and Cy complained of the lost. "As far as I know, Cy's men weren't able to collect, neither were the full-bloods he hired."

The words tasted bitter on his tongue. Storm would probably kill him the next time they met. Finding a mate was the gold ring, something they all wanted. Once Storm told him of his mate, Romano tried to release him from this job. Carlotta threatened to destroy his den the same way Adolfo's den had been destroyed if he didn't continue as planned. He hated being their tool but would do anything to save his mate and pups, even betray a friend.

Yesterday, feeling the noose tighten around his neck, he confessed all to his mate, begged her forgiveness for the man he'd become. His days were numbered, she needed to know that. Either Storm would kill him for endangering his mate, or Razor would lose control and rip him apart. His mate forgave him and had him write a letter to Storm, explaining everything. She was certain Storm would understand.

Romano knew better but wrote it to appease her. If something happened to him, the letter would be sent to Storm. Not to avenge his death, but to apologize and offer closure. Romano spent three hours writing the letter, and gave it to his mate, who would make sure Storm received it.

"Pity, we could use that money," she said, glancing at Razor.

"We should go after him, collect it ourselves," Razor said, his eyes bright with a hint of madness.

She patted his arm. "In due time, right now we need to take care of Trista." She glanced at Romano. "She needs our help. I'll give her a call and suggest she remain wherever she is until we find out more information."

"Sounds good," Razor said, his eyes clearing. "We can't let anything bad happen to Trista. We have to help her."

"Nothing bad will happen to my twin." Carlotta's narrowed gaze said completely the opposite as she stood, held out her hand for Razor to take. "Everything spoken in this room is confidential, to repeat anything is a death sentence to you and your den. Don't make the same mistake, Adolfo did."

A chill raced down Romano's back as he stared into the face of evil. Unable to speak, he nodded.

"Good, we understand each other." She walked toward the door. "Don't forget to make that deposit into our account before the end of business tomorrow."

"I'll take care of it," he said grateful to live one more night and angry at the condition of his life. These two leeches demanded money just because they could. They used Adolfo's murder as an example of what they'd do to him and his den if he didn't do what they requested. In the past year, they'd given him names of people who'd done previous jobs for them and ordered him to tell

Storm those men were involved with Adolfo's death. Most had bounties, which Carlotta collected.

"Make sure that you do." She looked over her shoulder at him. "We'll take care of this matter for now. Go spend time with your family in the country. I'm sure they miss you."

Terror slammed into him as chills raced up Romano's spine at her knowledge of his mate and pups whereabouts. He sought his mate's link and breathed easier when she responded.

"Thank you, I may do that."

CHAPTER SEVENTEEN

RENEE RAN THROUGH THE woods. Howls rent the air in the background as clouds covered the moon. Heart racing, she kept going, as long as she moved she would be safe. Safe? It hurt to breathe. She jumped over a fallen limb and continued as a stitch plagued her side. Do not stop, she warned herself.

Something dark leapt across the path in front of her. Dark, insidious with long, sharp claws dipped in blood. Unable to push down the terror squeezing her throat, she bolted upright.

"Are you okay?" Storm asked.

Caught in the horror of her dream, she jerked from him, pulling the covers with her.

He held out his hands. "It's okay. I won't touch you."

As her breathing leveled out, she dropped the sheet and reached for him. "Storm." She inhaled his masculine scent, allowed his warmth to fill the cold spots left behind from the nightmare.

"It's alright, I'm here. Nothing's going to bother you. I promise."

Hearing his promise, she melted against him and took several breaths before banishing the dream. "I'm sorry."

"Don't be sorry, you didn't do anything," he murmured and kissed the top of her head.

She cuddled closer as they laid down and wrapped her arm around his waist. It had been weeks since she had a nightmare.

"Want to talk about it?" he offered.

On one hand she did, he might be able to give insight on nightmares. On the other, she didn't want him to think she couldn't handle something as simple as a bad dream.

"Sometimes it helps if you share," he added.

She looked up at him. "Yeah? Have you ever followed that advice?"

He tweaked her nose. "Yes I have. With my Alpha and with you."

Storm had given her access to his memories, even the new ones grandfather released. Together, they reviewed several. She understood his love and loyalty to his former Alpha. It became evident to her the Alpha doted on Storm as well, they were more like brothers, than Alpha and beta.

"It's weird, I haven't had a nightmare in a while. I'm not sure why it happened tonight."

"We've been back in the condo for a couple hours since Mexico, maybe that has something to do with it? Or leaving Trista at the hotel? The two of you talked all the way from the airport."

Renee and Trista had more in common than they originally thought. "She's an artist, a glassblower for almost 24 years. She wants to go to Weston to the Glass Museum."

He frowned. "Is it made of glass?"

"No." She chuckled, feeling better. "They make glass art there. I've been. It's not the kind she makes but she still wants to see it. I think she's going to rent a car and go tomorrow."

"She's not leaving right away?" He sounded confused.

"I don't think so." She paused. "Portland, to Chihuly Garden and Glass Museum, is where she really wants to go. If she can swing it financially, I wouldn't be surprised if she went there. For glass blowers and artists, it's a Mecca experience. One of them at least," she corrected.

"Hmm." He rubbed her arm and squeezed. "Tell me about your bad dream."

Renee exhaled and told him what she remembered. During her description of the beast attacking her, he stiffened and then relaxed.

"In one of your dreams it bit you?" he asked.

She nodded. "Yeah. Long, yellow fangs, and it stank." She shook her head. "Stank really bad."

"These happened before we met?"

"Yeah. It had nothing to do with you, seriously," she said watching him.

He kissed her forehead. "Maybe not, but the similarity of the beast to mine makes me wonder what's going on here. Grandfather mentioned the timing of our meeting. When you connect the dots, especially with this Razor in the mix, it's an interesting coincidence."

"So, you're saying my dreams of a black wolf attacking me was to warn me of your arrival?" she sounded doubtful.

"No. I'm not the only black wolf with a wolf from the old man. I'm thinking the wolf in your dreams could be Razor. Our beasts probably look alike."

She shuddered and moved closer. "That makes more sense. He really was awful, and mocking and he talked as if he wasn't alone."

"He's mated."

"So am I," Renee said.

"Indeed." He paused. "Would you mind me discussing this with Grandfather and your father. I'd like to see what they think, if you received a warning about Razor or if he's a threat to you, I need to know how to kill him."

"We've got to talk about your go-to plan for eliminating problems, Niklas. You can't kill everyone who doesn't like me."

"This is more than that, and as long as they don't touch you or say bad things about you inside my hearing, I don't care. But he attacked you in a dream, repeatedly. That's something I want to look into."

"Okay. But just the three of you. I don't want everyone to start treating me like I'm falling apart. Plus, I have to plan our wedding."

He groaned.

She laughed. "Talk to Daddy tomorrow when we go to the Compound."

He started to object, but realized the sooner the better. "Sounds good."

Renee released a loud yawn, putting a damper on his rising manhood. "Sorry. Long day." She nestled against him and soon her breathing normalized.

Storm held her in his arms as he stared at the ceiling. Did the Goddess protection of him extend to his mate? He would find out tomorrow from the old man. Was there anything they could do to stop these nightmares? He didn't know but would seek answers. Why had the beast attacked her? Did that mean they were coming for her? Or for him? Not knowing the answer to that last question robbed him of sleep.

STORM STOOD NEXT TO a smiling Renee as more and more people entered her parents living room for lunch. He forced himself to remain still as she introduced him to her litter mates and their mates. He had met David, and had seen the two older ones at the challenge. They spoke of their pups being in school as they hugged Renee, and shook his hand.

Bella, Adam's mate teased Renee about understanding why she missed the performance at the museum. Quinn, Jackie's mate gave him a sympathetic glance as Renee introduced her Nana and her mate, Jacques. Asia and Hawke hugged Renee, wished her the best as they were introduced as her godparents. Hawke took Storm's hand, shook it and said. "I forgive you."

Renee and those nearby laughed along with Hawke at Storm's expression. He realized Hawke was joking and forced a smile. He doubted he would ever like the man. Asia looked him in the eye and nodded. He wasn't sure what to make of that other than it was obvious she loved Renee like her own and he couldn't fault her for that.

Storm had met Angus but not his mate, Shyla, until today. Alpha Cameron and his mate, Lilly were the last to arrive and were introduced as her uncle and aunt.

"Everybody, Niklas Storm is Renee's mate, a gift from the Goddess," La Patron said as he looked at them. "They have bonded and are here to be greeted by the family." He looked around and took his mate's hand. "At least the family who is here today. I've been told my Princess is planning her wedding, for which I'm sure her siblings are grateful."

Jackie and Adam clapped.

"Stop it," Renee said with a grin. "You're still having a wedding, right Bella? Quinn?" Bella, ran and hid behind Adam. Quinn walked to the side of Jackie and did a slow shrug.

The others laughed, including Renee.

"Mating supersedes everything," La Patron said. "If there were problems before, they're covered beneath mating, and family." He stared at Storm.

Storm's gaze flicked at Hawke and back at La Patron. He nodded.

"Welcome to the family, Niklas."

"Call me Storm, everyone," he said before they started cheering. He only wanted Renee to call him Niklas.

"Storm it is," La Patron said. "Welcome."

"Lunch is ready," La Patroness said. She took Storm's hand and held it as the others walked off. Renee took Storm's other hand. The three of them stood together for a few moments.

"I don't know you, Storm, but I know my daughter. I see how she looks at you and know that you're a good person, a good man, someone she respects. And that isn't easily done, especially in the short time the two of you've been together. She's intuitive, probably because of her gifts, and sees things others miss. I don't have to tell you how special she is, I can tell you already know, you already care deeply for her and have linked your life with hers. That's a comfort to me." She patted his hand with her other one. She glanced at Renee and then back at him. "Be good to each other, become one. Storm, for now call me Jasmine, but one day I hope you call me Mom." She rose and kissed his cheek. "Welcome to the family, son."

Storm's throat clogged with emotion. Unable to speak, he nodded and watched Renee embrace her Mom. Parts of him broke and lay fragmented on the altar of his pride. He didn't know what to do with his feelings, how to act.

"*Renee*?" he turned and took her in his arms, stealing a necessary moment to pull himself together. His world had changed too much, too fast. Family? He had no idea what that meant, even when Renee mentioned it before. He thought he'd be an occasional invited guest to an event, someone who stood against the wall watching everyone. Never in his wildest imagination could he conceive calling anyone, Mom. He'd never uttered the word, had no real idea what it even meant. For some unknown reason, Jasmine's words, her sincerity and willingness to include a mercenary, with bloody hands, like him, almost brought him to tears.

"It's okay, baby," Renee said through their link. "*Mama's like that. She said the same thing to Quinn. She's going to treat you like her son, it'll take time, but you'll get used to her. I should've realized this might be too much for you. Are you alright?*"

He pulled it together. Stuffed that emotional outburst away and straightened. Renee was his first responsibility, after lunch he had a meeting with her father and grandfather.

"*Yeah. I'm fine. I didn't expect this, that's all.*" He stepped back and took her hand. "*Let's go eat, they're waiting for us.*"

Smiling and looking radiant in jeans and a royal blue and white sweater, she nodded. They headed toward the dining room when someone else entered the foyer.

"Am I late?" Grandfather asked. Dressed in black slacks and a white shirt, he looked dapper.

La Patron walked out. "You're early, I said we'd get together after lunch."

"In that case I'm on time. Add a seat for me," he told La Patron.

"Okay, but we talk after lunch," La Patron stressed.

Grandfather waved him down and approached Storm and Renee. "Hello, you're still as beautiful today as the day you were born. Your aura is glowing, I'm happy things worked out." He placed a kiss on Renee's cheek.

"Thank you." She looked up at Storm.

"Everyone's waiting," Storm said.

"Hello, Niklas," Grandfather said.

"Hello," Storm said not bothering to correct the old man. "Will you join us for lunch?"

Grandfather smiled. "Yes, I will, thanks for the invitation. I don't get out much."

Renee offered him her hand, he took it. Storm took her other hand. The three of them entered the dining room amid cheering and clapping.

"Good, now we can eat," Adam said rubbing his hands. "Mama baked."

Moans of appreciation rose from the table. La Patron and Jasmine sat next to each other at the head of the table. Storm and Renee took the two empty seats in the middle, while Grandfather sat in the chair next to David at the end. For the next hour and a half they talked, laughed and consumed huge quantities of food.

Storm listened and learned.

Every man at the table would give their life for La Patron without hesitation. The man had earned their trust, saved their lives on multiple occasions and their sanity. Storm's estimation of La Patron rose.

La Patroness was the jewel at the table. She gave birth to the twins in her teens and raised them almost alone while her husband was deployed most of the time. It was her belief in the strength of family that changed La Patron, who lovingly gave her the credit for shaping their large, extended family. Her children adored and respected her.

Storm had never seen or experienced anything like this and wasn't sure he could survive these large gatherings where jokes flew across the table with ease. No one took offense at the good-natured teasing over their physical skills.

"*Are you okay*?" Renee asked from time to time.

"Yes, this is fine, everyone seems to be having fun." Now that he finished his meal, he wanted to get the meeting over and done so he and Renee could be alone again. "*Would it be rude to ask if we could have our meeting now?"*

"Yes. Relax. Daddy wants the answers too, but this is important to us. Being together, talking, it's important."

"Why?" he didn't understand.

"*Pack is social. We strengthen our bonds when we're together, talking, touching, caring for each other.*"

"*This is a part of who you are?*"

"*Yes, to be honest, most Packs are like this. They hunt together, travel together, find provisions for the group together...*" she trailed off.

For decades he had been a lone wolf, unable to show his true self among humans. When he went hunting, he went alone. Things just worked better that way. At first Alpha sent a few Pack members with him, but they had been untrained, and he left them behind most times.

"You never did any of that, did you?" she asked.

He wished he could say yes. Wished he could be this pack person she desired, and perhaps in time he would. "N*o, not yet,*" he said, meeting her gaze. "*But I will try.*"

Grandfather pushed back from the table. This time it didn't surprise Storm when the old man didn't eat anything. "Thank you for everything, Jasmine, Silas."

Jasmine smiled. "You're welcome and thank you for honoring us with a visit."

He nodded. "You're more than welcome." He looked at La Patron. "Can we get started a little earlier, I've got a few things I need to check on and time is slipping away."

La Patron nodded. He kissed his mate and stood. "Storm, you ready?"

Storm nodded and looked at Renee. "*Don't get into trouble, save it for me.*" He tugged her close.

She laughed, leaned forward, and kissed him. "*Trouble you will get, Sir. I'll be here with Mama, talking about our masterpiece wedding.*"

He groaned and stood. Looking at Jasmine, he said. "I've asked for a relatively small wedding."

Everyone laughed.

"No help here I see." He bent and kissed Renee again.

"Storm, we'll try but Renee's been planning this for a very long time," Shyla said.

"Yes she has, but we'll keep it to one day, how about that?" Jackie said, with an evil grin.

Storm looked at Renee, she looked so happy. Hadn't he thought he'd walk on water to keep that look on her face? "Whatever you want, I'll do it for you."

Renee squealed, jumped up and hugged him.

Jackie covered her face while shaking her head.

Bella groaned. The other women grinned.

"Just do it all in one day," he added as he walked off.

"Smart man," Tyrone said.

CHAPTER EIGHTEEN

STORM LOOKED ACROSS the table at the other two men and told them what Renee shared with him. A spasm of pain flashed across her father's face, followed by rage. Good. He then told them what he suspected, regarding Razor.

"Is that a possibility?" Storm asked grandfather. "Could she have received a warning about him through her dreams?"

La Patron looked at the old man and waited.

"It's possible. Dreams are a vehicle I've used on occasion to communicate with Pack. He could've inherited that gift from me." He rubbed his chin. "But why Renee? I didn't know she was your mate, neither did you. These dreams started before you arrived."

"What if Razor knew about Storm? What if he had something to do with him showing up here?" La Patron looked at Storm. "Is it possible Romano knows more than he's saying?"

"Definitely possible." He hadn't shared what happened in Mexico but he no longer trusted Romano. "But the Goddess assigns mates, right?"

Grandfather nodded.

"Did She tell Razor Renee would be my mate? Meeting Renee wasn't a coincidence, like you said it was perfectly time." He looked at the old man and snapped his fingers. "What if Razor has no idea who Renee is and was simply allowed to terrorize a victim in her sleep?"

For several moments, no one spoke. "The beast looked like yours?" La Patron asked.

"Based on her description, yes, minus a few things. But the basic similarity was there." That still rankled but he would get over it and find a way to keep Renee safe.

"Sounds like foreshadowing but in a way that doesn't help you and your mate. More like sowing seeds of distrust," Grandfather said. "I don't know if the Goddess had anything to do with this."

"But you're not saying She wouldn't do it," Storm said, growing frustrated.

"No, I can't say what a Supreme Being would do or not do. I can only talk about what I know," Grandfather said.

"Goddess will do whatever brings the necessary results She desires, even if it means wiping memories of loved ones, taking you from one place to another or whatever. I don't know if She's involved, but I know it's within the realm of what She'd do," La Patron said. "What can we do about Razor? Is he a threat to my daughter?"

"I don't know," Grandfather said a few moments later. "I thought this was about Razor wanting Storm out the way so he and his mate could take over the world. In retrospect, that seems unlikely. Razor doesn't care about things like that." He snorted. "There's something going on there. I have someone looking into it, seems there's another one, a twin."

"How's he targeting Renee in her sleep?" La Patron asked.

Storm held up his hand. "What did you say?" he asked Grandfather.

"There's a twin." Grandfather moved closer to the table while looking at Storm. "Remember I mentioned the wolf who raised Razor found his mate?"

Storm nodded.

"Seems she has a twin."

"So?" Storm asked.

"Twins have the ability to use the other's personal energy, like a signature. Maybe I'm in left field, but I can't accept the Goddess would mate Razor and Carlotta. If she has a twin, it's possible the twin is his mate and Carlotta is masking the bond."

"What?" Storm shook his head. "That makes no sense."

"When Rose came to us, she met Tyrese first," La Patron said. "He and Tyrone both thought she was their mates, she liked them both, was attracted to them both."

"What?" Storm couldn't imagine being confused over Renee.

"Grandfather's right. Twins have a different bond, different energy. They merge, take on each other characteristics, at times it's hard to distinguish one scent from the other," La Patron said nodding.

Grandfather slapped the table. “Exactly. I think that happened here. At least that’s my hope and prayer.”

“Rose and Tyrone are mated; how did they fix the problem?” Storm asked.

“My mate told them to separate. As soon as they did, Tyrone and Rose recognized each other. It was a moment of sheer brilliance,” La Patron said.

“Indeed,” Grandfather said.

“Okay, suppose that happened, and this sounds like a huge leap to me, how is Carlotta pulling it off? Why does Razor believe she’s his mate if her sister isn’t around?”

Grandfather sighed. “Like I said, he’s damaged. Chances are they were all together at first, Carlotta may have claimed him, genuinely thinking they were mated. Once separated, over time she would know the truth, but convince him they were mates since he experienced the initial pull. I agree, it’s a stretch but it’s all I’ve got.”

“If you met the sister, could you be more certain?” Storm asked, ignoring La Patron’s interest.

“Yes. He’s of my blood. Do you know her?”

Storm thought of Trista. “We rescued a woman in Mexico, she was the package I was supposed to pick up.” He looked at La Patron. “I thought Renee would kill her.”

He nodded. “The mating heat was too new.”

“Yes. I put everything in her hands and she handled the entire situation. This woman has a recently mated sister named Carlotta.”

The two men looked at him.

“Turns out this breeder didn’t like using her pheromones on men, she begged Renee to help her escape. She’s in town at the hotel, although she may have gone to a glass art place today. Turns out she’s an artist, creates glass art.”

Grandfather slapped the table again. “Good thing you saved her and brought her here, without her, Razor would be lost.”

“That’s if she’s his mate,” Storm said amazed by how this played out. Maybe the Goddess was directing this after-all.

“Wonder who was behind her kidnapping and who would’ve taken her in Brazil since Romano is mated. The breeder wasn’t for him,” La Patron said.

“You’re right,” Storm said thinking it through. “I could ask him straight out if Razor’s bitch had anything to do with Trista being held in Mexico.”

"Trista? Is that her name?" Grandfather asked.

Storm nodded while waiting for feedback on his question.

"There's another thing," La Patron said, meeting Storm's gaze. "You said your Alpha was ripped apart?"

"Yes," Storm said and didn't elaborate.

"Another Alpha, Ricardo in Honduras, was ripped apart. At the time we thought it was the three men I told you about. But it's strange two Alphas, Ricardo was a black wolf, died the same type of death."

"There was no scent? Renee said the wolf in her dreams smelled bad," Storm reminded him.

"I didn't track the killers; Ricardo's Pack members did. They called me after they found them." La Patron sighed. "It's possible he masked his scent."

"But you would've picked it up?" Storm asked curious.

"Yes, I would have." He shook his head. "It never occurred to me that they missed something. Then again, I didn't know his close kin walked the earth either." He pointed at Grandfather. "If Razor is killing Alphas, we should have heard something. It's a big deal."

"You hadn't heard of Alpha Adolfo," Storm reminded him.

"No, you're right. I admit I thought it was an isolated incident, now I'm not so sure. If Razor is in South America, he may have left a trail of bodies on his way. Where was he before?" La Patron asked Grandfather.

"Romania down to Italy. He must have left the country from there."

"Trista lives in Italy somewhere. They may have met there," Storm said.

"I'll have Barticus look into it," La Patron said.

"I've heard of him," Storm said, pleased they'd have the Alpha's help to get answers.

"He's a good man, and Asia's father."

Storm choked on the water he'd been drinking. "What?"

La Patron chuckled. "There's a story about that, have Asia or Hawke share it with you."

"Her father? Are you serious? Barticus had a son and daughter, I don't remember hearing Asia's name connected with his." Very few things surprised Storm, but hearing the rich, powerful Alpha was related to a top-notch assassin hit the mark.

"Very serious. There are a lot of things you don't know, in time you'll learn some things are neither black or white. I've asked Barticus to send out feelers in those areas. We'll know something soon," La Patron said. "Tyrone contacted the hotel, Trista rented a car this morning and left the hotel. She asked for directions to Weston."

"That's where the glass place is. It might be a good idea to have security keep an eye on her. If she's attacked, she will release the pheromones and they're strong. Make sure they keep their distance, I'll have Renee call her at the glass place and tell her about security watching over her so she doesn't panic and run."

La Patron nodded.

"One thing puzzles me," Storm said. "How are they functioning? I wasn't able to separate from Renee for an hour, let alone being on separate continents."

Grandfather frowned. "You should be able to."

La Patron and Storm looked at him. "Why? Is the mating heat different for your direct seed?" La Patron asked.

"I never suffered from separating from all the mates I've had." He shrugged. "Made differently, I always thought."

"Didn't you die?" Storm asked. "Maybe that had something to do with it."

Grandfather's brow rose. "Possibly." He shrugged. "Maybe she's using her pheromones on him to keep him thinking they're mated. It's completely different but he wouldn't know the difference. I've always thought she was the one to watch, really pretty girl, but mean. Unbalanced."

"Two unbalanced people with a lot of power, bent on undermining our way of life?" La Patron asked.

Grandfather shrugged. "Could be." He looked at Storm. "I'll meet Trista today to verify she's Razor's mate. I should point out, if she is, it'll be important to keep her safe from her sister. Carlotta will not want Trista around Razor; the mating bond is stronger than the pheromones she uses to keep Razor bound."

"Do you think she will send someone after Trista?" Storm asked, although he suspected they would. As long as Trista was free, Carlotta's hold on Razor was in jeopardy.

"Yes, she may have done that already," Grandfather said.

"Renee talked to Trista, explained the reason for security. She said Trista sounded happy and agreed to be careful," Storm said.

"That's good. We have to keep her safe. She's the key to controlling Razor," Grandfather said. "Maybe you can find a place for him after he settles down with his mate." He looked at La Patron.

"No," La Patron didn't say anything else.

"Storm will you keep her safe?" Grandfather asked.

"That's up to my mate. I'll tell her what we suspect, and she'll decide how we go from here. Let me be clear, I refuse to do anything that will create a problem in my den. We're learning each other and I know my mate does not like unattached females around me. I would rather fight Razor every day for the rest of my life than cause Renee discomfort."

"I understand, that's as it should be. You've learned a lot in a few days on keeping your den happy," Grandfather said, sounding pleased.

"Renee is an excellent teacher. She doesn't leave room for me to guess," Storm said. "Why not keep her in the Compound?" He looked at La Patron.

"We could. I'll talk to Jasmine." He smiled. "Don't be surprised if you and Renee return to the Compound. She's been planning weddings for everyone, and no one ever took her up on it. Now that she's planning her own, she's going to spend a lot of time with her mom and sisters."

Storm's gaze widened and then he shook his head. "Okay, we'll move Trista into the condo."

La Patron laughed.

Grandfather chuckled. "It won't be that bad, chances are Razor is searching for Trista without knowing why. Shouldn't take long."

Storm stood and left the room.

CHAPTER NINETEEN

YESTERDAY, GRANDFATHER timed his visit to Trista at the same time Storm and Renee met the woman for dinner. Storm had been surprised how cordial and funny Grandfather had been, entertaining the young breeder with stories of a bygone era. Trista and Renee both laughed and seemed to enjoy themselves, asking questions and egging the old man on.

Storm had wanted Grandfather to get to the point so he and Renee could return to the condo. They hadn't spent much alone time and he wanted to rectify that.

When Grandfather finally got around to discussing Razor, Trista's eyes lit up. She spoke highly of the man, made excuses for his bad reputation and fully believed he was misunderstood. She genuinely loved her sister and wished the best for the couple, although it was obvious she cared more for Razor than a brother-in-law.

Grandfather took his time explaining twins and mates and how things worked with breeders and half-breeds. By the time he finished, even Storm believed it was possible Trista and Razor were mates. Trista grabbed the straws of hope and admitted she thought of Razor more than she should, and was ashamed. The trip to Puerto Vallarta was to help clear her head, and put more distance between them. She hadn't spoken to her sister but would let them know if Carlotta or Razor contacted her.

Last night, Renee invited Trista to stay with them for safety reasons. Trista declined, stating their newly mated status but agreed to move into the Compound the next day. Which prompted Renee to ask him if they could move into her bedroom or a suite in the Compound.

Storm hadn't said no.

This morning, all three of them moved to the Compound. Renee's mother assigned Renee and Storm a suite similar in size to her condo, so he couldn't complain about the lack of space or privacy.

During the drive to the Compound, Trista talked about Razor, Pack protocol, asked Renee how mating worked. She had accepted Razor as her mate without really saying the words.

After getting settled in their rooms, Renee, Storm and Trista walked down the main street in the Pack community several miles from the Compound. "Pack lives everywhere," Renee said. "A lot live here on Pack lands. We have our own grocery stores, restaurants, meat markets, specialty stores, schools, libraries." She pointed to a four-story building. "That's a business center. A lot of our college graduates have ideas for businesses or are interested in research. They apply for scholarships, and if it benefits the Pack it's funded. They get office space in a building like this. Every Alpha has two in their state. They're always on Pack lands for privacy."

Storm heard the ring of pride in her voice as she gave him and Trista a tour of this Pack community.

"Only Pack members are allowed here?" Trista asked looking around.

"Yes. The prices are so much lower if you shop here that Pack comes from all over the state if there's a sale or to go to the nightclub. But only Pack members who live in the housing area or their guests are allowed there."

"Nightclub?" Storm was surprised.

Renee laughed. "Yes, Bella's performing tonight. I want us to go, support her." She looked at him biting the corner of her bottom lip.

Storm shrugged in agreement. He'd hoped they spend the evening in bed, just the two of them but as long as they were together he would be okay.

"You too, Trista. You'll love it." Renee smiled at the woman.

"I'm sure I will." She looked at Renee. "This is all so... so... normal, civilized." She covered her mouth. "I'm sorry, I don't mean to offend you."

"You didn't," Renee said with a grin.

"It's just I never thought this was how wolf-people, like the ones who kidnapped me, I never thought they lived like this." She waved her hands. "Stores, schools, clubs, libraries, homes." She shook her head and smiled. "Living with my wolf one day doesn't seem so bad."

"Not all are like this," Storm said quickly. "This is the first time I've ever seen anything remotely close to Pack living like this. But La Patron has a world-wide reputation for taking care of his Pack. Seeing this, I can understand why his Pack thrives. The infrastructure is amazing. Pack supporting Pack. They shop and live here." He pointed to a butcher shop. "Makes good economic sense."

"So, it's not like this in Italy?" Trista asked.

"No," Storm said before Renee responded. "I think La Patron's Pack is the only one in the world with this type of consistent set-up."

"Daddy requires every Alpha to offer Pack-owned food stores, medical centers, business incubators like that one, schools, a college, credit union and a car dealership," Renee said ticking them off with her fingers.

"Car dealership?" Trista asked surprised.

"I didn't know that," Storm said. The rest of the list dealt with basic needs for growth and survival. But a car dealership? That was odd.

"Pack can't use credit reports, so unless you have cash, you can't buy a car. Same with houses. If a Pack member lives away from the lands, they either use a Pack credit union or pay cash," Renee said. "In every state there's at least one place Pack can go and get something to drive without dealing with humans. This helps keep us hidden."

Storm was impressed. Of course, La Patron had been doing this a long time, but the level of organization and care his Pack received was top notch.

"I hope Razor and I can live in the states on Pack lands." She looked at Renee. "Is that a possibility?"

"Talk to my Dad when we return to the Compound, he can tell you what's involved." Renee glanced at Storm. "We can drive through the residential area if you want to see it."

"I'd love to see it," Trista said.

"*Whatever you want is fine with me*," Storm said as they walked back to her car. *"I'd like to spend some alone time with you before we go out tonight."*

"Most definitely. After this, I promised to take Trista to the art museum and then we're done for the day. Do you think she's Razor's mate?"

"Either that or she's in lust with her sister's mate."

"Ewww," Renee said.

"*Exactly*."

The drive through the residential area was interesting. Storm was impressed how the areas were separated, single family homes in one section, apartments in another and town homes in another. Parks, schools and an office building that oversaw everything in the Pack community were in the middle for easy access.

"Definitely want to live here or in a place like this. We're going to join this Pack," Trista said as they drove past a park where several children played, and parents sat on nearby benches talking. "This is what I want." She wiped her face.

Renee's heart dropped in dismay. "*Maybe we shouldn't have brought her here,*" she said glancing at him.

"You brought me, to show me how your Pack operated. She's along for the ride," Storm said and winked at her.

"Of course, you're right." She smiled. "Next stop the art museum. Storm and I have to be back for lunch, so we only have a couple hours to do this." She looked at Trista.

"Thanks, I understand. I can always come back, right?" Trista looked at her.

"Of course. It's only open to Pack but I'll put you on a waiver list. It's my baby," Renee said glancing at him. "I'm thinking of having my wedding reception here."

Storm inhaled slowly and looked at her.

Renee grinned.

"That's awesome. Show me where and what ideas you have. I'd love to make something that matches your theme as a wedding gift. Are you excited?"

"I am. I've always wanted to have a big wedding. Now I will." Renee reached over and covered his hand.

Storm lifted hers and kissed the back. "Whatever you want is yours." How big is big, he wondered?

Renee's smile widened.

"That's so sweet," Trista said. Her eyes filled. "I want that one day."

Renee glanced at him.

"*Not my problem, he said. Don't know Razor and don't care what they do. I just want you to be happy and know you're my sun and moon.*"

"You say that while I'm driving and can't kiss you," she complained.

"Stop the car."

Renee looked at him and pulled over. As soon as the car was in park. Storm reached over and kissed her. *"I need to be inside you right now. I'm burning up with need for you."*

"I feel it. At the museum," she promised.

They broke apart. She stopped breathing almost immediately as her gaze locked with his. *"Soon, baby."*

He nodded and sat back in his seat.

She pulled onto the highway.

WHEN THEY ARRIVED AT the museum, Storm exited the car, opened Renee's door and pulled her close for another kiss. Trista slid out and waited a few feet to the side. Renee loved the way he tasted, all sweet and spicy. The way his muscles bunched beneath her hand and how he completely focused on her.

She was falling for him, big time.

They separated, she stared into his dark eyes and saw her future. Her fingertip stroked his full lower lip. *"I'm so lucky to have you."*

His brow rose, followed by a large grin. With one arm still around her waist, he turned and they headed toward the walkway for the museum offices. "*You just made my day,*" he said.

"And your night." She winked and unlocked the door. Storm held it as she and Trista entered.

"I love the way it smells in here," Trista said twirling slowly while taking deep breaths. "If you point me in the direction I need to go, I'll give you guys some privacy." She smiled at Renee.

"One second, Crystal, my assistant is on her way, she'll get you started. We're going to my office and will meet up with you." Renee tugged on Storm's hand while moving down the hall.

Crystal came barreling down the corridor and stopped. "You're here? Everything okay?" She looked at Renee, Storm and then Trista. "Hello Storm. Hello, I'm Crystal." She extended a hand to Trista.

"Hello."

"Anybody ever said you look like Beyoncé?"

Trista smiled. "Yes, yes they have. I assure you I don't know her and am flattered by the comparison which will fade the longer I'm in your presence."

Crystal laughed.

"She's a glass artist, start her there and then give her a tour of whatever she wants to see," Renee said. "She's my guest, visiting for the moment. Place her on the waiver list for me, please." Renee looked at Trista. "Crystal will need to make a copy of your ID for the waiver, it will remain on file."

"That's fine, I appreciate this." She moved to follow Crystal. "Thanks."

Renee and Storm entered her office. He turned, placed his hand above her head, leaned down and kissed her. Delicious shivers rippled up her spine. Her purse fell to the floor as she wrapped her arms around his neck, needing more of him. His demanding lips slanted over hers, his tongue sought entry into her mouth, she accepted him and moaned at his taste.

So fucking sweet. Her body shuddered as his fingers tweaked her nipples, while his other hand held her in place, completely vulnerable, ripe and ready to be taken. Those thoughts sent a tremor through her. His palm covered her breast and squeezed, lightly at first and then harder. She moaned, throaty and shy-like, deepening the kiss, her tongue dragged along his.

He moaned and squeezed her breast tighter. Pulled her nipples. Pain, pleasure increased her heat, her pussy throbbed. Her body melted into his as they continued to kiss. They broke apart on a gasp. His eyes had lightened, his beast was near the surface. For a moment she stared, mesmerized by the magnificent beast. His heat enveloped her, but they didn't break the connection. Storm peeled the clothes from her body, while holding her gaze captive.

"Fucking beautiful," he murmured watching her and removing his clothes. "My bitch." Naked he pulled her close and whispered in her ear. "My sexy bitch. Mine."

She heard the claim in her soul. His words reverberated through her, strengthening their bond. Bathed by his heat, she swayed, her head rested on his chest. The steady beat of his heart called to her beast and moments later they beat in sync. His lips kissed, and licked a path from her mouth, down her neck and across her breasts, stopping to suckle her nipples. Her thoughts slowed and stopped beneath the sensual onslaught. Tingles shot to her core. Juices wet her thigh as he continued playing with her sensitive nipples.

His fingers traveled lower. He growled when they reached her apex. "You're so wet for me." He licked his fingers and moaned. She loved the sexy sounds he made. Chill bumps raced across her skin as he placed her hand beneath her breast. "Feed me," he demanded as he slid fingers into her slippery pussy. Each suckle at her breasts sent little jolts of electricity straight between her legs. The double assault, nipples and finger penetration ripped her focus. She forgot where they were, and yelled her pleasure as he brought her close to the brink.

"*Niklas*," she cried, needing a little more to go over.

"*I love how you say my name.*"

"*Niklas, please.*"

"*What do you want?*"

"*You. More of you.*"

"*I'm yours, forever yours. You already have me.*"

"*Stop playing and get me off.*"

"*As you command.*" He increased the speed of his fingers, sucked harder and did something with her clit.

Her thoughts scrambled as overwhelming sensations wreaked havoc all over her body. She cried out and clenched her internal muscles as pleasure ripped through her body.

"So sweet," he murmured while removing his fingers from between her legs. He cleared her desk and sat her on it. "Feet up." He sucked her juices from his fingers while she leaned back and placed her feet on the desk. Moving slowly, he held his cock in his hand, lined it up with her and pushed forward.

Instead of moving immediately they stared at each other. Her fingertips touched his handsome face. Her gaze roamed his scar riddled body, her man had been through the so many battles.

He leaned forward, and moved side to side slightly.

She moaned at the exquisite feel of being full of him. Tugging his hair, she pulled him close for a light kiss, hoping to see his beast again.

"*You are my world*," he said.

Just when she thought she had her emotions under control, he says the unexpected. Fighting tears, she swallowed hard, opened her mouth to tell him what was in her heart and he kissed her. His hips moved slowly inside of her.

Her heart overflowed with love and happiness. How was it possible he knew what to say and when to say it? Vulnerable, she opened her links and showed him what she hadn't had the courage to say. She filled their link with all the love in her heart for him.

"Renee," he said on a long-agonized gasp. Their gazes met. His beast looked at her and left. "I love you so much." He pulled almost out and then slammed back into her. "Hold on to the edge of the desk." He cupped her ass, holding her in place as he thrust harder...deeper. Her vaginal walls grasped and squeezed constantly, grasping his cock as he pulled out and squeezing as he pushed in.

"Niklas!" Her breath caught. This man, was like a drug. She needed him like she needed air. Sounds of their hips slapping against each other echoed in the small office. They were fucking the living daylights out of each other, grunting and moaning like they were the only two people in the world and she loved it.

Her breasts jiggled like crazy. Groaning, she wrapped her legs around his waist, holding on tight as he increased to a faster, harder pace, pounding into her, sending sharp bursts of pleasure careening through her body. She growled her consent to him loving her in such a primal fashion. Her body strained with her release. She rasped out tortured groans as wave after wave of bliss crashed through her.

Storm drove deep into her over and over, again and again. He stiffened and spewed loads inside her. He jerked with each jet of seed, emptying himself until she overflowed with it. Still connected, he pushed her legs down and stepped closer between her legs.

"Mine," he growled and released her hips.

She smiled at his caveman antics and touched his chest with her fingertips. Slick with sweat, his chest hairs lay matted beneath her fingers. *"Now that you've had me screaming your name at the top of my lungs in my office, I think we've officially had sex everywhere."* She pushed against his chest.

He moved, grabbed the box of tissues off her desk and placed a few against her. He wiped his cock while leering at her. "*Thank you. For loving me. I will always hold this moment, when you accepted me and my beast, sacred.*" Leaning forward he brushed a kiss against her lips.

Her heart melted at the adoring look he gave her. She ran her hand through his thick hair and held him. *"Thank you for loving me."*

His eyes brightened, as he gave her a boyish grin. He looked relaxed, approachable, she liked he could be that way with her. "*You own my heart, loving you is my main goal in life. Now get dressed so we can finish this in a bed.*"

She groaned. "*I need a shower.*"

"*Is there one here*?" He looked at her.

"*Yeah, there's one down the hall for staff. I never thought I'd do anything like this here, so I didn't need one.*"

"*But you expected your staff to have sex at work*?"

She pushed his chest and moved off the desk. "*No. Sometimes we get dirty uncrating items for display. The staff have lockers and the showers.*"

He picked up their clothes. "*Let's go.*"

Her brow rose. "*I can't go like this. My Mama's human, we weren't raised to be naked around strangers.*" She snatched her clothes from him. "*Let me see if I have a lab coat or something here.*" She looked in a desk drawer, pulled out a paint stained lab coat. "*Found one. Let me see if I can find something for you.*"

He pulled on his pants. "*I'm good. Cover yourself.*"

She put on the coat. He picked up their clothes. Renee told Crystal and Edmund to make sure no one came into the showers.

Crystal laughed and agreed.

Edmund didn't respond immediately. "*Will do,*" he said a few moments later.

Renee peeked out the door, inhaled. She waved Storm forward and ran down the hall, holding her coat closed. They reached the staff area and headed for the shower. They were two super small stalls where you washed one side at a time. No wonder no one hardly used them. Clean, she glanced at Storm who pulled on his pants and shirt while it took her a few minutes longer to fasten her blouse and tight skirt.

"*I left my shoes in my office, after I get them, we can meet Trista.*" She looked at her watch. "*I have time to show her my ideas for the reception.*" Thinking of the wedding was exciting. "*The real reason I'm so excited about the wedding is you.*"

He looked down at her.

She moved closer, appreciating the warmth of his palm on her hip. "*I'm marrying you, a man I respect, who makes me smile just thinking about my day, a man who will father my children, a man I'm crazy about. On my wedding day, my Daddy will tell the whole world, not just Pack, but everyone, that he's giving me to you, to love and cherish for the rest of my life. That's the meat of the wedding. Everything else celebrates our commitment to each other.*" She paused, bit her lower lip again. "*It's important to me to do that. To make a public declaration that you're mine.*"

A smile inched slowly up his face, softening hard lines. "*Thank you for explaining it that way, I didn't know.*" He kissed her gently and brushed her hair from her face. "*We'll both be telling the world we're taken. You're mine now and forever, just as I'm yours.*"

"*Absolutely.*" She turned and headed back to her office. "*Someone's near my car.*" She stopped to look out the glass facing the employee parking lot. "*I don't know them.*"

"*Stay here.*" Storm strode out the door and called the men across the parking lot.

"*Daddy, is there a security team following Trista?*" Renee asked her father.

"*No. Since she's with you and Storm I pulled them, why?*"

She told him about the men outside.

"*Storm is out there?*"

"*Yes.*" She moved to get a better look.

"*Ask him not to kill them all, it'd be good to question them, find out why they're here.*"

"*I'll ask him but that seems to be his default for dealing with problems,*" she said and told Storm what her father said.

"*I was the same way until your mom came into my life. You'll be good for him, Sweetheart.*"

One of the men shot Storm.

Renee's heart dropped. She ran to the glass, pressed in close to the pane.

Storm flew into action. He zipped from one man to the next to the next in a ball of black fur before dropping on the ground.

She couldn't see him. Heart in her throat, she called to him. "*Niklas?*"

"*Trying not to kill this last one but he's talking shit.*"

She released a breath. "*Daddy if you want to question the last one, send security to get him. He's talking trash and Storm's on the edge.*"

"*On my way. I'll send a team to clean up. How's Trista?*"

Renee told him about their morning and Trista wanting to live with Razor on Pack lands.

"I'll talk to her about it after Razor gets here."

"He's coming?"

"If she's his mate, he won't be able to stay away."

"It is a strong, all-consuming pull," Renee said thinking of her and Storm. They'd been together a week and already he owned her heart.

"Yes, it is. But it's necessary to temper the beast."

"Temper?" She watched Storm return to each body and search them.

"We're never truly tamed, but we learn to temper our responses, take a step back to think before acting, that kind of thing. Our beasts need to remain true so that we can hunt, protect and provide."

"You think he'll always be like this? Ready to kill?" She wasn't sure she liked that.

"With the right trigger, yes. He'll temper the desire over time. All of us are that way. If anything happened to my den, I would be the same blood thirsty wolf I was when I met your mom. My wolf didn't die, or change as much as he realizes there are times we don't kill. The ability is still there, beneath the surface, he's not tamed, tempered."

She chuckled. *"Sounds like tamed to me, but okay. Not going to argue semantics."*

Her father drove up and directed security to remove the dead. Uncle Angus touched the man lying on the ground next to Storm's feet asking him questions.

"What's going on?" Crystal asked.

"I'm not sure." She told her about the men around her car.

"Storm's fast. Lethal. We watched him out the window," Crystal said.

"Yeah, he is." She hoped he'd tell her what was going on.

"Hope I meet someone like that," Crystal said.

Renee didn't respond. The only person remotely close to Storm was Trista's man.

"Does this mean you guys will be leaving? Trista is in heaven, she can't believe everything here is from Pack. I think she drooled over a couple metal pieces in the garden," Crystal said.

"I'll let you know when I'm on my way." Renee opened the door, walked outside and stopped.

Storm looked over his shoulder and extended his hand to her.

Renee moved quickly and took it. "Who are they?"

"They were sent to retrieve Trista," her Uncle said.

"I'm not telling you anything," the bleeding man on the ground snapped.

Angus stood, wiping his hands on a small clean patch of the man's shirt.

Her father waved toward security. They grabbed the man from the ground and took him away with the others.

"They were after Trista?" Storm asked in a doubtful tone.

Renee looked at him. "*You don't think that?*"

"Yes, but that's not what that asshole said. He claimed he wanted the bounty on my head. I'm wondering why they don't believe the guy."

"Maybe they could smell him lying?" She looked at her car, hoping they hadn't done anything to it.

"*He was lying, but why jump to Trista? Why not you? You're La Patron's daughter, a much bigger prize.*"

She looked at him.

"Yes, they were sent to re-capture her and take her to Lima, South America," Uncle Angus said. "Have you been there?"

"Over the course of years, I've visited. Lots of people, not the best place for a wolf," Storm said. "You're certain they're after Trista?"

"Yes," her father said. "How much longer will you be here?"

Storm looked at Renee.

She shrugged. "Almost done, Trista's in the sculpture garden. I told her she could return when she had more time."

"You think it's a good idea encouraging her like that? We don't know much about her," her uncle asked.

"Maybe not, but she's an artist," Renee said.

Her dad smiled.

Storm squeezed her hand in support.

"Would a mate send those guys to kidnap his mate?" Storm asked.

No one spoke for a few moments.

"I hope not," Renee said into the lingering silence.

"I wouldn't," her uncle said.

"Me neither," Storm said.

"That means someone else wants Trista. Probably her sister, or someone who wants to control him using his mate." Her father looked at Storm. "I think I'll give Romano a call, see what he knows about all this."

"I could go pay him a quick visit," Storm offered in a low, deadly tone.

"Now's not a good time for me," Renee said. "Jackie's not sure when she's leaving, and I need her input on the wedding."

The three men looked at her.

Renee stared at Storm.

"I would go alone," he said.

"I'm not ready for that, to be separated."

"Renee, there will be times I will leave you behind —"

"I know. But not now. It's only been a week."

He pulled her close and kissed the top of her head. "I withdraw my offer, for now."

CHAPTER TWENTY

LATER THAT NIGHT THE Club was packed. Storm sat with Renee, Trista, Jackie, Quinn, David, Bella, Adam, Rose and Tyrone at a large table in the VIP section. During his life, Storm hadn't spent much time in nightclubs, or any type of club for that matter but it was obvious someone spent big money on the sound system and décor in this place. He leaned back with his arm over the back of Renee's chair, playing with strands of her hair. A few hours earlier, he'd been holding a fistful of the silky strands while taking her from behind. He sent her an image of their earlier play.

She shuddered and looked at him from beneath her lashes, appearing shy when he knew better. His mate matched his beast thrust for thrust and demanded everything he wanted to give. They were great together.

"*When you look at me like that, everyone knows what you're thinking,*" she said and took a sip of her drink.

He shrugged and continued playing with her hair between his fingers.

"What time are you on, Bella?" Rose asked.

"First set's in 20 minutes." She looked at Adam and leaned her forehead against his shoulder. Adam placed his hand on her head, closed his eyes as if the moment was perfect and kissed her.

"Have you decided what you're going to do?" Tyrone asked. "Play ball or stay here?"

"Both," Adam said, giving his brother the side eye. "We've worked our schedules so we're here during the off-season, and Europe the rest of the time."

"Does that mean you'll perform over there?" Rose asked.

"No. I don't want... they don't have the same type of clubs over there," Bella said. "I'll be a ball-player's wife, maybe do one of those reality shows." She chuckled at Adam's look of horror. "Adam's hired an assistant to handle scheduling for me and everything."

"That's awesome," Renee said. "Make sure my wedding is on your schedule."

"Oh no, please Bella sing, do something to stop the wedding talk," Jackie said.

Renee elbowed her. "Stop. I only said one thing."

"You promised an evening free of wedding talk," David said.

"I'm not talking about it, you guys are." Renee pointed at them.

Storm smiled at the friendly banter, something he was beginning to understand they did often. How would his life be if he had grown up with his mam, sire or litter-mates? The idea was so weird he couldn't fathom it.

"Storm? Storm?"

He looked at Renee's hand on his arm, pushing.

"*Daddy wants to talk to you, says it's urgent.*"

Storm nodded. If La Patron wanted to talk, he could come to the Club.

"He wants to see you at the Compound," she said.

Obviously, she thought he should go. *"Okay."* Would Renee stay or go with him? He wasn't sure how he felt about her remaining. Not that her kin were lightweights, he was sure they could hold their own. But protecting Renee was a responsibility he took seriously.

She handed him her car keys. "*If you finish soon, come back or we'll ride home with David or Rone.*"

Dismissed, he took her keys, nodded to the others and left the Club. Outside, he inhaled the fresh night air, listened for heartbeats and strode to the car.

What did La Patron want? Did it have something to do with Grandfather? Probably not. Maybe Trista? Or Razor? He didn't know, nor did he appreciate being called like some school boy to the Principal's office. They would need to come to an understanding.

Storm passed through security and parked in the family area. Angus stood near the elevator and greeted him as he approached.

"What's going on?" Storm asked him as they entered the elevator.

"Jasmine received a message for you, she thinks it urgent."

Storm slid his hands into his pants pocket and digested that information. What kind of message could Renee's mom have for him and from who? It made no sense.

The elevator opened on a floor Storm hadn't been on before.

"This way," Angus said pointing down the corridor. Several offices were dark with closed doors. Light flowed at the end of the hall. When Storm and Angus reached the open door, he saw Jasmine sitting on a sofa looking at a large digital tablet and La Patron standing near a window looking outside. Thick tension filled the room.

Storm looked around. He sensed no immediate threat. So why the tension?

"You wanted to talk with me?" Storm asked. Renee wanted him to return and he planned to do just that.

La Patron turned, glanced at Jasmine and then looked at him. "One of Jasmine's contacts was asked to forward a letter to you. It came an hour ago and we've just verified its source is legitimate. It's from Alpha Romano's mate."

A heavy sense of dread filled Storm's stomach. He had met the woman once, but didn't remember her name or what she looked like. For her to reach out to him… something must have happened.

"Okay." Storm looked at Jasmine.

She met his gaze with a sad smile. "The women in the Nation band together to keep an eye on things. We have a simple structure in place that goes up the chain from neighborhood watch, to local chairs to regional chairs to the Alpha house. If it's something that can impact the entire Nation, it's sent to my office and we work to neutralize the threat. In most cases the Alpha's are on top of it and we never hear about it." She paused. "My New York Chair-person, Betsy, is the sister of Alpha Romano's mate who contacted Betsy with an SOS message." She inhaled and then released a breath. "Romano and his Beta are missing. His mate thinks they're dead and fears for her pups. She wants you to get them out the country, bring them to Betsy for safety."

Storm's brow rose. "Romano's missing? Dead?" He would've killed him, probably, maybe, but the idea the man might be dead, stunned him.

"That's what Betsy says her sister, Anita, believes," Jasmine said.

"How do we know this isn't a trap?" Angus asked.

Storm glanced over his shoulder at the man, he'd forgotten all about him.

"Verified it through Lucian's guy. I sent him in to get the woman. She refused to leave with a stranger. But it's true, Romano's missing," La Patron said.

"Why does she want me? I don't know her," Storm asked the next question rolling around his head.

La Patron shrugged. "She says Romano wrote a letter explaining everything, but she can only give it to you. She's scared, and Lucian's guy can't stay in that area much longer. What do you want to do?"

"Nothing I can do, I promised Renee to remain here." He met La Patron's gaze.

"Renee will understand," Jasmine said, in a strong voice.

La Patron shook his head and faced the window again.

"Ma'am?" Storm didn't want to get involved with whatever was going on between these two, but he wanted to hear Jasmine's point of view.

"This woman and her three young children are petrified of being killed by whoever took her husband. Her mate. The only reason she's probably still alive is because of her pups and she may lose them." Jasmine looked at him. "Renee will understand that you need to save those children and their mother, because one day she'll be a mother and will not want anyone to ever abandon her den. Reaping and sowing is a spiritual law. If this woman believes you're the only person she can trust to save her babies, then you're the only person."

Storm opened his mouth and then shut it. Swallowing hard, he didn't bother looking at either man. No one was going to argue with the determined glint in her eyes.

"Yes, Ma'am. I'll let my mate know of the emergency. When would you like me to leave?"

"The plane is fueled, the pilot is waiting for you," she said in a demure tone that fooled no one. Jasmine Knight was a force to be reckoned with.

"And Renee?" he asked to hear how she planned to handle her daughter.

"Will stay here with us and work on your wedding. Try not to stay too long." She winked at him.

"Do I bring them here or are they going to New York?" Storm asked wondering if he was looking at his future. Jasmine's soft, appearance belied a core of steel.

"Betsy will meet the flight here and they will continue to New York to meet with the Alpha there." She offered him the tablet. "This is the message if you want to read it."

"No, Ma'am. I'll take your word on it. Just give me the instructions where I'm supposed to go, and I'll leave."

La Patron handed him a sheet of paper. "I'd like to link with you."

Storm didn't know what to say. He wasn't sure he wanted more links.

"I need to tell my daughter we're linked and that I'm available to help if you need me." He stared at Storm.

Storm nodded. "Okay."

La Patron placed his hand on Storm's shoulder. Moments later, he looked at Storm. "Your shields are like mine. You have to let them down and initiate the link."

Storm thought about it and opened a link.

"Good, we're linked. Renee's mom has always been better at dealing with the girls than me. I tend to give them whatever they want and was against you leaving because it's going to upset my Princess. Jasmine's not having it and will deal with Renee, thank the Goddess."

"I won't see her before I leave?" Storm hadn't thought about that.

"You can, but it'll be harder. Contact her now, tell her what's going on and the need to leave immediately, see how she handles it," La Patron said.

Storm read the location, and stuffed the paper in his pocket. "Jasmine?" Storm glanced at La Patron. "Should I see Renee before I leave?"

"No." She shook her head and stood. Diamond's winked in her ear as she pointed at him. "Contact her, tell her you have to leave to save this woman and her kids, and that I will fill her in on the details." She waved at him. "Just go. If this woman dies because we were too late, I don't know what we'll say to her sister."

Storm nodded, turned and walked out.

Angus left behind him. "I'll take you to the pad. Do you need to pack a bag or anything?"

"Just need to get a few things. I'll meet you at the elevator in ten minutes. I've got to talk to Renee."

Angus nodded as they entered the elevator.

Storm waited until he was in their suite. "*Renee?*"

CHAPTER TWENTY-ONE

STORM BREATHED A SIGH of relief as the plane taxied onto the runway of the airport. The nine-hour flight hadn't been pleasant. Renee hadn't been happy or understanding. She accused him of lying, demanded he not leave, questioned his love for her and called him a "mama's boy" for bowing to her mother's wishes over hers. This mating thing had taken a dark turn and he wasn't sure what to expect next.

His explanations of saving the pups fell on deaf ears. She refused to compromise and stopped speaking to him three hours ago making the long trip harder. His beast didn't like the friction with their mate, and wanted him to turn around and go fix things. By the time he walked off the plane he hoped some asshole would fuck with him, so he could release his frustration.

Duke met his flight.

Storm nodded a greeting and slid in the front seat.

"I'll get you close to the location, you'll need to go the last few miles on foot," Duke said.

"How do I get them out? You expect pups to walk that far?" Storm looked at Duke.

"They'll have to, maybe they have transportation, I don't know. I'll wait here until you come back."

Storm nodded. The rest of the drive was in silence. Bright lights dotted the countryside. For all the criminal activity, it was a beautiful country.

Duke pulled over on the side of the road and handed Storm a shirt. He inhaled. The fabric smelled of a variation of Romano and someone else. Could be his mate or his pup. Three pups.

Sliding out the car, Storm zipped up his black hooded jacket, pulled the hood over his head and bolted. It didn't take long to leave the paved road and hit the rain-dampened earth. The aroma of the soil called to his beast, the freedom of running in the wild clawed at him. But they were too close to human eyes to shift. Faster, he ran and started climbing a well-worn path. Someone had been here recently, blades of glass were crimped and flattened, mud, was smeared on the rocks, and grass.

Searching the darkness, he sifted through scents and sounds as he continued running in the direction of the home hidden in the hillside. The moon hid behind clouds Darkness prevailed along the path for several moments as he veered to the right following the scent Duke had given him.

Slick with perspiration, his jacket clung, his hair lay matted against his head. Insects bounced off his face, several stuck to his sticky skin. Rivulets of sweat rolled down his neck and back. His heartbeat picked up as he climbed and the air thinned.

Inhaling, he picked up several scents, filtered through them and found the ones he needed. Legs pumping, he ran up the path, jumped over a fallen log and slowed as he heard voices.

Human hunters. He cursed and changed directions. Moving quietly, he ran around a curve that should've taken him beyond their campground.

A bullet whizzed past him. Storm kept running. More bullets whizzed by. One slammed into his right arm. He veered left into a copse of trees and jumped on a high branch. It didn't take long for the bullet to push through his skin, fall into his palm and his arm to heal but the delay pissed him off.

Now he had to deal with humans. He leaned against the trunk and waited. In the dark, he would look like a part of the tree and if necessary he could blend further, become a part of the tree.

Noiseless, two men moved forward, using hand-signals as they spread out. One stopped, held his finger to his ear and looked around. "Team B is at the house. We stop him here, and leave."

Storm wasn't surprised it was a trap. He spared a hope for Duke and hoped Romano's mate was at the house, preferably alive or Jasmine was going to be pissed. He didn't think that would be pretty. Inhaling, he searched for full-bloods or breeds. He found four heartbeats.

Good. Romano's mate and pups still lived. There were five human heartbeats, two close, two a little further out and one close to the pups.

Identifying the location of his enemies, Storm crafted his strategy. A light moved slowly through the trees. Storm remained still as it passed over him and moved on. One human walked toward him. Storm prepared to attack.

"Storm?"

He watched the human continue to search.

"*Storm I'm sorry,"* Renee said. *"Mating, the heat, all of it's new to me. I overreacted like a spoiled child, having a tantrum."*

Were those her words or her mom's? Either way he couldn't afford the distraction right now. Any second the human would be close enough to take out.

"I don't want you to think I'm like that," she continued, *"I'm not. Most of the guys I've dated said I act like I don't care what they do."*

"Renee." He didn't want to hear about her past relationships.

"*Sorry. That was stupid. The point I'm trying to make is I'm sorry and I support what you feel you need to do. Forgive me?"*

"Yes. Of course." Storm jumped, landed on the human, and knocked him out. He removed the weapons and searched the man's pockets. He found plastic ties and cuffed the man's arms together.

"*Thanks, Baby,"* Renee said. "*When you get back—"*

"Renee, can we have this conversation later?" He ran through the woods, jumped and landed on the second man, knocking the wind out of him. Before the hunter could respond, Storm punched him, and hit him with the butt of his gun, knocking him out. He cuffed him with a zip tie and inhaled to locate the others.

"*What? Oh yeah, you're in Brazil? Already?"*

"Yes." He moved sideways to avoid the hunter who had turned back to look for the others.

"I'm sorry. We'll talk later... after you're done... okay?

"Okay." He lunged forward, grabbed the automatic and swung it around. The hunter went airborne, slammed into a nearby tree and slid down onto the moist ground. Someone spoke on the ear-mic, demanding the others report. Three down, two to go.

"*Love you,"* Renee said.

"Love you, too." Storm jumped and landed on a thick overhanging branch to wait. It didn't take long. Two men walked slowly toward him from different directions. He listened intently, identified the heartbeats of Romano's den and

searched for more. Where was Razor? Was he somewhere watching? Did he kill Romano?

Storm shut down those questions and focused on the mission at hand. He morphed into his beast and leapt forward. Within seconds he was on the closest hunter and bit him in the leg and arm. The fifth hunter fired a shot and hit the hunter on the ground.

"Stop shooting, asshole, you shot me," the hunter gritted.

Storm leapt and landed on the fifth hunter, biting his arm and leg as well before running into the woods where he returned to human. Storm strode back to the men, he'd bitten, grabbed their guns and tossed them aside. Ignoring a stream of curses and their pitiful attempts to fight him off, he searched their pockets. He took their phones, keys and wallets. Turning, he ran to the house and slowed as it came into view.

After another scan, he walked inside.

Romano's mate sagged in her chair with an expression of relief and gratitude. She opened her mouth.

Storm shook his head and placed his finger against his lip as he moved quickly and untied her. She helped him untie the kids. He pressed his mouth to her ear. "Luggage? Bags? Anything you want to take?"

She nodded and placed backpacks on each child before placing one on her back.

"Car? Truck?" he asked.

A sad expression crossed her face as she shook her head.

They eased toward the door, he inhaled, heard the five human heartbeats and nothing else. Looking over his shoulder at her, he nodded and stepped outside first. When there was no gunfire or attacks, he waved for them to come. They walked in silence down a path a distance from the one littered with human hunters. The terrain roughened. Storm picked up the two oldest kids and motioned for her to pick up the youngest.

Then they ran down the hillside toward Duke.

They had been running for 15 minutes or so when the woman called out. "Wait."

Storm stopped, turned and saw Romano's mate changing the child's position on her waist. She took large gulps of air. He realized he'd pushed too hard, too fast.

He stood waiting for her to catch her breath and calm the pup in her arm for several minutes.

"Thank you, I understand the urgency to leave the area and apologize." She caught up to him. "I'm Anita."

"You're welcome, Anita. There's a car waiting for us, I'd like to reach him before sunrise, it's not much further."

She nodded and started running again.

Storm caught up, passed her and soon the terrain changed as they left the hillside. He slowed to a brisk walk as they came closer to the area he left Duke. In the distance he saw the vehicle parked in the same place. He held up his hand and stopped.

"*La Patron?*" He waited a few seconds. "*La Patron?*"

"*Storm?*"

"*Can you contact Duke, ask him his status?*"

"*Yes.*"

Storm remained still, trying to identify Duke's scent and couldn't.

"*He's not answering, where are you?*"

"*I can see his vehicle but didn't scent him. I have the woman and pups with me.*"

"*Solo is on his way. This can turn into a fucking nightmare if they've done something to another Alpha.*"

"*Solo? I met him at the Alpha's house in Brazil.*" Storm glanced at Anita and the pups, they were exhausted, asleep on his shoulder. He needed to get them to the plane and out of this country.

"*Duke is coming, he was... let's say he thought he had more time and found a way to distract himself.*"

Storm shook his head but was relieved. "*Have him flick the lights when he's back in the vehicle.*"

Minutes later, Duke walked fast to the car, unlocked the door, slid inside and flashed the lights.

"*Did he scan the vehicle?*" Storm asked La Patron.

Duke stepped out the car, walked around it and after a few minutes slid behind the driver's seat. He flashed the lights again.

"*Have him drive forward, I'll stop him when he's close. I don't want this group to walk any more than they must. Is the plane ready?*"

"Working on it. You were faster than anticipated, the pilots who flew in can't fly out, so they're at the hotel. I've got two others on the way. We'll get all of you up in the air as soon as possible. Any word on Romano?"

"I haven't spoken to her, there were human hunters who objected to her leaving. Once we're in the plane, I'll question her," Storm said.

"*Human hunters?"* La Patron whistled. "*How many? Did you kill them?*"

"*No. At least I heard five heartbeats when I left them. They will need medical care, but they are breathing and lack proper identification.*"

Duke drove forward slowly. Storm released the two kids in his arms to their mother and told them to wait. He stepped out the shadows and flagged down the car.

"Sorry, I didn't expect you back until later," Duke said, sounding apologetic.

Storm glared at him, looked around and opened the back door. He returned to Anita and the kids, and walked them to the car while praying no one would shoot these small babies. Once inside, Storm slid in the front seat. "Airport, please."

"Sure thing." Duke wasted no time getting them to the airport.

AT THE AIRPORT ANITA pulled out passports and other paperwork for the authorities. Storm didn't ask questions on her preparedness, and was relieved when they boarded the private jet. He settled the three pups in the bed and returned out front to sit with Anita.

"You have lots of questions I'm sure," she said.

"No, just one. What happened to Romano?" Storm asked as he took the seat across from her.

She sighed, pushed her hair behind her ear and sat back in the seat. Without lines of fear etched across her face, she didn't look as old or plain as he initially thought. "I can't reach him. He may be dead, I don't know."

"Or drugged," Storm said relieved she hadn't said the Alpha was dead. A mate would know.

Her brow rose. "Drugged? I hadn't thought of that, you could be right." She sat back and crossed her leg. "That would explain it." Her face brightened.

He didn't add his Alpha had been drugged and helplessly watched as his mate and pups were slaughtered.

"Thank you again, Romano always said you... oh, he left something for you." She stood, grabbed her backpack and a few moments later handed him a sealed envelope.

Storm looked at it for a few seconds, took and read it. At first he couldn't believe the tale Romano wrote. Fighting to keep his beast under control, Storm closed his eyes, took several deep breaths and when he could think past the reddish haze of anger he read it again.

Were there no more trustworthy Alphas? Did their words mean nothing? How would he know who to trust?

"They threatened to kill our pups if he did not cooperate. Over and over they show him pictures of what they'd done to children, what they'd do to ours if he refused," Anita said in a soft tone.

Storm shook his head. No. No. Fucking hell no. The bastard used him. Sent him all over to kill strangers who had nothing to do with Adolfo's death. Looked him in the eye, asked him to join his Pack and all the while he was someone's puppet?

"You are now mated," she said.

A low growl rumbled from Storm's throat that she would dare mention Renee.

"If someone threatened your pups, your mate, what would you do?"

"Kill the bastards," he snapped, angry at her defense of the indefensible.

"And if you know you can't win? That you would die and leave your pups alone? What then?" she asked watching him.

"Why didn't you give me this before? At the house?" Storm glared at her.

"I forgot until now." She looked at him. "Would you have done things differently if you had known?"

"Most definitely. I would not be here now."

She sighed. "You would allow innocents to die because of his mistake."

"If his den is lost, it's because of what he did, not me." He fumed over her attempt to paint him as the villain when had been royally used. Unwilling to remain in the cramped space with her, he strode off the plane to wait until the pilot was ready to leave. Fuck it, from now on, he wouldn't trust any of the bastards.

Storm did a mental tally of all the places Romano sent him, the people he killed. At the time he had no idea there were bounties on their heads. He'd been blinded by vengeance, a perfect patsy. He stuffed his hands in his pockets and stared at the ground wishing he could find Romano and wrap his hands around his throat.

If he and Renee had pups... when they had pups, he'd protect them. But what if you couldn't? What if something happened to you? The questions persisted.

Jasmine would take care of them, La Patron wouldn't allow anything to happen to his grandkids, especially from his princess, Storm thought.

What if you had no La Patron to help you? What would you do to protect your den? How far would you go to keep your mate and pups safe?

Those questions ran in circles in his mind. He knew the answer. But to admit that, meant forgiving Romano and he didn't want to do that. Probably would never truly forgive the man, but in some far corner of his mind, he understood the difficult position he'd been in.

Romano said Alpha Adolfo had met with Razor and Carlotta a few times and never mentioned them. Storm never picked up weird scents or anything that would alert him of strangers in their territory.

They asked Adolfo for information on Storm. Adolfo refused. That last time, his Alpha sent him away intentionally so that they wouldn't see him. What the fuck was his Alpha thinking, sending the one person who could protect him away? This whole thing, everything Romano said read like a bad, cheap, novel.

All of this, for what? It had to be more than wanting information on him. None of it made sense. An hour and several minutes passed before the fueling tanks left and the pilot called out to him.

"We're ready to get underway, Mr. Storm."

"No mister, just Storm," he said as he turned and walked back to the plane. When he entered the cabin, one of the pilots locked the door behind them and headed to the cockpit. Storm ignored Anita as he retook his seat, fastened his seat belt and closed his eyes.

Now that the mission was completed, all the hours he'd gone without sleep slammed into him. He fought a yawn as he settled in for the long flight. For the next eight hours he planned to sleep as much as possible and forget the letter in his pocket that flipped his world upside down.

CHAPTER TWENTY-TWO

CARLOTTA SAT ON THE sofa of the large suite in the five-star hotel in Rome, Italy staring at a video feed of Romano and Henri, Trista's former boyfriend. Both men were drugged and lying on mattresses in an abandoned stable in the Italian countryside. She glanced at her watch and then at Razor who sat in front of the TV watching some show in Italian he couldn't possibly understand.

She placed the tablet aside and picked up her phone. Henri's family were supposed to deposit 10 million dollars into an off-shore account for his return. Minutes after she placed the call to see if the funds had been transferred, she smiled. She was set for life. This money, coupled with all the bounties she had collected over the past few years were more than enough to keep her in the lifestyle she had been born to live.

What to do about Romano? He'd kidnapped Henri to save his Beta who would eventually recover from the damage Razor did to him. Killing Romano at this point wouldn't benefit them. She couldn't threaten to destroy his den again after discovering Storm was in the hillside to rescue them.

It still pissed her off that he had been contacted and arrived before she could move the family. The best she could do was contact some bounty hunters who'd been in the country and send them the information where Storm would be heading. Romano's den was out of the equation for now.

She tapped her fingertips on the tablet. Romano might come in handy and if not, he'd make a good distraction. Camera footage showed him carrying Henri into the shack but nothing inside. If she sent the information of Henri's whereabouts, Romano would be implicated.

She grinned. Would they place him in a human prison? Take a sample of the Alpha's blood? What would the human press make of Romano? What would La Patron do about that she wondered? Not that he had jurisdiction in Italy. She sent an encrypted message giving Henri's location to his family.

She glanced at an unsuspecting Razor, picked up the tablet and scrolled to another scene.

Storm was thorough, she had to give him that. According to her helpers, it hadn't taken more than an hour and a half to reach the house and remove Romano's den. Unfortunately, he left the humans alive. That would never do, they may want more money or start asking questions or try to contact her again. She had made it clear to the men under her control, to kill the hunters in a way that made it look as if Storm was as out of control as Razor. Now that she had the gruesome photos and video, they would toss the bodies into the forest like road-kill.

Once more, she looked at the ghastly pictures and nodded. Razor would identify with this, hopefully it would be enough to convince him to leave and go after Trista. Carlotta would take that time to disappear. If he and Trista found each other, great, otherwise, fuck them.

Yesterday, Trista surprised her by completely withdrawing her energy. For the first time in years, Trista's presence was gone. Worse, Trista knew Carlotta hated when she did that. Fuck Trista for bailing when Carlotta needed her most.

Although twins, they were very different. Their mom died when they were in college, leaving them very little. Carlotta dropped out of school and went in to retail management. Most of their lives, Trista had been the aloof, goofy one who saw the world through abstract thought and vivid meanderings. It came as no surprise she wanted to be an artist. Everybody knew artist barely survived financially, but that never bothered Trista. She remained in school, preferring to be a starving artist than getting a real job. Over the years they argued about it constantly but never separated.

Carlotta swallowed her anger, refused to allow it to overwhelm her. She took a deep breath to steady her nerves, to stop thinking about Trista.

Like an old black and white movie, history replayed itself within her mind. Nells, the old man had been wrong, Razor belonged to Trista and Storm was not her mate. Carlotta leaned back in her chair, remembering the day she met Nells, the man claimed Razor as his son. He'd been so sure she and Trista were

Razor and Storm's mates. The stories he told of their fighting skills, how no one could win against them.

Her first impression of Razor wasn't favorable at all. He was dirty, with long matted hair on his head and face. He looked crazy to her and she mentioned it to Nells. She knew Trista wouldn't be interested in the man. Nells must've known she was about to leave because he mentioned money. He believed Razor could win large bounties or rewards with the right assistance. He claimed Razor could become a millionaire within a year. The idea of having access to that kind of money, living wherever she chose, and escaping her dead-end job appealed to her. She agreed to bring Trista to meet Razor after Nells cleaned him up.

The man cleaned up well and he'd been drooling over them at the restaurant. Nells had been happy and later reminded her that Razor had a kinsman named Storm, someone just like him, and he believed either she or Trista was his mate as well.

That proved to be false.

When Carlotta realized Razor might not be her mate, she began searching for Storm. He was everything Nells said and better. He wasn't crazy. She walked by him in the airport and then again when he was in town on a job she had set in motion, just to be sure. Storm showed no interest in her, worst she wasn't interested in him. Not in the way of mates. After Razor, she knew the difference.

One of the side-effects of Trista's withdrawal was Carlotta knew with certainty Razor wasn't her mate. It wouldn't take long for Razor to sense something different either. She hoped and prayed she could control him with her pheromones long enough to get him to leave and go after Storm or La Patron. She didn't care as long as he left her behind. Maybe she would reach out to Trista, tell her Razor was coming to rescue her.

The thought of her sister living happily with Razor curled her stomach. It wasn't fair that those who don't want the finer things in life, get them anyway. Time was slipping away. The stage was set, it was time to play her part.

"Shit," she said flipping to the screen with the bloody bodies. "This is getting ridiculous. We need to do something." She waited for Razor to take the bait.

"What?" He looked at her over his shoulder and then turned around fully. "What happened?"

"Look at this. I sent some men to watch over Romano's mate and pups to keep Storm from taking them. Look what he's done." She held up the tablet and looked at him.

He stood, walked over and looked at the picture. He flipped through them all and looked at her. "He killed all of them?"

She nodded.

He looked at the pictures again. "He took the mate and pups?"

"Yes, they weren't there. They're gone." Experience taught her she would need to say this again at least three times to get a reaction.

"Maybe they're hiding under the blood?" he looked at her with a slight smile which shocked her. He was joking. Razor never joked. He was single-minded in his quest, whatever it happened to be at the time. He should be licking his lips at the idea of beating someone for this atrocity.

She eyed him warily and released her pheromones while he looked at the tablet.

"Something stinks," he said as he flipped through the tablet. "Lots of blood. Who did this?"

"Storm or La Patron, or someone who works for them." She hoped the pheromones kicked in and he became pliable again. This couldn't be happening, she was so close to the end.

"They took the mate and pups?"

"Yes, they aren't there."

"Why?" he asked looking at her. "To kill them?"

"I don't know," she said watching him act out of character.

"You want to help them? Get them back, protect them?"

"Yes. He can't keep taking mates and pups. It's not right." She watched and debated if she should mention Trista. It would be risky, he tended to get flustered whenever her name was mentioned. But if the pheromones didn't work, she might have to.

"We need to help them," she said and released more pheromones.

He looked at her and blinked a few times. That crazy glint reappeared in his gaze as he twitched his nose and wiped it. "Okay."

She released a breath. "I will book a flight for you to fly into Charleston, West Virginia."

"Where's Trista?" he asked looking at the tablet.

Carlotta fought to remain calm as she spoke. "In Charleston, West Virginia."

He looked at her. "That's where we're going? To this place?"

"I will meet you there, I have to take care of some things first," she hedged.

"No. We will go and get Trista first." He wore the stubborn look of a toddler. She tried to reason with him even though she doubted it would work.

"Once we find Trista and bring her home, we need a bigger house. That's what I need to take care of while you go and bring my sister home, so we can have our own den." She reached out and touched the back of his hand.

He met her gaze for a few seconds and shook his head. "No. Find Trista first."

She wanted to scream her frustration to the heavens. Why now? She wondered. Was it because she and Trista were separate? Had he spoken through Trista by mind-link? She doubted it. Something had happened.

"Let's go." He returned the tablet to her. "Let's go to the airport."

"I need to see if there are flights," she stammered.

"Rent a plane like you did the last time." He crossed his arms and looked at her as if he knew she was stalling.

She did a quick search and wanted to throw the tablet at him. A flight from Rome to West Virginia would be 11 hours, and the only planes they had available cost a little over 100 thousand dollars. Since she had an account with the company it didn't take long to make arrangements. But she didn't want to be on that plane. Maybe she could ditch him at the airport and he'd leave without her. She weighed her options. He probably wouldn't leave her and would be furious at the delay.

"We leave in four hours." She stood, walked to the bedroom to start packing and planning. If she had to go to the States to face her sister, she would make sure she left a mark.

CHAPTER TWENTY-THREE

RENEE SAT ON THE SOFA in the suite she shared with Storm and watched her Mom flip through pages of a wedding magazine. Every now and then, she would make a comment or smile or frown. On the one hand Renee wanted to be a strong woman of character, efficient and well loved, like her Mom, on the other hand, the verbal spanking her Mom gave her over Storm leaving to save kids he didn't really know still irritated her. Storm was her mate and her feelings mattered and should come first.

Despite what her Mom said, and her siblings co-signed, she wasn't throwing a temper tantrum. In her mind, Storm broke a promise. Promises should be sacred between mates no matter what. Plus, he just left. He could've returned to the Club, talked to her about it and then left.

Goosebumps raced across her skin. She missed him so much, it had been over 15 hours and she hadn't been able to sleep for more than short periods of time. This part of mating held no appeal to her.M mom said without looking at her.

"I'm not pouting."

Her Mom glanced at her with a raised brow.

"I miss Storm. He's been gone a long time." She tried to keep the whine out of her voice as she rubbed her arms.

"The flight is nine hours," Mom said.

Renee knew that. Storm was on a plane headed home. Her Dad claimed he rescued the family so quickly they had to wait for new pilots and fuel. When Storm contacted her, he had been so tired, she told him to get some rest and promised to take care of him when he got home.

"What if..." Renee pulled her legs beneath her, and bit her lower lip.

"What?" Mama asked.

"What if this is all he can do? I mean, can I live with someone whose only skill is killing people?"

"Do you believe that?"

If it was anyone other than her parents, she would feel she was betraying her mate but she needed to talk to someone and met her Mama's curious gaze. "In a way I do, and it scares me." Renee pulled her hair behind her ear as her thoughts formed. "Mom, he's... his beast... it's vicious, like nothing I've ever seen. He moves so fast, faster than the twins or Asia, like a blur of darkness."

Mom's brow rose, her lips quirked. "Blur of darkness?"

Renee sighed. "I don't know how else to explain it. When he stopped, bodies were everywhere. Honestly, I was shocked watching him, so shocked I didn't see the full-bloods approach the truck until they were almost there. I shot one of them, but they never should've gotten that close." Mentally she revisited the trip to Mexico. "He leaps really high." She raised her hand as she spoke. "Like he has bounce shoes on or something, then he flips in the air, lands and runs, and he does it so fast."

"Sounds like that was quite a fight, were you scared?"

"At times. Kinda reminded me of my nightmares, you know? His beast looked like the one in my nightmares," she added.

"Really?"

Renee nodded and explained Storm's thoughts regarding Razor in her dreams.

"No matter what, I'm sure Storm will take care of it, both of you will work to fix it."

Her Mom's reassurance went a long way in easing her concerns about her mate. "What do you think of him? Of Storm?" Renee asked.

Closing the magazine and laying it aside, her Mom met her gaze. "He seems like a complicated man with a difficult past. But then the same could be said about my mate, or Angus, Jacques, Cain, Abel, Hawke, Asia—"

Renee held up her hand. "I get it." She smiled.

"The point I'm making is this. Our pasts are important, we learn lessons and gain experience that can affect our lives. But it's not our future. We shape our futures with every decision we make today. You and Storm can acknowledge his past, accept it and move forward. Right now, being an assassin may be the only skillset he has. From what I've learned, he was created to protect and defend wolves. If that's where he is now, he can add things that interest him, learn new skills." She paused. "But you can't punish him for being who he is, no more than he should take exception to the long hours you spend creating your masterpieces."

"I didn't punish him."

"You called him a mama's boy for listening to me," her Mom reminded her. "He never knew his Mom, remember that the next time you start name-calling."

"I was mad." She had no justifiable defense for that and she knew it. Mama rarely interfered with Renee's or any of her kids' lives. For her to step in and tell Storm to go, knowing the potential fall-out, meant it was important. Everyone else recognized that immediately.

"Doesn't matter. Being angry is fine, inflicting damage is another thing. He's nobody's boy."

Renee nodded.

"Remember, Storm has no concept of family. He's never seen anything like what we have here. I saw it in his eyes at lunch the other day. He was overwhelmed."

Renee's eyes widened a bit. "He didn't say anything."

Her Mom smiled. "No. He wouldn't. You'll have to guide him through this new terrain gently. It's bumpy and filled with surprises like a stranger saying I want you to call me Mom and then treating him like a son. For a lone wolf, being around so many people who laugh and tease each other could be a bit much. So, if he doesn't want to be around us as much as you do, don't be offended. Take it slow. Remember this is his first time having a family."

Storm hadn't wanted to go to the Club, but did it because she wanted to. Had he said anything at the Club? Talked to anybody? No. He'd played with her hair, flirted with her, otherwise, he just sat there.

"Okay, I hadn't thought about that." She bit her lower lip, realized what she was doing and stopped. "I don't want to push or nag him about anything. But, I want to be honest how I feel too. I love being here, he's already said we won't live here. I want a den like the one I grew up in, kids, love, laughter, a sense of purpose. How do I do that with someone who's not sure who he is or what he wants? Storm has no direction right now. He's avenged his Alpha, that goal was his life. He has no back up plan."

"Being honest without laying on guilt or making demands is important," her Mom said. "Have you told Storm this is how you really feel? Maybe he doesn't understand the core, underlying issue for you."

"I told him he couldn't be an assassin," Renee said on a rushed breath. "He agreed and offered to work with me."

"And?" her Mom said when she didn't say anything else.

"And he needs to find his own hobbies or work, not tag behind me. He —"

"Isn't your father, or your brother, or any other man you know. He's your mate. Period."

"That's not fair, Mama. I know he's not like anyone else—"

"Drop the like. He's not anyone else you know, don't compare him."

Heat flew up Renee's spine and filled her face. "I'm not comparing him."

Her Mom's brow rose.

"I'm not. I just don't want him hanging around while I paint."

"He offered to work with you at the museum or while you paint?" Mom asked.

Renee's brow's furrowed. What had he meant? She'd dismissed his comment without giving it much thought. Why? Why had she done that? Storm was interested in art, she knew that. But the idea of him working for her bothered her on some level she hadn't realized. Quinn was a doctor, Jackie helped him, not the other way around. Mama helped daddy. Rose worked for daddy. Shyla helped Angus and sometimes helped Mom. None of the mates of women close to her worked for their women. Some worked together, but the man was typically in charge.

"We didn't discuss it. Now that I think about it, you're right. I was comparing him and that's not fair." She would keep her recent revelations to herself and work with Storm to fix this. If he wanted to work at the museum, at least they would remain here, and that was fine with her. "Should I apologize to him?"

"You tell me?" Her Mom crossed her leg while watching her.

"I could, but he didn't seem offended. I doubt he gave it a second thought. Seems like I'd be making a new sore or something."

"Or you could ease his mind on finding something to do while searching for new interests. I don't know if you heard me earlier, so I'll repeat it. He was created to protect and defend wolves. That's an awesome job description. You can call him an assassin every second of every hour of every day of the week but that doesn't change the fact the Goddess and Grandfather gifted Storm with talents no one else, not even your father, has. Correction, one other person may have."

Renee had been about to mention Razor.

"That's nothing to be ashamed of. I'm not. I'm proud he's my son and on our team."

Renee's heart dropped at the accusation. "I'm not ashamed." She held up her hand when her Mom started to speak. "Not like that. I'm not ashamed of him as my mate, but I don't like his job. I just don't." She refused to lie to herself or anyone else. "Hearing you say the Goddess and Grandfather made him the way he is… seeing it from that perspective helps. Doesn't change my feelings, but it helps make it better. Kinda like he can't help being who he is."

"It is who he is, but he can be more. So much more," her Mom said. "Be patient, this is a marathon with the finish line decades away." Mom knocked on the wood end table. "Listen and encourage him to be the best he can be, honey. The rest will work itself out. People blossom in environments where they feel safe in failing."

"Huh?" Renee didn't understand.

"Create a den, a home, that both of you feel safe trying new, wild, different things without being afraid to fail. If something interests you, try it. If it bombs, it bombs, no one will make you feel bad. Instead, you should be praised for trying. That's what I mean by blossoming in that kind of atmosphere."

Renee thought of her childhood and how her parents encouraged them to all try different things, with lots of praise when they went outside their norms. In hindsight, Renee hadn't been afraid to try sculpting, basket and tapestry weaving or even glass art, all things she now knew held no appeal for her.

"Thanks, that makes sense." Renee doubted she would be as good as her parents had been, but she would try. She started to ask another question when her Mom's eyes widened, and her mouth opened and snapped close.

"What's wrong?" Renee asked, certain something happened to Storm. Fear choked her.

Her Mom looked at her. "A bomb went off at the museum."

Relieved it wasn't Storm, Renee almost relaxed until the words slammed into her. "My museum?"

Her Mom nodded.

CHAPTER TWENTY-FOUR

RENEE, WITH JACKIE'S arm wrapped around her, walked toward the yellow caution tape surrounding the museum. Pack firefighters cleared rubble from the opposite side of the charred building. Glass, stone, and pieces of art littered the ground. Twisted and bent iron beams stood defiantly near the blast site.

"A whole side of the building is gone," Renee whispered brokenly.

Jackie's grip tightened.

A covered body was rolled out and placed into an SUV. "Who was that?" Renee stopped and watched the truck drive off.

"Daddy has to identify him or her," Jackie answered.

Renee had spoken to Crystal and Edmund, they had both been at home and were devastated by the news. She told them both to stay home and to contact the rest of the staff they would be closed until further notice.

Renee inhaled as they approached Hank, the Security Chief who'd been around forever. He looked at her, opened his arms and she walked into them. With her head resting on his chest, she accepted his comforting pats on her back before speaking.

"How bad is it?" she asked.

"Northeast side's completely gone. No damage to the back, all in all, it's not as bad as it could've been. The insurance company will have that side rebuilt good as new, don't worry."

Intellectually, she knew what he said was true, Daddy had said the same things. But this bypassed her mind and drove an arrow into her heart. This museum was her baby. As much a part of her as anything else. She'd been intimately involved with every decision since she saw the first architectural rendering.

"Who did this?" Renee didn't think she was a vengeful person, but she wanted whoever did this punished.

"We may never know, that was his body, they just rolled out of here. Your dad's going to try and identify him but it's a long shot," Hank said releasing her. "Give us an hour or two to make it safe for you to go inside and look around, okay?"

Unable to speak around the ball of misery choking her, Renee nodded and watched him walk away. Jackie returned to her side, along with Quinn, David, Adam, Bella, Tyrese and Tyrone. They stood and watched the smoldering building for several minutes. Bella hugged and kissed Renee on the cheek before moving away.

Adam hugged her. "*It's going to be okay, we'll do whatever you need to fix this.*" He placed his finger beneath her chin and turned her to face him. "*We're here for you, whatever you need.*"

She nodded.

"*Want to go have breakfast? Bella's cooking.*"

Renee loved Bella's cooking. "*Maybe later, not right now. I need to absorb this. I still can't believe it and I'm looking at it. Love you guys.*"

Adam nodded. "*Love you too.*" He walked away, took Bella's hand and left.

Tyrese wrapped his arms around her. "*You're going through too much. Tell me what you need.*"

"*Niklas. I need Niklas.*" She hadn't realized how much she wanted her mate standing here with her until that moment.

"*Done. Soon as he touches land I'll be there waiting and will bring him to you. What else? Anything else you need?*" He placed a kiss on the top of her head.

"*Not right now. Thanks, Rese. Love you so much,*" she said.

"*Love you too, Peanut. Stop crying, you're breaking my heart.*" He wiped her tears with his thumb. "*We'll fix this. Whatever it takes, we'll fix it.*"

She inhaled to stem the flow of tears and wiped her face. "*I know. Still hurts, though.*"

"*I know it does. I know.*" He hugged her again and released her.

Tyrone placed his palms on her cheeks and stared into her eyes. "*I'm so sorry this happened. So sorry.*" He wiped her tears and pulled her close. "*Haters and assholes, I can't stand them,*" he said.

She nodded.

"*I know how much this museum means to you, and I promise we'll fix it, make it better than before. Okay?*"

Throat tight, she nodded.

"*Good.*" He kissed her forehead. "*Go ahead and grieve, just know this is a temporary setback, nothing can hold you down for long. You're a fighter, the Comeback Kid.*" He pinched her chin and stood aside.

David placed his arm around her. She leaned her head onto his shoulder. In silence they watched the workers. Tears rolled down her cheeks as her heart cracked and crumbled. Incomprehensible pain pressed against her chest, making breathing difficult at times as they hauled chunks of stone and glass away. Renee refused to leave, refused to abandon her baby despite many requests that she do so. She needed to see everything.

An hour or so later, Jackie returned. *"Here, Bella cooked and sent food. She and Adam will be here in a bit.*" Jackie handed Renee and David, who remained the entire time with Renee, two covered dishes. Quinn set out four lawn chairs for them to sit. They took seats, ate and watched.

"*Daddy wasn't able to identify the guy. He was a full-blood, not from around here. Daddy think he was from another country or something,*" Jackie said.

"Think this had something to do with Storm rescuing that family?" David asked Renee.

Emotionally drained, Renee shrugged. At this point anything was possible.

"*Why wait until after the largest annual event the museum has to blow it up? What does that prove? That we're vulnerable? That our security sucks?"* Jackie said.

Renee was happy this happened after the event, she would be devastated to lose the works of artists all over the country. Presently there wasn't much stock since everything had been shipped out days ago.

"*All of that will change,*" David said joining their link. *"After what happened here yesterday, Daddy made calls to have it fenced with security.*"

"*Asia went to talk to Trista,*" Jackie said.

Renee frowned. "*Trista? Why?*"

"Timing, I guess. Nothing like this ever happen before. She's in town less than 48 hours and we have two incidences here." Jackie shrugged. "*Coincidental? I doubt it.*"

Renee hadn't given Trista a thought since they returned from the Club. "*Hmm, I hope this has nothing to do with her.*"

"Probably not, but it's best to be sure," David said.

TRISTA SAT ON THE BED reading a text from Henri, her ex-boyfriend. She ignored his pleas to get back together. Claimed he needed her after his recent ordeal. He'd been kidnapped, his wealthy family paid the 10 million ransom and he was back home.

She found the whole thing hard to believe. Henri was no lightweight when it came to martial arts and street fighting, plus he handled weapons as if they were an extension of his arm. Who was able to get the drop on him, she wondered?

"Glad you're okay and everything worked out," she typed. There was a light tap on her door. "One minute," she yelled as she pulled on a dress and opened the door.

"Hi, I'm Asia, I work for La Patron in Administration. Can I ask you a few questions?"

Trista looked at the tall, toned, woman who wore her hair pulled back in a neat bun, fitted jeans, a short-sleeved shirt and half-boots. "Of course. I'm Trista. Did you want to come in? Or talk in the hall?"

Asia extended her hand.

Surprised, Trista took it and shook the woman's hands a few times. When Asia didn't release her hand immediately, Trista grew uncomfortable. She wasn't interested in women, no matter how attractive they were. Easing her hand from Asia's she took a step back. "What do you want to know?"

"First, I should tell you someone used explosives on the museum a couple hours ago."

Trista frowned. "Museum?" Then it hit her. Her hands flew to her face. "No. Not Renee's museum?"

Asia nodded. "Renee is there now, in case you wanted her for anything."

"She's expecting her mate, so we had no plans today. I planned to go into town later, do some shopping."

"That's true. Storm should be here soon," Asia said watching Trista.

Trista exhaled thinking of the beautiful building and artwork. "I hate that's happened, that place is amazing. Is there a lot of damage? What about the sculpture garden? I hope that's okay; those pieces can't be replaced." She paused thinking of the canvases, glass work, and ceramics and shook her head. "That's a damn shame."

"Do you know anyone who might attack the museum?" Asia asked cutting through Trista's mental rant.

"Huh?"

Asia repeated the question.

Trista's eyes widened when she realized she was being questioned about the bombing. After the attack yesterday, she shouldn't be surprised. But she was a little hurt that she was a suspect.

"Maybe the guys in Mexico? They were rough around the edges and moved me around a lot. The Alpha's name was Cy. Alpha Cy." She exhaled and pushed through her feelings to search for clues that could help Renee. "My brother-in-law, Razor. But he's more hand to hand than explosives."

"Would he hire someone to do it?" Asia asked.

"I doubt he'd think to do that," Trista said. Carlotta would hire someone to blow-up a building in a heartbeat.

"Do you know where he is at the moment?" Asia asked.

"I separated from my sister the other night, so I don't know where they are now. They move around a lot."

"Anything else?" Asia asked.

"Just this and it probably doesn't have anything to do with anything." Trista turned and walked back inside. "Come in." She picked up her phone while Asia closed the door. "My ex-boyfriend was kidnapped, he lives near Rome. Anyway, his parents paid a high ransom to get him back." She read the text and clicked on the link her ex sent. "One second." She read the article and looked at Asia.

"They found him with the man who kidnapped him. Both were drugged. The police arrested the kidnapper. His name is Romano, the same name of the guy who sent Storm to pick me up in Mexico." She showed Asia the phone which showed Romano's picture.

Asia looked at the picture. It matched the one in the file La Patron had on Romano. She wondered if Trista knew Storm left to rescue Romano's family. Asia hadn't picked it up when she did a quick scan of Trista with the chameleon bracelet which read thoughts and could change her form to match Trista's if Asia wanted.

"Henri is your ex-boyfriend who was kidnapped by Romano, his family paid someone money, probably a lot of money and then left Romano to take the fall," Asia said reading the article.

"Which means he's exposed to the police," Trista said.

Human police, Asia thought. Her father, Barticus, would need to be notified. Hopefully, they could get him moved before things got out of hand.

"Problem is, Henri's family is old school rich. Things must be done a certain way. They're real snobs and won't let this slide. Especially if Romano doesn't repay the money. If it wasn't for his family, we may have had a chance, but they didn't like me." She shrugged as if it didn't bother her, but Asia heard the hurt in Trista's voice.

"Thanks, I'll pass this on to La Patron. I know you want to leave the Compound today, but I'm going to ask you to stay here until we get a handle on what's going on."

"Am I under arrest or something?" Trista asked.

"No. Not at all. You're Renee's guest, she's at the museum. If there's something you really want to do, that's fine. We'll need to assign security to go with you in case this Alpha sent someone for you, that's all. I'm sorry if I made you feel that way," Asia said.

"Thanks, there's no place I need to be, I'll sit in the courtyard and read. It's just... I want my life back. I want all of this to be over, so I can move forward. I feel like the sky is about to fall but I don't know when or how." Trista shrugged and sat on the edge of the bed.

Asia smiled. "I understand, La Patron doesn't think it'll be long, he believes your mate is on his way to find you. How did your sister respond when you separated from her?"

Trista frowned. "She never mentioned it. Strange."

"Why strange?" Asia asked.

"Strange she didn't mention it though, Carlotta hates when I do that. Normally she would've questioned me about it by now."

"Would it have made her mad? Angry?" Asia asked.

Trista nodded. "Most definitely. The few times we've separated our energies, I was the one who pulled out and she always gets angry. Not a yell and scream kind of thing, Carlotta goes cold. Does things to get my attention and then she'll reach out and reconnect us. Most times I was over whatever made me do it in the first place, so it didn't matter. But she hasn't reached out and by now, which is strange."

Or she ordered someone to bomb the place where you spent substantial time yesterday, Asia thought. She needed to discuss all of this with La Patroness and the others.

"If you want to leave the Compound or need anything, let me or someone know. Renee showed you how to contact Security?"

Trista nodded. "Yes, we went through that last night. I'll probably talk to Henri, he's sounding spooked." She looked at her cell phone.

Asia turned to leave. "Nice meeting you, Trista."

"Same here, Asia."

Asia closed the door behind her and headed toward the elevator. *"Mistress I'm on my way."*

"Good. Silas and the others are in their offices, I'll call them. Storm is an hour away thank God. Renee's falling apart but won't leave the Museum," Jasmine said.

"*Who's with her*?" Asia asked.

"All the kids. Tyrese and Tyrone just returned. They're sitting out there until Hank signals she can go in. They'll go with her for support. I couldn't be prouder of my kids than I am today with how they stuck with Renee over this."

"I agree, Ma'am. Anyone who knows Renee knows this struck a blow to her heart. When we're finished meeting, Hawke and I plan to go over there, pledge our support, let her know she's in our thoughts," Asia said.

"She knows," Jasmine said.

"I want to give her a hug like I did when she was a wee one running around the nursery with a new picture she'd just drawn." Asia chuckled. Renee knew what she wanted the moment she was old enough to hold a crayon. Art was her world.

"*She'll never outgrow those, Asia. Silas is on his way.*"

Asia stepped off the elevator and strode down the hall to Jasmine's conference room. She nodded to Jacques, who entered as well. Inside the conference room, Jasmine, La Patron, Hawke, and Angus waited.

Asia went to a keyboard, typed in the website with the information regarding Romano's arrest and waited for it to load. She repeated the highlights of her conversation with Trista.

When Romano's face appeared on the screen the room went silent.

"Have you informed Alpha Barticus?" Angus asked.

"No, I haven't," Asia said. Something like this should come from La Patron, he would decide how much information to share with her father.

"This could be a cluster fuck of major proportions," La Patron said. "Let's hope they don't examine him. I'll give Barticus a warning and a few highlights. I'm thinking Carlotta and Razor did this. They used Romano's family as leverage, forced him to kidnap the human and then left him to hang. If Razor understood Pack dynamics he should never have allowed it to happen."

"The way I see it is all of this will come to a head soon," Jasmine said. Everyone looked at her. "Storm is on his way home and he's going to flip out because Renee's grieving. That's not the best time for Razor and his mate to appear but I think we'll be seeing them within the next 48 hours."

"After seeing that article, I've checked to see if any charted flights have left the airport headed our way," Jacques said and looked at them. "There is one headed from Rome to Charleston, West Virginia with a scheduled re-fueling stop in New York, and will be here in two or three hours. We could meet their flight, give them a real West Virginia welcome."

"We will, but not at the airport," La Patron said. "We need a place away from cameras and humans. I think we need to keep this fight between Storm and Razor quiet. The fewer wolves who know about them the better."

"Excellent thinking, Silas," Grandfather said walking into the room.

"Thank you, I try," La Patron said watching the older man take a chair and sit. "Why is it you seem to be around all the time when centuries went by without ever seeing you?"

"Things are changing, with technology and new enemies, the Pack as a whole is more vulnerable than before. I'll be more hands on to help navigate the murky waters of change," he said.

They all stared at the old man for several moments.

"To the situation at hand, things have progressed, I've learned more of the matter," Grandfather said. "They can be killed. Not by anyone in this room, unfortunately, but by their mates."

"What?" Jasmine said. "I didn't think we could do that."

"You can't," La Patron said clearly making a personal statement.

"You know what I mean, Silas. I thought if one mate died the other could die as well."

"That's full-bloods and if they're children, they may not perish," Grandfather said.

"So other than Carlotta killing Razor he's unstoppable," Angus said.

"I didn't say that," Grandfather said and then lapsed into silence.

"Can Razor be stopped?" La Patron snapped, obviously growing frustrated.

"Yes he can," Grandfather said, "but the Goddess hasn't shared how. She only said both could be stopped."

Jasmine threw up her hands and glared at Grandfather. "The purpose of your visit?"

"To help in any way I can," he said as if it should be obvious.

"Do you know anything about Romano?" Angus asked.

Grandfather frowned. "Alpha Romano?"

Angus nodded and turned on the overhead monitor again. The article regarding the kidnapping appeared. Grandfather read it and shook his head. "Has Barticus been informed to get Romano out of there? If they examine him, draw his blood..." He looked at La Patron.

"He's been told of the situation. I didn't give him orders or instructions what to do," La Patron said in a dry tone.

"I guess that's the best we can do for now," Grandfather said. "Storm is going to be upset when he returns."

"We know," La Patron said.

"No, you don't, not really. He learned what happened to his Alpha during this trip and is having a hard time reconciling all the deceit that went along with it." He held up his hands to stop their questions. "He hasn't shared it with his mate yet, it's only fair that she knows before everyone else. I hope he sees the real villain and victim in this whole game. I don't want the last two pups from my line to constantly try and kill each other."

Asia sensed his sadness and looked at Hawke. "*The next few hours are going to be long.*"

Hawke nodded and looked at La Patron. "Where did you want them to meet? Is Trista the bait?"

"We need to decide how to do this. Storm is not going to leave Renee, she won't leave the museum. Can we clear the town by then?" La Patron asked.

"If we started now, we might be able to move 80%," Angus said. "What if we moved those within five miles of the museum, will that be enough?"

"Once they engage you could cover them in one of those opaque bubbles like you did in Honduras, so no one could see," Hawke said.

"That's if you can move fast enough," Angus warned.

"That might work," La Patron said.

"It would work better if Trista was at the museum helping Renee sort through things. Razor would go there, and we can deal with Carlotta," Asia said.

"Make sure Carlotta comes with them," Jasmine said. "If she orchestrated that kidnapping and collected the ransom, there's no reason for her to stick around. I'm sure her sister would like to deal with her."

"Don't forget she uses pheromones, which limits who can be in her presence." Angus looked at La Patron. "Make sure David returns to the Compound when Storm arrives."

"Anyone who's unmated must leave that area when Storm arrives," Jasmine stressed. "History will not repeat itself today."

"Agreed," Jacques said. "I'll alert Hank, I'm sure he remembers when Arianna wreaked havoc here years ago. La Patroness is right, we'll prepare for this breeder and anyone she corrupts on the way."

"One more thing," Grandfather said drawing everyone's attention. "You cannot help Storm in any way, Silas. The Goddess forbids it." He snorted. "I'm not sure She will permit those two to fight even though it amounts to them just blowing off steam."

La Patron looked at the older man and nodded. "How do we fix this so these two peaceably co-exist?"

"I don't know," Grandfather said. "Different continents? Send Storm to handle Mexico for you, he does speak Spanish," Grandfather said.

"And is mated to my daughter," La Patron said with a determined glint.

Grandfather shrugged. "Once he chooses you as his Alpha, that will work itself out."

"Stop. Just stop talking," La Patron snapped.

Grandfather sighed and sat back in his chair with his hands clasped over his belly.

La Patron pointed at Jacques. "Have Hank clear the area of town within a five-mile radius of the museum. Tyrese is picking up Storm when he arrives and taking him to Renee." He looked at Asia. "When should Trista be invited to the museum?"

"After Storm and Renee have some time alone. Trista doesn't know anyone else," Asia said.

"She spent time with Crystal, Renee's Admin," Jasmine said. "Scratch that, Renee said Crystal took it real hard. She's probably not the best person to interact with Trista at the moment. We don't want her offended or anything."

"As long as she's at the museum before Razor's plane lands," La Patron said.

"After those two battle, then what?" Jasmine asked.

"Let's hope Razor gets hit with the mating heat and can only see his mate," La Patron said.

CHAPTER TWENTY-FIVE

"DAMN," STORM SAID LOOKING at the museum as Tyrese pulled into the parking lot. "Who did this?" he glanced at Tyrese.

"Some guy who died in the explosion," Tyrese said opening his door.

Storm stepped out the car. *"Renee I'm here."*

"Niklas, I'm on the second floor in the back. I'll meet you near my office. It's bad, really bad."

"I know, we'll fix it." With Olympic worthy strides, he moved across the parking lot to the employee entrance. Security opened it for him and Tyrese. Storm followed Renee's scent and turned right. She was running toward him and leapt into his outstretched arms. His chest tightened as she shared her pain and heartache with him. Turning, he strode toward her office, hoping it was still there. Miraculously, it was.

Storm closed the door behind them and rocked her from side to side in his arms. "*I'm so sorry, so sorry this happened.*" He repeated the words over and over, feeling them from the depth of his soul. "*Give me your pain, let me carry it for you.*"

She shook her head against his shoulder, leaned back, teary eyed, and met his gaze. "*No. We'll share it. I don't want you to hurt alone either.*" She sniffled and brushed her lips across his.

He hungered for more of her and held her head in place while deepening the kiss. She was water for his thirsty soul. "*I missed you so much,*" he murmured against her mouth and kissed her again.

"*Missed you too,*" she said on a gasp when they broke for air. *"Sorry, this is what you came home to."*

"You're home. Wherever you are. I came to you." He stared into her eyes, saw the sadness, the pain and determination. His mate had a core of steel. He wiped

the tear from her cheek with his thumb and kissed her forehead. *"What do you need?"*

"Right now, I need you. Time to hold onto you and talk. So many things have happened since you left."

He wanted to sink balls deep into her, but he'd sit and talk if she wanted. Storm pulled up a chair, sat and pulled her onto his lap. For several moments they hugged and kissed. It wasn't sexual, more like she said, reconnecting skin to skin. He'd never done anything like this but found it soothed his beast in a profound way. Tension rolled off him as she placed kisses along his neck and stroked his arm.

"Umm, this is nice. You smell so good," he whispered.

"Just being with you makes me feel better, not as tense," she said looking into his eyes. *"What happened on your trip? You said you had something to share before you fell asleep."*

Storm had forgotten. "*I'll show you.*" He pulled out the letter from his pocket and handed it to her. "*It's in Spanish.*"

"I can read it better than talk, I mean speak it." She unfolded the letter and looked at it. Frowning, she handed it to him. *"I made good grades in Spanish class but that's not any Spanish I've ever seen."*

He smiled as he took it and read it to her. When he finished, she had wrapped her arms tightly around his shoulders and buried her face against his neck. Several moments passed in silence.

"Carlotta and Razor killed your Alpha? His pups?"

"That's what Romano claims."

"You don't believe him?"

"In a way I do, but he could've been lying."

"What did his mate say? He can't lie to her," Renee said.

Storm hadn't thought of that. "*Said he told the truth.*"

"Sounds like he's warning you about Carlotta more than Razor. Kinda like he's her puppet, does what she says. Wonder how you got on their radar?"

He'd missed the underlying warning about Carlotta until he read it again just now. La Patron and Grandfather thought the same thing, that Carlotta had some kind of hold on Razor, used him to do things he might not do otherwise.

"There are a lot of evil people in this world," she said.

Surprised and unsure where this was going, he nodded.

"That letter makes me realize I've lived a sheltered life." She leaned back and stared at him with glassy eyes.

His heart squeezed at the sorrow etched on her face.

"Remember our conversation about your work?"

"Yeah. I told you I would find something else to do." He thought that was settled.

"I know. But this... this is what you do best. It's a big part of who you are, what you're equipped to do best."

He tried to read her expression, to understand what she was saying beyond her words. *"What happened?"*

She frowned. "*What do you mean?*"

"Before, when we had that conversation, you made it clear you didn't want a mercenary as a mate. Now you're saying... what? That it's okay? That it might not be a bad idea for me to go after evil people?"

"I just thought —"

"There's a multi-million-dollar bounty on my head, Renee. Plenty people think I'm evil. Every person I killed probably had someone, somewhere who's heart is broken over that person's death. There's more blood on my hands than I can ever scrub off. I'm no hero, Renee. Let's be clear on that."

"I didn't say —"

The floodgates were opened, and he couldn't stop. *"Every day, I fight to keep my beast and my sanity in check otherwise, my beast would attack at the smallest infraction or injustice. You once asked if killing people was my default, it is. It is,"* he stressed wanting her to know his deepest, darkest shame. *"Hobbies? Hunting my enemies and killing them. That's what I do in my spare time. You're right, though. My beast... he's built for that. His skills permeate my human side, making me lethal in either form. In battle, I fear nothing. Nothing."* He wiped the sweat from his brow and looked at her. "*Some days I wonder if I'm the monster I've been called or worst.*"

She pulled him close and rubbed his back.

Feeling unclean, he resisted until she poured words of love and acceptance down their link. Tears pricked his eyes, but he refused to allow them to fall.

"I guess that makes me a beast-lover," she said.

The ridiculousness of her words broke through the last shield protecting his soul. Completely vulnerable, he spoke of his love, commitment and dedication to her through their link. She returned with a volley of sweet words, promises to love him, to accept him as he was, to build a life together. Back and forth they loved on each other without spoken words, strengthening their bond, entwining their hearts closer together.

"*Niklas?*"

"*Hmm?*"

"*You do realize that because it bothers you, the killing, your beast's hunger to go after people who've done wrong, or those who commit an injustice... that's a sign of who you are at your core? You were made to defend those who can't defend themselves. You're special, not a monster. The Goddess gave you specific gifts for a specific reason. Maybe it's time to talk to Her, get some clarity so you have peace about who you are.*"

Storm looked at her for several moments. Special? He never saw himself or his fighting abilities that way. Through the years, he alone survived ambushes, raids, and suicide missions. He'd been told he was lucky, but what if Renee was right. What if the old man was right? He'd have to apologize, probably put up with more interference but it was worth considering.

"*Most of my life I never thought She was real.*"

"*She's very real. Mama has met her a few times,*" Renee said.

He raised his brow. "*I shouldn't be surprised your mom is a determined woman, but I am.*"

Renee nodded. "*Maybe, and I'm no expert, but it's possible your beast is so unsettled, ready to go off so easily because he needs a solid connection, a purpose. Which leads me back to the Goddess since She gave you the gifts. I think we should try and talk to Her.*"

"*You say that like it's as easy as calling her on the phone making an appointment.*" He wasn't sure if Renee was serious or not, but her idea made sense.

"*Daddy will teach us,*" she said snuggling against his chest. "*Oh, Jackie said Trista's here.*"

"*She is?*" He didn't care one way or the other. "*What do we need to do here? Are you going through each floor? Is it safe?*"

Smiling, she stood. He missed her warmth immediately and fought the urge to pull her back down. They had work to do. He stood and took her hand.

"*It's safe, they wouldn't allow us to come inside until they removed a lot of the debris. Have you seen where the bomb went off?*" She walked toward the door holding his hand.

"Just from the outside." They walked toward the taped off area. Acrid odors itched his nostrils, he dialed down his scent factors. The entire front corner was missing. Storm wrapped his arm around her shoulder, pulled her close and kissed the top of her head. *"We'll stay here until the museum is rebuilt and restored to your satisfaction. I'll do whatever I can to help. I promise,"* he said.

She turned, wrapped her arms around him and held tight. *"Thank you, Niklas. I know you don't want to stay here, but I really want to make sure the museum is operational when we leave."*

He rubbed her back and let go of his desire to have her all to himself in some remote part of the world. Renee's bright light would be shared through her work and generosity to Pack. Charred steel beams, wood pieces, glass and dust were everywhere, but it could have been worse. Three quarters of the museum was still standing.

"Put me to work, Renee," he said.

She nodded and looked up at him with a light smile. "Yes, sir."

STORM PLACED UNBROKEN ceramic pieces into a box after Renee scanned them for the data base. They had been working a couple hours with Bella, Adam, Trista, Jackie, Quinn, Tyrese and Danielle. Rose, David and Tyrone had left with a promise to return with food and drinks.

"*Razor and Carlotta arrived in town a half hour ago and are on their way to the museum,*" La Patron told Storm.

"*What?*" Storm asked looking for Renee. She stood on the other side of the room talking to Trista and Jackie.

"*We've been tracking them since Trista's ex-boyfriend was kidnapped.*" La Patron gave him a quick update on what happened and his suspicions. Storm wondered why he was just being told and then realized it wouldn't have mattered. No way would he have insisted Renee leave the museum. Chances are, her father realized that as well.

"He killed Adolfo." Storm hadn't meant to blurt it out, but the scab had been pulled off that wound with Romano's letter, and it bled anew.

La Patron whistled. "*Any idea why?"*

"Something to do with me. I don't know what interest he has in me, but I want it to end today, after I kick his ass for what he did to Adolfo. Did he have anything to do with the museum?"

"Honestly, I don't know," La Patron said. "*If the two of you fight, I cannot interfere. The Goddess forbids it."*

"You've never interfered in a fight for me, why would you do it now?" Storm didn't understand the logic behind that.

"*Because you're my son through mating. You're family and She knows I'll never let anything happen to you. Never leave you to fend for yourself if things go wrong. Grandfather nor I can interfere,"* La Patron said.

Storm walked toward the exit and stared at the door for a second. Son? The word sounded strange. Storm couldn't digest La Patron's statement right now and left it alone. "*How much time before they get here?"*

"My sister just contacted me," Trista said wild-eyed from the other side of the room looking at Renee and then Storm. "They're here in town and want to see me. She wants me to come to the hotel." She gripped her hand's tight together and looked at her cell phone again.

Storm told La Patron what Trista said.

"*They're on their way to the museum, Security is following them,*" La Patron said. "*I'm out front waiting. It might be a good idea if you come outside. He may attack you and that could cause more damage to the museum."*

"What do you want me to do?" Trista asked.

Storm glanced at Tyrese before answering. "The truth is they're on the way here. I don't know why your sister is lying to you. Maybe she's telling Razor lies to get him to attack when they arrive." He shrugged and looked at Renee. "Not that it matters, he and I have a score to settle."

"The Mexico trip?" Trista asked.

Renee wrapped her arm around Trista's shoulder. Trista grabbed her hand and watched Storm.

"That and more," Storm said not wanting to discuss what happened to his Alpha again. He looked at Renee. "*I need you to stay safe."*

"I'll be nearby with everyone else. Promise I won't go walking off by myself like they do in the movies." She winked at him.

"On my way," Storm told La Patron as he left the second floor and headed downstairs. Outside, he wasn't surprised to see Grandfather standing next to Angus and La Patron. Storm walked to the three men and nodded. He looked at Grandfather. "When this is over, my mate thinks we should talk to the Goddess about the gifts I received."

Grandfather's brow rose. A slight smile lit his face. "Sounds like you've been blessed with a wise mate. Cherish her, she's the real gift."

"I know." Storm nodded and looked at La Patron. "What's the plan?"

"No plan. If the two of you decide to fight, I'll enclose you in an opaque bubble so outsiders can't see what's going on."

Storm frowned and looked around. "Outsiders?"

La Patron looked up at the sky. "Yes. We're always being watched and recorded by satellites, remember that. No need for them to see what the two of you can do."

Storm hadn't thought of that. "Appreciated."

"Any chance the two of you could talk and work this out?" Grandfather asked.

"Zero," Storm said thinking of his Alpha's pups.

"There's a chance he didn't do the things you think he did," Grandfather said.

Storm looked at Grandfather. "I have to do this." He beast demanded he go after the people who killed his Alpha and den. The circumstances of why Razor did it, didn't matter.

Grandfather held his gaze a few seconds longer and nodded. "Maybe you two can talk afterward, have lunch or something."

Storm glared at him. The old man didn't know when to quit.

"What? You're family. My closest kin. It's not wrong for me to want you to get along," Grandfather said returning Storm's glare.

A black SUV pulled into the parking lot. Jasmine and Asia stepped out the truck and walked toward them. "Hello, Niklas," Jasmine said.

"Ma'am," Storm said, deciding he would allow her to call him by his first name.

"They should be here soon, are we ready?" Jasmine asked Silas.

"Yes. I didn't know you planned to be here," he said.

Jasmine shrugged. "It was a last-minute decision. The Goddess said you couldn't interfere but didn't say anything about me."

"Jasmine," La Patron said in a low warning tone.

She waved her hand. "As long as they play fair, I won't get involved," she promised.

"We are one, Jasmine. Our energies are combined, you can't become a separate entity when you want to go rogue," La Patron argued.

"Silas, as long as they play fair," she said again, matching her mate's stare.

Storm's gaze flew between the two. They were arguing over him. Over helping him. He tried to remember when anyone offered to watch his back and couldn't recall.

"Ma'am, if you would make sure Renee is within my sight at all times that would be greatly appreciated. My concentration would be shot if I didn't see or sense her nearby."

"Of course." She looked at La Patron. "Have the kids come down."

"Yes, ma'am," La Patron said shaking his head before pulling her close into a loose embrace.

Minutes later, a blue, late model car drove toward the parking lot and came toward them. Inhaling, Storm picked up a familiar scent. His beast didn't like it and a low growl rose up his throat. Turning, he faced the car, waited until Razor stepped out and raced forward to meet him.

Razor leapt up in the air, barely missing being clawed from the attack.

Storm continued forward and hit the wall La Patron erected. He bounced off, flipped and went at Razor again.

Razor met him in the air. The two slashed at each other with sharp, extended claws. Blood flew and hit the wall and bystanders who moved away from the two combatants.

Wounds healed as quickly as they were made.

Storm punched Razor in the jaw so hard, the sound of breaking bones echoed in the confined space. Razor shook it off and punched Storm in the stomach, robbing him of air. Punch for punch, kick for kick the two went after each other with a dizzying frenzy. Storm shifted and freed his beast.

Razor shifted as well.

The two animals fought with a ferocity that exhilarated Storm. Fur flew everywhere as they battled for supremacy.

Renee watched with baited breath, praying that Storm would be okay. She looked at Trista. The woman had tears in her eyes.

"What's wrong?"

"He's an animal, a real animal." She looked at Renee. "How can we be mates?"

Renee wondered if Trista remembered both men were animals and one was Renee's mate.

"Shut up," Carlotta yelled, walking toward them. Her loose dark blond hair flew behind her as she glared at her twin pointing.

Asia, Jackie and Renee's mom moved closer. Danielle, Tyrese and Quinn stood behind them.

"Why is everything about you? He can hear you," Carlotta said standing a few feet from her sister.

"You shut up, I wasn't talking to you," Trista said frowning at her sister.

"I heard you, which means he can hear you. Do you know what it took for him to come here? To find you? And you're here with them? Which one is your lover? Storm?" Carlotta glanced over her shoulder and looked at the two fighting. "Is he fighting your lover?"

"No, he's fighting my mate," Renee said, becoming heated.

"Mate? Storm's not mated," Carlotta said staring at Renee as if she was a bug or something lower.

"What-the-fuck-ever," Renee said and turned to watch Storm. He moved so fast it was like watching a dark ball fly around the room.

"Why didn't you link back up with me?" Carlotta asked Trista.

"I didn't want to," Trista said.

Carlotta's mouth opened and closed. Her cheeks reddened as she balled her fists. "You didn't want to?"

Renee stepped in front of Trista and looked at Carlotta. "Whatever you start be prepared to finish, because I will kick your rotten smelling ass if you start some shit in here today."

"And if she misses anything, I assure you I won't," Jackie said placing her arm around both Renee and Trista.

"We got your back too," Danielle said looking at Bella who approached with Adam.

"This is between me and my sister," Carlotta said, not backing down. She stepped forward, brushing against Renee.

"Not today, bitch. Not today." Renee swung and punched Carlotta in the stomach and then in the face. Carlotta dropped to one knee. Looked at Renee and ran forward, grabbing Renee around the waist and pushing her backward until they hit the wall. She punched Renee in the stomach and tried to scratch her in the face.

Renee ducked, lifted her knee and hit Carlotta in the stomach, followed with another punch in the face. She grabbed Carlotta by the hair, pulled her upright and twisted her arm behind her back. "Who killed Alpha Adolfo?"

"Fuck you," Carlotta said through tight lips.

Renee twisted her arm harder, causing Carlotta to stand on her toes. "I get that on a regular basis from my mate, so I'll have to pass on your offer. Who killed Alpha Adolfo?" Renee realized the fight between Storm and Razor had stopped, both men moved toward them.

"I killed him," Razor said.

"Wait, Storm," Renee yelled when he dove toward Razor. Storm stopped.

"Razor," Trista called. Frowning, he walked toward her.

"Why did you kill him?" Trista asked.

Razor opened his mouth and closed it. "He did something wrong, something to his mate and pups."

"You're a fucking liar," Storm yelled pointing at Razor. "You killed him, his mate and his pups."

"I've never killed pups. Never," Razor said.

"He watched the men kill his mate and his pups," Storm said.

"I killed him, the pups and mate were dead, already dead because he killed them," Razor said.

"Asia, take Carlotta into custody," her Daddy said. "There are some questions she needs to answer. And stop releasing those rotten pheromones, everyone here and within a five-mile radius is mated."

Renee released Carlotta to Asia. Carlotta kicked Asia in the leg. Asia backhanded her.

"Why are you letting them do this to me?" Carlotta yelled at Razor.

He looked confused. "I don't know. I really don't know. Why are you here Trista? Why didn't you meet us in Brazil or Rome? We've been everywhere trying to find you."

"Carlotta had me kidnapped in Mexico," Trista said meeting his gaze. "She's done everything to keep us apart, she's not your mate, I am."

"She's lying, Razor. Lying," Carlotta yelled.

"This one has been busy," Asia said. "Razor's telling the truth, he didn't kill the pups or his mate. Men under her spell acted on her orders, killed the mate and pups. When Razor arrived, she convinced him Adolfo was evil and blamed the death of his den on Adolfo who was drugged."

"You rotten bitch," Storm said taking a step forward. Renee took his hand and walked with him to the other side of the room.

"*Now we know what happened, chances are you killed the men who did the work for her. She's a corrupt breeder and for everything she's done, chances are she'll be put to death.*"

"*Chances are?*" he sounded outraged. "*Did you hear what that evil, stinking bitch did?*"

Renee rubbed his chest to calm him down. "*Yes, so did everyone else. I only say chances are because I'm not in charge, Daddy is. Breeders have been put down for less.*"

He moved back and forth in front of her, breathing hard, looking at Carlotta.

"*Baby look at me,*" she said. "*Niklas, look at me,*" Renee demanded.

He stopped and looked at her.

"*You're not going to kill her, so bring your anger down a notch, put it on simmer or something. This battle, this fight is over. I've had a long day and we're not going to extend it with you breathing fire over some dead-beat breeder. We have too much to do to expend this much energy on her.*"

They stared at each other for several moments until he exhaled and shook it off. Storm took her hand. "*You're right. You've had a bad day. Let's get this over with.*"

"One question," Renee said as they returned to the small group. "Why Storm? You went looking for him, why?"

"Fuck you," Carlotta said and then winced as Asia tightened her grip on her arm.

"Tell them," Asia said. "Tell them you were told by Nells that you and your sister were Razor and Storm's mates."

"Fucking lie," Storm yelled.

"Not a lie, asshole," Carlotta screamed. "He told me that. Nells told me that."

"He told you a lie," Renee said, in a cold tone.

"Yes, he did," Carlotta said. "Nells started all of this. Made promises, set things up for Razor to make money."

Asia pushed Carlotta so hard she fell to the ground. "He may have started Razor on that path, but you sent someone to blow up this museum."

"What?" Renee screamed and ran toward Carlotta with outstretched hands. Claws split her skin as she tried to slash the woman across her face. Storm caught her around the waist and walked off with her.

"Let me down, Storm. Let me... I'll kill that bitch." Tears ran unchecked down Renee's cheeks. A red haze clouded her gaze as she tried to free herself from his iron grip. "I said put me the fuck down now, Storm."

"Not yet," he said. *"You can't kill her, Renee. You don't want blood on your hands, or the stain of taking a life."*

"Why? Why did she do it? She didn't know you were mated." Renee's head dropped on his shoulder as she cried her frustration and pain.

"Let me go, Quinn. See what that bitch did to my sister? I'll kill her myself," Jackie screamed.

"I will put my foot so far up your ass, you'll be tasting leather for breakfast," Danielle said in a low threatening voice. "Get the hell out the way, Rese. I'm gonna fuck this bitch up."

"Move Adam," Bella yelled, her voice hit a high note. "I just want a few minutes with this bitch."

All four women tried to reach Carlotta but were held off by their mates. Carlotta scooted backward to her sister. "Help me, Razor." She looked up at him.

Razor moved forward but stopped when Trista placed her hand on his arm. "Wait a minute."

He stopped and stared at her.

Trista pointed at Carlotta. "You're responsible for this?" She pointed to the museum. "You had someone bomb it?"

Carlotta glared at her but didn't answer.

"If Asia said she did, she did," Danielle yelled, trying to walk around Tyrese.

"Why? Why would you do that? This place is amazing, you have no idea what you've destroyed. Most of those pieces can never be replaced." She stared wide-eyed at her sister.

Carlotta's expression clearly said she didn't care.

Trista looked at Razor. "I'm sorry."

He frowned. "Why?"

Trista exhaled. "When Carlotta told me one of us was your mate, and then we met you, I thought it was me. But I was scared. You're too violent, and fight too much, that wasn't the life I wanted." She shook her head. "In a way I gave you to her. But I had no idea she would take things this far. Hurt innocent people for money... I didn't know she would use you like that."

Razor took her hand and held it for a few seconds. "You're the one. I've always thought it was you but wasn't sure. Things were confusing for a while but now I'm sure. I can't change what I've done, things I've done, not directly." He took a deep breath, cupped her cheek. "You're my mate, no more running, my beast cannot handle it. We'll fix whatever we need to make this right."

Tears ran down Trista's cheeks. "Not this. There's no way to fix Renee's heart, it's broken because she helped me. She and Storm saved my life, gave me a safe place to stay and wait for you. And this is what happened." She pointed to the museum. "Carlotta did this to the museum because of me."

"Saved your life? You were in danger?" Razor asked, his voice deepening.

Trista nodded, wiping the tears from her face. "Yes. But that's not the point right now. We hurt Renee, my friend. We have to make this right."

"How?" he asked.

"Apologize and pay for the repairs," Trista said looking at him.

"NO," Carlotta yelled, trying to break free. "That's my money."

Razor looked at Carlotta for several seconds. She backed up, closer to Asia. "My mate was in danger because of you?"

"No," Carlotta said. "She's my sister, my twin, I wouldn't ever put her in danger."

Trista placed her finger beneath his chin, turned his face toward hers. "Carlotta is lying."

Razor held her gaze for several seconds.

"But you cannot kill her," Trista said when he started to move. "La Patron is law here. He and his mate will decide what happens to her."

"Trista!" Carlotta screamed. "Stop this. Everything I did, I did for us, so we could live free and independent of anyone."

Trista shook her head. "You killed pups, innocents, that's got nothing to do with Razor and I." She looked at La Patron. "Please test my words for the truth. Whatever Carlotta has done, I had no part in it other than denying my mate."

"We know," La Patron said.

Razor turned and faced La Patron. He looked at everyone. "Who is Storm and Renee?"

Trista took his hand and walked him to Renee, who was crying in Storm's arms. "Razor this is my friend, Renee. She saved my life, we owe her and her mate a great deal. The museum is her baby, it means a lot to her," Trista explained.

Razor and Storm looked at each other for several seconds. No one would ever guess the two had just tried to kill each other moments past.

"Razor!" Carlotta screamed as Asia pulled her toward the SUV. "Trista, I'm sorry, we can fix this."

"Maybe before you tried to have me taken again, yesterday," Trista said turning her back on her sister.

Razor's gaze flew to Carlotta. Trista patted his arm. "That's over, fixing this is more important."

The others moved closer to Renee and Storm. Jackie wrapped her arms around Renee's back. Bella placed her cheek on Renee's arm. They all touched Renee, offering comfort.

"Renee and Storm," Razor said in a low voice. "I apologize for the destruction of your property. I should've paid more attention to everything going on around me and did not. We will pay for the repairs. As my mate has said, many things are irreplaceable and for that I am truly sorry. Whatever else you need from my mate and I, we will give."

He bent his head and then lifted it.

Trista hugged him and laid her head on his shoulder. "Thank you," she whispered.

Razor kissed her cheek.

Trista reached out and touched Renee's cheek. Their gazes met. Renee released Storm. She and Trista embraced. Soon they both were crying.

Razor looked horrified and patted Trista's back awkwardly. He looked at Storm who stood back and watched the two women.

"I'm so sorry," Trista said.

"Not your fault," Renee said. "Carlotta's a bitch."

Trista chuckled. "Yeah, she is."

They broke apart with watery grins. Renee looked at Razor. "I'm Renee, Storm is my mate. These are my sisters, Jackie, Bella and Danielle. My brothers, Quinn, Adam and Tyrese."

Razor nodded but didn't speak.

"Daddy?" Renee called.

La Patron, Angus and Grandfather walked over. "Mama left?" Renee asked.

"She went with Asia and Carlotta," La Patron said.

"He is your father?" Razor asked, looking at La Patron.

"Yes," Renee said holding Storm's hand. "Is Security staying through the night?" Renee asked.

"Yes. You can start first thing in the morning." Her father looked at all of them.

Renee nodded and stared at Grandfather who seemed to be fighting a grin. "Are you happy?" Renee asked him.

"For the most part, yes. The Goddess keeps surprising me, but in good ways." He patted Razor on the shoulder. "I'm your Grandfather."

Razor looked at Trista. She nodded.

"Let's go eat and get to know each other," Grandfather said to Razor.

"He's a ghost, ghosts don't eat," Storm told Renee.

She elbowed him as they walked to the car. "*Behave*."

CHAPTER TWENTY-SIX

RENEE SAT IN THE PASSENGER seat as Storm pulled out of the parking lot behind Jackie and Quinn. Trista and Razor sat in the back seat in a deep embrace. Storm took Renee's hand and kissed the back of it.

She smiled. "*This was one of the worst days ever.*"

He looked at her and nodded.

She glanced at the back seat. "*And one of the best. I met your cousin.*"

Storm frowned. "*What? Who?*"

Renee laughed. "*Razor.*"

Storm shook his head and turned onto the main road. "*Don't start.*"

"Guys can we drive through that community we saw yesterday? I want Razor to see it," Trista said.

Storm looked at Renee. She shrugged. "Okay." Renee contacted Jackie, told her what they were doing and asked her to pass the word that they would be about an hour late.

"Will you tell me everything that happened when you rescued Trista? How did that come about?" Razor asked Storm.

Storm nodded and started with Adolfo's death. By the time they reached Pack lands, Razor had added what he recalled filling in the blanks. Carlotta had been busy.

"I'm sorry," Razor apologized to Trista. "I trusted the wrong person and didn't seek answers beyond her explanations." He kissed the back of Trista's hand. "What will happen to her? Carlotta?"

Renee wasn't sure why he asked the question but answered honestly. "I don't know. Breeders have been put down for less. I'd be surprised if she sees the sunrise, but it's not up to me," she said.

"La Patron is the law in this country, I've heard of him," Razor said. "What is this?" He pointed to security station they approached.

"Pack lands," Trista said in a soothing voice. "It's for Pack only, not humans. I'm Renee's guest."

"I see."

They drove through the gate, Trista explained everything to Razor. Gushing over the stores, business center, nightclub, everything. When they reached the residential area, she sat forward in her seat.

"You like this?" Razor asked.

"Yes. Just wait until you see it. It's great." She looked out the window as they drove around. Once again, she explained to Razor the housing, schools, park and recreation.

"Look at the children," she said pointing at the kids playing beneath bright lights on the park.

"Very nice," Razor said.

"Should we stop?" Storm asked Renee.

"No. We don't know him well enough to allow him to walk around near the pups."

Storm nodded. They drove around again and left the residential area.

"This means a lot to you?" Razor asked Trista. "This is the way you want to live? The reason you were afraid to mate with me?"

Renee glanced at Storm and kept staring ahead. "I'm so glad we mind-speak," she said.

"Is there any way to not hear this conversation?" Storm asked her.

"Yes, in a way. I'd seen you fight and the idea of being with an animal... I couldn't handle it."

Storm squeezed Renee's hand. "*I'm an animal.*"

"Me too," Renee said as she looked out the window.

"I'm both," Razor said simply. "Man and wolf."

"I know. I know," Trista sighed. "My mind got in the way. But seeing Renee and Storm, and all the others, seeing this neighborhood, how happy and normal everything is, helped me understand that you have two sides. I kept focusing on just one side. Does that make sense?"

"*Maybe we should pull over, go for a walk, give them some privacy,*" Storm said.

"*No, I need a shower and food and you,*" Renee said.

He kissed the back of her hand. "*Not in that order I hope.*"

"Yes, it makes sense. But I am who I am. Will you continue to run?" Razor asked.

"No. I won't leave you again, I promise. I'm your mate and I want..."

"*Please don't mention us again,*" Renee said.

"I want to mate with you, have your pups, create our den," Trista said.

"Good. Because I will not let you leave me again," Razor said. "I will learn of this life you want, maybe the Grandfather can help after you explain what that means."

Trista explained families, and Razor's connection to Grandfather and Storm. "We are the last two?"

"Yes, that's what Grandfather said. That's why you couldn't win against him," Trista said.

"I won against him," Razor said. "He did not win the battle."

"You did not win the battle," Storm said looking at Razor in the rear-view mirror.

"No one won," Renee said raising her voice. "You guys can fight all day, but you can't kill or seriously hurt each other, get over it."

"That's right," Trista said. "It's obvious they're related."

"Girl, for real," Renee said, turning to look at Trista.

"I know I explained their relationship, but egos got stuck on who won the fight." Trista rolled her eyes.

"Huge egos," Renee said, opening her hands wide.

Storm pulled onto the side of the road, grabbed Renee and kissed her until her thoughts scrambled. They gasped for air when they separated.

"Yeah," Trista sucked in air as Razor allowed her to take a breath from their kiss. "Definitely related."

CHAPTER TWENTY-SEVEN

SILAS, JASMINE, ASIA and Angus sat in the room above the operating room watching as Dr. Passen checked the IV in Carlotta's arm. He looked up at Silas for permission to administer the lethal drug.

"Continue," Silas said.

Jasmine held his hand and remained at his side until the doctor informed them it was done. Security removed her body for incineration.

"Why don't I feel bad about this?" Jasmine asked the others.

"She killed babies, mates, innocent people for money. Razor doesn't know she had Nells, his adopted father killed. No doubt the man realized he made a mistake and she stopped him before he could ruin things for her," Asia said.

"Yeah, that would kill any guilty feelings," Jasmine said as they turned to leave the room. "What about Razor?"

"Grandfather's downstairs with David and the others waiting to welcome him to the family," Silas said. "I'm not sure I'm ready to throw out the welcome mat."

"Would he have attacked Carlotta?" Jasmine asked. "For a moment, when he learned Trista had been in trouble, I thought he would attack Carlotta."

"I would have," Angus said. "If it was Shyla and she did half that shit, I'd put my foot on her neck."

Jasmine snorted. "Shyla would've handled Carlotta before you got a whiff of anything."

"Renee wants Storm to meet with the Goddess," Silas said before they walked out.

"Why?" Jasmine asked.

"To explain his gifts."

No one spoke.

"Gifts?" Angus said choking back laughter. "Is that what she's calling it?"

"Hey, whatever helps her accept her mate," Asia said.

Silas looked at Jasmine. "Did you tell her that? That his killer wolf was a gift?"

"I may have mentioned, it was highly possible he was sent to protect Pack," Jasmine said.

They stopped smiling and stared at her.

"Seriously?" Angus said. "You told her that? Why? Is that what you think?"

"Yes, I do. But they need to talk to the Goddess for confirmation or not." Jasmine walked into the hall and looked back at them. "Come on, Renee and the others are here." She strode toward the elevator.

Angus looked at Silas. "Grandfather did say things were about to get worse and he would be around more."

"Yeah, but two of them?" Silas shook his head.

"Maybe one is for my father and Europe. He's on his way to New York with Romano to reunite the Alpha with his den," Asia said.

"Could be," Silas said. "But which one?"

"Ask the Goddess and come on Silas," Jasmine called from the elevator.

"*On the way, Sweet Bitch*," he said as he headed out.

CHAPTER TWENTY-EIGHT

A WEEK LATER, RENEE, Storm, Trista and Razor sat in La Patron's prayer room after being washed, dressed and briefed on the proper way to meet the Goddess. Storm's interest had been peaked when Grandfather announced the Goddess would meet with them after Razor and Trista's mating heat ebbed some.

He and Razor hadn't talked since the day of their fight. That day after lunch, Trista accessed their bank information and gave Renee a million dollars for repairs of the museum. Renee said it was too much, but both Razor and Trista insisted she take it. The architect and contractors had been making plans all week and should begin repairs once the steel beams arrived.

Renee insisted Razor and Trista stay at her condo, the two accepted the offer and hadn't been seen until this morning. Storm doubted they would have contacted anyone if they hadn't run out of food.

The prayer room hummed with energy. Renee, dressed in a white loose gown rubbed her arms constantly while listening to last minute instructions from her parents.

"This isn't the time to spout off smart remarks," La Patron said. "The Goddess may not directly answer your questions –"

"She doesn't do that often," Renee's mom said earning a frown from her dad.

"Perhaps, but remember this is an honor, treat it as such. Ask your questions and remember everything She says. Every word means something," La Patron said.

Storm nodded. He had one question, but Renee had several.

"Do we have to leave?" Trista asked La Patron.

"Ask the Goddess what She wants you to do, where She wants you to go," La Patron suggested.

"We have no choice in the matter?" Trista asked looking at Renee.

"You always have choices," La Patron said. "You don't have to obey." His tone said there would be consequences if you didn't.

Razor held Trista's hand and kissed the back of it. His eyes appeared alert, his manner less aggressive and he spoke less now than he had before.

"Thank you, Sir," Trista said. "After being pulled back and forth, the idea of being a puppet holds no appeal, I'll tell you that."

La Patron frowned. His mate placed her hand on his arm.

"We'll wait outside, so you can begin," Jasmine said. She smiled at Storm and they left the room.

The aromatic scent of the incense tickled his nose as the four of them held hands. Renee began the prayer of petition seeking an audience. Storm followed her lead, introduces himself as her mate and respectfully requested a meeting with the Goddess. The other two did the same. They sat connected for several minutes before a cool breeze whipped around the room.

Kneeling, Storm bent from his waist, the tip of his nose touched the floor. Power as he'd never sensed before hovered above him. Renee's hand tightened on his, reminding him of their connection and he was indeed grateful.

Sounds of a trickling stream and bubbling brook arose. Storm picked apart the scents filling the air, lavender, vanilla and damp earth. His beast relaxed and rested, something it never did while Storm was awake. He tried to lift his head and could not. His legs, arms and fingertips refused to obey his whim. Concerned, Storm tried to rouse his beast unsuccessfully.

"Renee?" She didn't respond. He tried to turn to look at her and couldn't. Why couldn't he sense her through their link? His heart raced at the thought something happened to his mate while he sat next to her. "*Renee? Renee? Answer me.*"

"She cannot. All mind links are canceled for now."

"What? Why?" Storm demanded.

"Because I require everyone's full attention." With that proclamation, Storm regained the use of his limbs, but his beast remained unresponsive. He looked up and closed his eyes at the bright light.

"You're the Goddess?" Stupid question. Rattled because She was real, Storm forgot everything La Patron said regarding protocols. "*Where's Renee?*"

"Standing next to you. For this meeting, every person stands on their own. I'm talking to each of you as individuals, not as pairs. You asked for this meeting."

Now that the moment was at hand, Storm was speechless. Unrelenting power bathed his skin but didn't hurt him, quite the opposite he felt empowered. "*What do you want from me?"*

"Live a prosperous life serving the Pack."

"Which Pack? Do I stay in the States or go somewhere else?"

"Alphas give directions to Pack."

"I don't have an Alpha," Storm said, he didn't particularly want one.

She didn't respond.

Did that mean he needed an Alpha? That his future was in someone else hands? He hoped he wasn't supposed to be an Alpha, he didn't want the job.

"*What should I do with the gifts you gave me?"*

"Use them to honor Me."

He hadn't expected that. "*I… I don't know you, how do I honor you?"*

"Finally, you ask the right question. Listen to Grandfather and learn, I will help."

Warmth rolled over Storm's skin and invaded his being. His beast chuffed as if bathing in the feeling. A sense of acceptance he'd never felt before, filled him.

"Stand strong, be who you are, at the appropriate time be ready." Those words rang in his ears as he opened his eyes and realized he was back in the prayer room. Renee stared at him and then looked across to Razor who was just opening his eyes. Trista leaned against Razor staring at the floor.

"What's wrong, Trista?" Renee asked.

"I have been in the presence of a Goddess, someone I never believed in until now. It's mind-boggling to have come to this place where I want to change, to serve Her," she said looking at Renee. "Know what I mean?"

Renee nodded and squeezed his hand, reminding him of their connection. "Yeah, I do." She looked at Storm. "*Did you get the answers you needed?"*

He nodded for the others who looked at him. "*That blew me away, I didn't believe until I couldn't do shit, I mean She controlled everything."*

"Did you ask your questions?" Renee asked.

"*Yes. Like your mom said, the last thing wasn't specific, but I got an idea of what I'm supposed to do.*" He kissed the back of her hand. *"I'm Her warrior, for the Pack, Renee. Something's coming and I'll be needed."*

She cupped his cheek. *"I know. It's an honor and privilege to be chosen as your mate. Our links are different, the way we function is slightly different. Now I understand why you needed to see me during your fights, I'm your anchor. No other wolf needs or has one."*

His brow rose. "*Anchor? I didn't know that.*"

"That's why Razor lacked control, control he now has with Trista."

Storm glanced at the couple. Razor's forehead rested against Trista's. Razor turned slightly and looked at Storm.

"We are different it seems," Razor said lifting his head while meeting Storm's gaze.

Storm nodded but didn't know what to say.

"Will you choose an Alpha?" Razor asked.

"It seems we need one or become one ourselves. I'm not interested in that job." Storm shook his head for emphasis.

Razor nodded. "I don't have the temperament for it either. In my life, I have met very few honorable Alphas. La Patron is one, Alpha Barticus another, there are a few more in Europe as well. What about the new Alpha in Honduras. You've met him," Razor asked Storm.

"At the time I met him, he was sniffing around my mate so my opinion of him is biased."

"Of course," Razor nodded and looked at Trista. "My mate would like us to petition La Patron to join his Pack. Grandfather says the Goddess tasked him to create a Pack for this continent, not just the States. He seems to think our help will be needed. What do you think?"

Storm recalled Grandfather's push for them to consider La Patron as Alpha at the lunch last week. "I don't know another Alpha I respect more than La Patron," Storm said slowly, thinking it through. "He cares for his Pack, meets their needs and shields them from humans which the Goddess requires." He looked at Renee and winked. "Plus, I am in love with his pup." He tapped the tip of her nose with his fingertip. "One thing, and this matters a lot to me for my den. I don't believe he, La Patron, will use us as cannon fodder just because of our gifts. He is an Alpha who gathers as much information as he can and then makes a decision. He's just as strong as we are with gifts and abilities we don't possess. If he sends us to handle a problem in Russia or some part of the world, he will make sure we return to our den."

"And protect them until we return," Razor said looking at Trista. "That is a most important benefit from an Alpha. I agree with you."

"Humans will be involved with the challenges," Trista said. "It'll be important to shield you, so they don't know your capabilities."

"That's right, the Goddess made that clear. As your anchors we have to help keep you hidden in plain sight," Renee added.

Storm frowned. "I don't want you traveling places to stand by while I do battle."

"No, the Goddess took care of that. She gave us a gift that will anchor you wherever you go," Renee said leaning into him. "*She took care of you, baby.*"

"Are we going to petition La Patron to join his Pack?" Trista asked Razor.

He looked at Storm for a moment and then at his mate. "Yes we will."

Trista hugged him and then reached over to hug Renee. "I'm so happy, I didn't want to leave you."

Renee returned the hug. "You just want to work at the museum"

"Well yeah, who wouldn't?" Trista laughed and offered Storm a light hug while Renee hugged Razor.

The three of them looked at Storm. "What?" he asked and then grinned, "I'm not leaving, Mom. No one bakes like that woman."

Renee hugged and kissed him. "Thanks, I'll call Daddy and Mama back in."

He nodded and took a deep breath. Life took weird curves. Masterminds in the heavens sent him around the world, fighting dangerous people, experiencing the Liege, meeting Alpha Adolfo and other things to bring him to this moment in time. His beast rested in the knowledge of their purpose, he found his mate, and looking across the room at Razor and then La Patron walk into the room, family.

<<<<End>>>>

HELLO,

By now you know my secret passion is paranormal romance where anything is possible. The world can be wacky, the men charismatic, strong and faithful, and the women courageous with inner beauty.

Thank you for taking the time to read Renee's story, Book three in La Patron's Den.

Renee's view of the world is shattered with dramatic results. She's lost faith and is struggling to find her way. Storm embodies the violent tendencies that keep her awake at night, afraid of losing her father and those she loves. The two navigate choppy waters as they come to realize life is a series of colors, and compromise.

You're invited to journey with me through all the books in this series. If you like fast paced action, suspense and great love connections like me, you won't be disappointed. Feel free to drop me a line, SydneyAddae@msn.com or join my Facebook group, La Patron's Den, where discussions regarding Silas and the Wolf nation abound. Also, you can find me at my website, SydneyAddae.com.

Knight Chronicles is a newsletter for my Readers Group from the characters of the series to keep you informed of what's going on in the Wolf Nation. Each issue has a personal message from Silas Knight, La Patron, or his mate, Jasmine. Character profiles with in-depth interviews and thoughts you won't find anywhere else. Also works in progress, new releases and special giveaways in every issue. If you would like to receive **Knight Chronicles** click this sign up[1] link! Thank you. (http://eepurl.com/bb3csz)

La Patron, the Alpha's Alpha is my first paranormal series and I'd like to ask a favor. When you finish reading, **please leave a review**, whatever your opinion, I assure you I appreciate it.

Thanks again

Sydney

BirthRight

BirthControl

BirthMark

BirthStone

BirthDate

BirthSign

1. http://eepurl.com/bb3csz

Sword of Inquest
Sword of Mercy
Sword of Justice
La Patron's Christmas
La Patron's Christmas 2
La Patron's New Year – w/Catherine Marsh, & Leigh West
KnightForce 1
KnightForce Deuces
KnightForce Tres'
KnightForce Damian
KnightForce Ethan
Angus
La Patron's Den – Jackie's Journey
La Patron's Den – Alpha Awakening – Adam
La Patron's Den – Renee's Renegade
Knight Rescue
Booksets
La Patron Series Books 1-6
La Patron Series Books 4-6
The Sword Series – Books 1-3
Vampires:
Last in Line
Bear:
Bear with Me
Jewel's Bear

www.ingramcontent.com/pod-product-compliance
Lightning Source LLC
LaVergne TN
LVHW010057110826
845155LV00028B/376
* 9 7 8 1 9 3 7 3 3 4 8 7 1 *